A COLLECTION OF
SHORT STORIES ABOUT
WOMEN MAKING
LIFE-CHANGING
DECISIONS

Carole Gift Page

*"Carole has caught the conflict and bewilderment of life.
Thank God, there are still answers when we turn to Him."*
JANETTE OKE

Regal Books
A Division of GL Publications
Ventura, California, U.S.A.

Published by Regal Books
A Division of GL Publications
Ventura, California, U.S.A.

Many stories in this book were originally published in such publications as: *Virtue, Moody Monthly, Bread, Power for Living, FAITH for the Family, Vista, Evangel, Standard, The Christian Home, Teens Today, The Lookout, Christian Living, Sunday Digest, The War Cry, Event, Live, Leadership Library, Touch, Presbyterian Journal, Say, Good News* and *Ministry.*

Library of Congress Cataloging-in-Publication Data
Page, Carole Gift.
Petals in the storm : a collection of 28 stories about women making life-changing decisions/ Carole Gift Page.
p. cm.
ISBN 0-8307-1483-9
1. Women—Fiction. I. Title.
PS3566.A3326P47 1991
813'.54—dc20

91-13343
CIP

1 2 3 4 5 6 7 8 9 10 / KP / Q3 / 95 94 93 92 91

To my mother
Millie Gift

The most beautiful woman I know.
Your love has sustained me for a lifetime.

Contents

Preface

My dear friend:

I know you.

You are a woman of the '90s.

Like me, you may juggle a full-time career with household chores, parenting responsibilities and marital commitments. You are concerned about recession, world unrest, drugs, dwindling finances, pornography, toxic waste, political corruption and the disintegration of the American family. You worry about your weight, your looks, your budget, your lack of time, your lack of faith. Your mind is stirred by memories—memories of SCUD missiles and terrorism, bombing sorties and desert storms, friends and loved ones in uniform, yellow ribbons and troops coming home in victory.

But you still carry on your own internal wars. In the middle of the night you wake up and brood about your children growing up and your parents growing old and feeble. You're balanced precariously in the middle. You wear entirely too many hats and try to do too many things at once, and you keep thinking that life was simpler in the innocent, tranquil past.

Mainly you're concerned about relationships. Your relationship with God. Your relationship with your husband. With your kids. With your parents. With your friends, colleagues and employers. You want to be all things to all people, but sometimes you have a hard time being anything to anyone. And then you stop and think about priorities and pray that God will give you wisdom to mete out parts of yourself where you are needed most. You want to please everyone. Yet often you find it hard even to please yourself.

So many choices! So many things waiting to be done, places to go, far countries to be explored, people to know and love, problems to solve. But perhaps what you yearn for most is significance, a glimpse of what the ordinary events of your life add up to. What sort of picture do the scattered puzzle pieces make? What does it all mean? You long to see a transcendence in the ordinary and mundane. You want long-term peace in a world gone mad. You want to see God's handiwork in the fabric of your life—His pattern, His design, His indelible touch.

And it is there. But often we miss the vision because our eyes have not been trained to see it.

In his book *The Orphean Passages: The Drama of Faith,* Walter Wangerin says, "In order to comprehend the experience one is living in, he must by imagination and by intellect be lifted out of it. He must be given to see it whole; but since he can never wholly gaze upon his own life while he lives it, he gazes upon the life that, in a symbol, comprehends his own."

What is that symbol? Perhaps a story, a parable, a tale created by the imagination.

According to Professor Matthew Dickerson, we gain wisdom and understanding about our lives when we see our experiences from another perspective. He says, "Good stories do this for us. They lift us out of our experience and allow us to see it whole...As our imagination takes us through the situation in the story, our intellect comprehends the experiences of that story."

In other words, through stories, imagination makes sense of experience.

Dickerson claims, "Good stories go beyond merely revealing Truth, they give meaning to the Truth...They reveal profound truths in simple ways which all of us, Christian believers and non-believers alike, can grasp. They make wisdom and truth available to the ordinary person. They deny the meaninglessness of modern life. In short, they teach us truth in ways that nothing else can."[1]

That, my friend, has been my goal in writing these stories. As an artist paints pictures on canvas, so I have attempted to paint with words heart-stirring portraits that capture the eloquence and pathos of women caught in the maelstrom of contemporary society and emerging victorious, by God's grace.

Now I invite you, friend, to come with me on an adventure. Step into my imagination and sample the variety of choices made by women like you and me. Women who have found themselves in every sort of dilemma, in crises big and small, laughable and tragic, sometimes even forced to make life-or-death choices.

This book is for you, today's time-strapped woman on the run. You don't have time to read or a moment to spare, so I give you these stories in bite-size pieces to savor in a single sitting or nibble on at your leisure. These stories introduce you to my fictional friends who confront and solve problems you yourself may be facing. Just as Jesus used the parable to drive home important truths, so may these contemporary stories with universal and enduring themes give you valuable insights and glimpses of eternal truths.

These stories are about women like you and me. Women in all walks of life—young and old, married and single, mothers and women without children—making life-changing decisions and coping with a multitude of challenges. These women struggle with husband-wife relationships, family conflicts, self-esteem, loneliness, illness, career problems, sexual temptations and spiritual crises. Some face the tragedies of child abuse, divorce, abortion, drug abuse, miscarriage, depression or death. Others are caught up in the tantalizing fantasyland of romance and first love.

Each story reveals a different facet of what it means to be an American woman in this unpredictable, topsy-turvy world of the '90s. In "Wednesday, 8:00 P.M." Joanie must decide whether to have sex with her boyfriend or lose him. In "Another Chance at Life," Shelley must choose whether her husband's infidelity will cost her her marriage. In "Stranger in My Home," Barbara must decide whether she can love someone else's child as her own. And in "The Healing of Annie Warner," Annie must determine whether her son's death will destroy her marriage or make it stronger. Through 28 stories you will meet women in conflict who ask, "What does a woman do when...?"

Ultimately, each woman in her own way catches a glimpse of God's transforming power, for if there is one primary message in this book, it is that God is at work today in the lives of women who trust Him. He is sufficient to meet their needs, whatever their circumstances.

Just as He is sufficient to meet *your* needs, my friend.

So I invite you to sample these stories and share the lives of women like you and me. And know that you are not alone in your predicaments and dilemmas, in your countless perplexing choices. We are together in this, you and I, together with millions of women whose stories we will never know, never have a chance to read. But, by sharing, we can learn from one another, be encouraged and challenged and comforted by one another—because we glimpse common truths and know by name the God of all Truth.

So read. Enjoy. Walk with me. Weep with me. Imagine with me. And rejoice with me in God's incredible love.

In His Love,
Carole Gift Page

Note:
1. Matthew Dickerson, "A Case for Fiction," *Christian Retailing* (Lake Mary, FL: A Strang Publication, Vol. 36, No. 10, October 15, 1990), pp. 39-40.

Wednesday, 8:00 P.M.

What does a woman do when the man she loves demands more than she can give?

Wednesday, 12:45 P.M.: Joanie Welles skipped lunch and spent the noon hour in her Manhattan Beach apartment nursing a cup of black coffee while her Carly Simon CD filled the empty room with wistful strains of "My Romance" and "When Your Lover Has Gone."

Usually at lunchtime she left the building where she worked as a dental hygienist to go next door to Denny's for a sandwich or some soup. Today, instead, she walked the two blocks back to her apartment. She needed time alone to think.

All morning she had peered into open mouths, taken X rays, cleaned and polished teeth. And smiled, her "Gleem" grin. Smiled at everyone in sight, when inside she felt sour with the memory of last night's confrontation with Alan.

Usually her dates with Alan evoked pleasant thoughts,

stirred her with delight. But today the memory was oppressive, nudging her with guilt, demanding something of her that she could not or would not recognize.

What it boiled down to was Alan. Alan Greer. Alan's demands.

1:30 P.M.: Alan Greer wore a perpetual frown today. Dave, the assistant manager of Hank's Men's Wear, noticed it first thing that morning and chided Alan with some remark about scaring away the customers with a face like that. Now Alan was tied up with several indecisive customers and was a half hour late for his lunch break.

He was ringing up a sale when Dave came by, slapped him on the back and said, "Go on now, before someone else comes in."

Alan nodded and was about to leave when Dave cleared his throat and asked, "Anything wrong, buddy?"

"Nothing I can't handle."

"Girl trouble?"

"You might say that."

"You mean that new one? Joanie somebody?"

"Yeah," said Alan, straightening his tie. "She has these weird ideas about—" He spit out the word. "—purity."

"Oh, man, don't waste your time on one of those kind," Dave laughed. "You know what they say—too many women, too little time!"

"I'm not worried," Alan smirked, forcing more confidence than he felt. "I have a feeling Joanie's going to see things my way—real soon."

3:15 P.M.: Joanie chatted amiably with the small boy cowering in the huge chair. Nothing she said could wipe away the look of dread on his face. Her voice sounded brittle and excessively bright when she said, "Now you just open your mouth wide when the doctor looks in, and afterward we'll have a surprise for you—a great big red balloon. How about that?"

Behind her words the thoughts churned darkly: *I have to decide. What do I want? What am I going to do?*

4:30 P.M.: Joanie's mother was busy in the kitchen and did not hear her husband Robert come in. When she turned from the stove to see him, she exclaimed, "Well, dear, you're early. Dinner won't be ready for another hour."

"That's okay, Alice," he said, kissing her. "I let Jim stay to close up the drugstore. I don't suppose we heard from Joanie, did we?"

Her face clouded. "No," she replied, wiping her hands on a towel. "It's been a month or more. Since she got that job in Manhattan Beach, it's as though our daughter doesn't exist anymore."

"I know." There was a hard, worried expression around Robert's eyes now. "Guess I'll go wash up," he said. "We have prayer meeting tonight, you know."

5:30 P.M.: Joanie peered without interest into the open refrigerator and noted that she had a choice of leftover spaghetti or a turkey TV dinner she could pop into the microwave. Automatically, she took the spaghetti, emptied it into a saucepan, and set it on the stove to heat. Then she went to the bedroom to change into Levi's and a sweater.

A harsh sputtering sound warned her the spaghetti was scorching, but she didn't care. Her only real concern was that Alan call her tonight. But that was impossible.

Hadn't he said just last night that he would not call again? Ever. "I'm not playing games, Baby," he had warned her. "If you decide you want to try things my way, call me."

And thinking of it now, it seemed she was on an inevitable

track, one-way, and in spite of everything she would finally call him. The lonely ache inside her demanded she say yes.

6:00 P.M.: "See you in the morning," Alan told Dave as he prepared to leave the store.

"You're looking better," Dave remarked. "Something happen?"

"No, I just got this feeling. Like the song says, 'everything's going my way.'"

"Oh, yeah? How come?"

Alan smiled, his eyes twinkling, as if he were about to share a secret. "Like I said before, I've been having some problems with my girl. She has these hang-ups. Some religious stuff her parents taught her. We finally had it out last night. I gave her a choice between that stuff and me."

"What's she expect—for you to marry her or something?"

"Yeah, right. But that's the last thing on my mind," said Alan. His eyes narrowed. "But if I know my Joanie, she's just about ready to dial my number. And if not, well—"

6:30 P.M.: Joanie settled for the TV dinner after all. She ate slowly, silently, listening for the phone, praying that Alan would call. While she waited, his words came back, bombarding her over and over. All the hot and heavy arguments. His seething anger. Women had been liberated decades ago, he insisted. Why should she live by rules that were meaningless, outdated? Why should she deny the pleasure they were both free to enjoy? This was the '90s, after all. Loosen up, he told her. Live! Be free!

He quoted every cliche, all the frazzled phrases. Yes, he spouted them all. Her own protests were air, nothing, swallowed up by his accusations. If she loved him, there would be no other way, he said. No other way.

Wednesday, 8:00 P.M.

7:15 P.M.: Robert Welles swung his car into the church parking lot and, looking around, smiled at his wife. "Remember how it used to be, the three of us like this? You and me and Joanie going together to church. Remember?"

7:30 P.M.: Joanie turned the radio on low and stretched out on her bed, careful not to muss the bedspread. Cupping her hands under her head, she stared mindlessly at the ceiling, at the fine mosaic of cracks fanning out across the expanse of white.

In her mind, she was reaching out for something, trying to understand how she had come to this particular point in time. How had Alan become so important to her? Why was she ready to toss away her beliefs, her standards, those qualities she had been taught to cherish? Was it simply a matter of trading one set of values for another? Alan talked about being free. But wasn't she already free—since she had accepted Jesus Christ as her Savior years ago? How could she have forgotten that freedom?

7:35 P.M.: The phone rang, and Alan whooped as he caught it on the second ring. "Hello. Oh, it's you, Dave." His voice sank. "No, I just thought it was—what? No, I figured I'd stay in awhile this evening. Oh, yeah? Some real possibilities, huh? Well, I'll give Joanie a few more minutes. Call back in half an hour, and I'll let you know."

7:40 P.M.: A man with a thick, husky voice was giving a commentary on the radio—something about automobile pollution. Joanie reached over and switched it off. She stared at the clock on the bed stand. The evening would be gone before she knew it. She felt a pang inside—a sense of loss, a feeling of need, an overwhelming confusion. Doubt. Desire. Shame.

7:45 P.M.: When Pastor Wilkins asked if there were any special prayer requests tonight, Robert Welles raised his hand as usual. "Just want to ask you to keep remembering our daughter," he said. "Joanie—" His voice broke.

7:55 P.M.: Joanie held the telephone receiver in her hand. *I have to decide now*, she thought. *Everything in my life is muddy. I have to take a stand one way or the other. Dear God, what should I do?*

7:59 P.M.: The phone was ringing, but Alan decided to wait a few seconds before answering. Good strategy, he figured. He gave himself plenty of time to put the receiver to his ear and offer a smooth, perfect hello. Recognizing Joanie's voice, he grinned broadly, triumphantly, and said, "Yeah, I expected it would be you, Babe."

8:00 P.M.: Joanie's hand trembled. "Alan?" she said, but her voice was so light that she had to repeat his name. "Alan, I just called to tell you that I've been thinking a lot about our talk last night. I realized you're right about me needing to be free. I was free once—yes, free—but somehow I let it slip away. Anyway, I've got some things to straighten out, so I'm going home. Well, for the weekend—or maybe longer. I don't know. But I wanted to let you know what my decision was—and, Alan, I wanted to say...good-bye."

Another Chance at Life

What does a woman do when she's expecting a child and her husband is having an affair with her best friend?

The apartment Shelley moved into during her separation from Chad seemed somehow determined to overwhelm her with its oppressiveness. She had come to this hole-in-the-wall—this dreary, airless prison—fresh from her disappointment with her husband. She had accepted the place without question, considering it perhaps another dirty blow dealt by the hand of fate in recent days. Even Chad's unborn, unsuspecting child—which by its gentle movements was making its presence known inside her—had become a travesty, a mockery of the sacred love bond Chad had so casually broken.

Nothing is as it seems, Shelley had noted ruefully when she first surveyed the apartment. *Not love or marriage or honor or fidelity.* But at least the apartment, by its very drabness and gloom, seemed not to make any pretense. It was honest in its unattractiveness. It offered no promises. Shelley took it on the spot.

There were certain things about the apartment that Shelley noticed as soon as she moved in. The walls, bearing yellowed wallpaper veined with a myriad of minute cracks, seemed to shun light and warmth. The rooms were always cold and damp, even when the days were sunny. Shelley dismissed the chill, however, reasoning that perhaps her own blue mood was reflecting itself in the atmosphere around her.

In the first few days Shelley managed to establish a certain schedule, a ritual of activity. Early in the mornings she called the two employment agencies in the city to see if there were temporary office work available. Twice she was sent to typing jobs that lasted two weeks apiece, and once she was sent to replace a receptionist taking a week's vacation. But most of the time there were no leads, no positions to step into temporarily. There was no sense, of course, in seeking full-time employment now. Who would hire a woman expecting a baby in five months?

Shelley was reluctant to admit that she didn't have to work now if she didn't choose to. Chad had insisted on paying her way. He made it clear that even when the divorce became final, he would support her and the baby. But Shelley was stubborn, refusing to accept help from a man she no longer trusted nor respected. She sent back his checks with the envelopes unopened. Every week a check arrived; every week she placed it in the return mail.

If she felt herself weakening, if she occasionally entertained the idea of cashing the check and spending the money (because the rent was due or there was only peanut butter and crackers in the cupboard or the gas tank was empty), Shelley had only to recall the evening she had confronted Chad with her suspicions about his relationship with Diana. Diana, the other woman. Her *friend*, Diana, who seemed not so different, and certainly no prettier, than Shelley herself.

Shelley had challenged Chad to refute her suspicions, but with his reluctant nod her nebulous fears became raw reality. It had been so ironic. Shelley, armed against Chad with her angry suspicions, had been knocked down, stunned by a mere nod. There were no denials from Chad, no lies, no attempts to cover up or blur the truth. Shelley could not even find it in herself to rant and rave, to scream or cry. She listened mutely until he finished. Then, in a dry whisper, she said, "But why? You're a Christian, aren't you? How could you do it?"

"I'm human," Chad defended.

Shelley had no reply. She moved out that night, driving the 20 miles to her parents' home outside of town. Her mother welcomed her for the night—her expression kind, sympathetic—but told her she must go home in the morning. "For the sake of the child, my grandchild, work things out with your husband," she advised Shelley. "Go home and pray together. God is bigger than your problems."

Outraged and indignant, Shelley had driven the next day into the city to find a place to live. This apartment. Whatever else it was, it was her own.

On the days when Shelley did not go off to her temporary employment, she spent the mornings cleaning and scrubbing the apartment. During her first days there, she had gone from room to room inspecting corners and cupboards and closets. She had been appalled by the filth, the dirt of strangers, which had accumulated over the years. There was a filmy scum on the shower door, the faded carpet bore dingy tracks of wear, and black fingerprints spotted the walls near the light switches.

Shelley cleaned diligently, relentlessly, scouring the walls and floors, polishing and waxing, forcing a gleam from the sinks and appliances. She was proud of the work she had accomplished.

Of course, there were certain things that Shelley could not control, matters over which she had no power. Her neighbors, for instance. On Shelley's left lived a man and woman with a small child. The child often cried at night and the man and woman fought. Shelley could hear them through the thin walls. It dismayed her to think of them so close, on the other side of the wall, going about their hectic, frenetic lives—the man drinking, drunk; the woman whining, bitter; the child caught in their fury, helpless, always bawling.

At times Shelley lay in bed listening against her will to the fights, the arguments, the angry words flailed back and forth. Revulsed by what she heard, Shelley confirmed in her own mind the rightness of her decision regarding Chad. It was better to end a marriage swiftly and neatly than to wallow indefinitely in a wretched relationship like the one next door. It was better to get out now than to subject her child to a father who could not be trusted or respected. Besides, didn't the Bible support her decision? Wasn't adultery considered sufficient grounds for divorce? Certainly there was no reason for Shelley to feel guilty over her decision. But why, then, did the Spirit of God seem so distant lately? Why did it seem that the presence of Christ had fled from her heart? Perhaps her life these days had become filled with too many distractions—including the man and woman next door.

If the family on Shelley's left was a matter of irritation and concern, the neighbors on her right were even more disturbing. Duncan and Peter, huge and menacing in appearance, with faces often unshaven and bellowing voices that made the walls tremble, lived on the other side of her kitchen. Shelley had no idea what the men did or where they went each day, but she could always hear them returning home, usually after dark. They inevitably slammed the door so that her entire apartment shook; and while she sat alone eating her evening meal, she could hear them laughing and cursing, banging utensils and pans and chairs in their gruff carelessness.

There was an ominous quality about the two men. Shelley instinctively feared them, and at the same time, chided herself for being afraid. She made every effort to avoid the men, being careful not to speak nor to meet their gaze should they happen to pass on the sidewalk.

But one night she was startled out of sleep by a loud, insistent pounding on her door. She groped her way through the darkness, flipped on the living room light and made sure the chain lock was in place.

"Who is it?" she cried.

"Me. Duncan," her neighbor answered. "I'm sick. Open up."

She opened the door a crack.

Duncan shoved open the door, snapping the chain, and exclaimed, "What's going on? Whatta'ya doin' here? Where's Peter?"

"What do you want?" Shelley gasped, stunned with terror.

The man stared at her quizzically, then blurted, "Whatta'ya doin' in my place?"

A sudden wave of comprehension and relief swept over Shelley. "Don't you see? You have the wrong apartment. You live next door!"

Duncan scrutinized her sharply, then muttered something under his breath and stumbled back into the darkness. Shelley, breathless and trembling, slammed the door shut and locked it. "He was drunk," she reasoned, quelling the terror, pushing it back down inside her chest. "He was drunk, that's all."

Nevertheless, the fear did not subside; and at last, in desperation, Shelley telephoned Chad. She needed to hear his voice again, needed the comfort only he could give. But it was not Chad who answered the phone. It was Diana.

Speechless, Shelley slammed down the receiver. Bitterness against Chad erupted afresh, bordering on hatred. Shelley vowed then that she would never telephone her husband again—in fact, would never again turn to him for help of any kind.

Days later, when Chad telephoned to see how she was feeling, Shelley found herself venting her anger over Diana's presence in their house the evening of her call. "It was the last time I saw Diana," Chad insisted. "When you telephoned I was getting my keys in another room because I was about to go out. I had just told Diana I wouldn't be seeing her again, that it's you I love. It's over with her, Shelley. I've prayed for God's forgiveness. I want us to try again."

"Just like that, your affair has ended?" she retorted

"It's true, Hon, listen—"

Shelley slammed the phone down abruptly, refusing to listen. How could she possibly believe anything Chad told her now? "Why, God?" she cried. "Maybe you can forgive him, but I can't."

During the days that followed, Shelley struggled frequently with her emotions. She caught herself staring into space, brooding or standing at the window watching nothing at all while the minutes escaped, leaving her puzzled by the sudden lapse of time. Occasionally she cried for no reason at all. The smallest incident could prompt her tears—the baby's unexpected kick, the song of birds outside her window, a nostalgic tune on the radio. Thoughts of God's forgiveness, her own bitterness.

In self-defense Shelley set up projects for herself: refinish the bassinet she had picked up at a garage sale, crochet an afghan for the baby, make a silk flower arrangement for the coffee table.

Shelley was busy refinishing the bassinet one afternoon when her mother telephoned—"just for a chat." But it was not difficult to detect the real motive behind her mother's call. "Your divorce becomes final soon, doesn't it, dear?"

"Yes," Shelley admitted cautiously.

"Have you considered talking with Chad?" the older woman questioned, her tone mildly accusing.

"No," said Shelley. "We have nothing to say; you know that."

"No, Shelley, I don't know that. Chad has called me several times. He wants you to come home. A divorce between you two is the easy way out. It's not God's way."

"You can't say that, Mother," said Shelley firmly. "There's nothing easy about it. You make it sound like the divorce is *my* fault. Chad is responsible for what happened. Not me."

Her mother's voice was edged with a pain that startled Shelley. "Chad's mistake—his sin—greatly wounded your marriage; but dear, the potential for your family is still alive. Believe me, I know. Chad has found God's forgiveness; now he needs yours."

"How dare you take Chad's side—defend him."

"Oh, Shelley," her mother said, "I want what's best for you and Chad and the baby. You're so unhappy these days. So broken—"

"It's no good, Mother," Shelley insisted. "Knowing what I know about Chad, I could never be happy with him again."

Her mother was silent for a moment before replying. "Well, yes, many couples today see divorce as the answer to their problems. But, Shelley, the success of a Christian marriage isn't measured by your own happiness but by your yieldedness to Christ. You're well aware of Chad's failure, but are you also aware of your own?"

It was all Shelley could do to keep from hanging up the telephone. Where was her mother's loyalty? How could she be so unsympathetic, so unfeeling? Shelley resolved that she must never again turn to her mother for emotional support or encouragement. Why, in fact, had she never before noticed her mother's shortsightedness and lack of compassion?

Shelley was in no mood that evening for the ruckus that occurred in the apartment next door. The man and woman argued and fought incessantly. Their baby screamed. Nothing could block out the shouts and accusations that filtered through the frail walls. Shelley sat in perturbed silence before her blaring television set, trying to concentrate on Peter Jennings' news report, but the opposing noises only gave her a headache. Finally she went to bed, but her tears of frustration kept falling. As she drifted off to sleep, she prayed, "Please, dear God, don't ask me to forgive Chad."

Hours later Shelley awoke to another sound. Fuzzy with sleep she reached across the empty bed. "Chad, Chad, where are you?" she cried. "I'm so afraid—"

Dazed, she perched on one elbow and listened. Strange creaking, snapping sounds came from outside. Someone was prying open her front door! Shelley slipped out of bed and threw on her robe. She stole quickly into the living room. Her heart pounded so loudly now that she could scarcely hear the peculiar scratching sounds—but no, wait, they were still there. Shelley's breath caught as she imagined one of her drunken neighbors breaking down her door. What could she do? Where could she run—in her condition?

Shelley opened the door just a crack, her chain lock in place, fully expecting to see a man outside her door. But there was no one. Instead, in front of the adjacent apartment housing the feuding family, a great orange glow cut apart the cool blue silence of the night. Smoke. Flames. She stiffened, terrorized. The baby kicked, protesting inside of her—stirring her to action. Her eyes smarted, her hands trembled as she dialed 9-1-1.

"Fire," she gasped, sucking for air. "Hurry—"

Shelley left the phone dangling, threw open her door and rushed outside. As the flames exploded from the neighbors' door, she raced to the landlord's apartment at the end of the complex and pounded fiercely. Momentarily the door opened, the landlord appeared—groggy and grumpy. Spotting the flames, she cried, "I'll get an extinguisher. Call the fire department!"

"I've already called them."

As Shelley raced back to her apartment, she could hear the commotion gathering—tenants shouting, people spilling out of their apartment cubicles, the terrible crackling, popping noises of hurricane-like flames mercilessly devouring woodwork and walls. She stared about wildly, aware for the first time that the fire could destroy her apartment too. What should she try to save? Which possessions should she take with her? Her mind was blank. She could think of nothing—except her wedding photo album in the bottom desk drawer. She yanked open the drawer, seized the album and stumbled back into the hallway.

Duncan was there, sober, his eyes dark, bleak. He grabbed Shelley's arm and hurried her along outside to the parking lot, choking as they ran.

Sirens split the air with their shrill, haunting wail, engulfing even the sharp, spitting noises of the flames. Shelley, shivering from cold, from fear, and from an agonizing sort of excitement, joined several other tenants who hovered together in bewilderment, watching the fire.

"It's terrible, terrible," moaned one woman.

"I heard several people screaming," murmured another. "That's what woke me up."

"That was only me," Shelley whispered shakily. "Just me."

"Was anyone caught in there?" asked a woman in a maroon robe.

"My next door neighbors—a man and woman and their small child," said Shelley.

Firemen were swarming over the complex with their hoses and ladders, darting about swiftly, moving with precision to quench the flames, urging everyone back away from danger. Through the darkness Shelley could barely distinguish the flurry of activity as several firemen slipped into the apartment. Minutes later she saw men reappearing, moving heavily, carrying—what? Bodies?

"Dear Lord, let them be alive," Shelley whispered.

Shortly, Shelley's landlady came bustling toward them, her hair fluttering about her head like wispy, gray bird wings. "They have them all out," she announced, her voice quavering slightly. "They're alive."

"Will they be all right?" asked Shelley urgently.

"I don't know. I overheard the firemen. The woman and baby weren't burned—only overcome by smoke. They were in the bedroom. But the man was seriously burned. He was on the living room couch where the fire started."

"How did it start?" asked someone nearby.

"The fireman said it could have been a cigarette in the sofa did it," replied the landlady. "Of course, he says there'll be an investigation, but I'm sure that's what happened. That man drank so much and he always had a cigarette in his hand. And, oh, the fights those two had—even tonight I heard them. But no...no sense in going into all that now."

"Is there anything I can do?" offered Shelley.

The landlady patted Shelley's arm and smiled. "No, my dear, you've already done it. You woke us before it was too late and probably saved us all. You worked a miracle."

"No," said Shelley softly, "it was God who worked the miracle."

"Maybe so. But if that poor burned-out family has another chance at life, it's because of you. Not that they're likely to appreciate it though; they're so bent on destroying each other. But then, who knows? Maybe a close call like this will make them see things differently."

Shelley clutched her wedding album against her chest. "Yes, another chance—another chance at life," she murmured, but she wasn't thinking now of the fire or of her neighbors, but of Chad and herself—and their baby. She touched her landlady's arm and said, "The fire is out now. Do you suppose it's all right for me to go back to my apartment?"

The woman looked surprised. "No, my dear. It's not safe yet. But check with the firemen. What is it? Are you feeling okay?"

Shelley nodded. "I'm a little shaky—but I'll be all right. I've just got to find a phone and telephone my husband."

"Your husband? But I thought—"

"I know. We're practically divorced. But it's possible, just possible, that God worked more than one miracle tonight."

Stalemate

What does a woman do when the man she loves doesn't share her newfound faith?

"It's not too late to change your mind, Beth," Jim says in that super cool offhand way of his.

I am smiling. Actually I am a Raggedy Ann doll with the willpower, the steel fabric of broadcloth and cotton stuffings. In other words, a powder puff! My smile is pasted on, brilliant, and my eyes remain wide open, unblinking. Button eyes. You will notice also that my heart is painted Valentine red for all the world to see. It reads, "I love you."

I shake my head determinedly. "No, I can't, Jim."

"Why not?"

"You know why not. You don't want to go into it here, do you?"

Jim glances around at the scores of people milling about, then looks down at his watch. He winks mischievously. "I have 15 minutes before boarding time. That should be long enough to persuade you."

I give him a look that says, *Don't do this to me!* He catches the glance all right, but tosses it right back at me. We stand there like dorks while passersby, pushing and shoving against us, cast glances that seem to say, "Move it or lose it." We move.

We are waiting at Gate 18 at L.A. International Airport on a crisp winter evening. Things are different these days. Fewer travelers. Too many delays. Security is tight. Baggage is guarded. No one—except passengers—can go beyond the checkpoint. In self-defense we decide to go sit down. Together we stare out the huge windows at the great silver planes coming in and going out. We gaze mechanically, not really aware of the planes. Actually we are still arguing vehemently, in our heads. Silently, where no one can hear. This whole confrontation thing is going on behind closed doors. In locked minds. We know it is happening but neither of us will speak of it.

"I hate airports," I say, plucking conversation out of the air.

"You said you love airports," counters Jim.

"When did I say that?"

"Two weeks ago, when I arrived."

"I like meetings, not partings," I reply, and realize too late what I've said.

Jim is aware of it too. He uses it as a weapon, to wound me. "The parting is your idea," he says accusingly.

I had it coming, so I don't retaliate. Ignoring his implication, I stare into space and absently twist my purse strap.

Jim won't let up. "I still don't see why we can't resolve things," he says with a tenderness that makes me want to weep.

I bite my lower lip. I don't dare look at him. "I've told you—"

Jim puts his arm around me. His touch is electric. "All you've told me is that you've become a—a religious person. Well, Beth—honey—that's all right. I believe in God too. I don't have anything against going to church, if that's what a person wants."

I give Jim a sidelong glance. There's no mockery in his expression. But I'm not encouraged either. He's come this far before. But that's it. From then on it's a dead-end street. Still, I pursue it.

"You say you believe in God. Well, what do you believe?"

Jim shrugs. I can tell he's trying not to show his irritation. "I believe He exists—"

"Well, what do you think of Jesus Christ?" I persist gently.

Jim's eyes turn icy blue. "That's your department, Beth. I have no opinion."

It still surprises me that my heart wrenches so when someone talks that way about my new Lord and Savior. I am struck by a disturbing realization: Jim and I are standing in two separate worlds shouting across to each other. We face a distance even greater than the miles to the desert sands where he is going, going without God. We are separated even more by belief and unbelief, distanced with God between us. There is no way we can communicate, no way to touch unless one of us steps across to the other. Resolutely I tell myself I cannot give up the world I have found in Christ. It is too precious, too wonderful. It is up to Jim to make a move, not me.

"You know I'm an agreeable guy, Beth," he remarks pleasantly, fishing for something in his jacket pocket. He brings out a little box and holds it toward me in the palm of his hand. "This is still yours if you want it."

My eyes steer carefully away from the shiny black box, but its contents are vivid, clear in my mind—a lovely diamond engagement ring to turn the plain little Raggedy Ann into a beautiful fairy princess, loved and wanted by the charming prince. "You already have my answer, Jim," I say in my steeliest voice.

"Beth, maybe you should keep it. I won't need it where I'm going," he says sadly. "Not in Saudi."

"No, Jim," I say again firmly, masking the pain I feel inside.

He shrugs and puts the ring away. "Just thought you might have changed your mind," he says, trying to sound nonchalant. But I know I have hurt him, and that hurts me.

Jim glances at his watch again. "About five minutes," he says matter-of-factly. We watch the people around us. Everyone moves in a state of great agitation. Businessmen stride briskly, carrying briefcases and overcoats. Mothers grasping the hands of small crying toddlers balance diaper bags and baby paraphernalia under their arms. I notice that their eyes seem to rove over the crowd in a silent plea for help. *I need help too*, I think wordlessly.

Families hover together in small intent units, locked in private conversations. Young lovers cling to each other in secret reverie, oblivious of the bustling world about them. Somehow only Jim and I fail to fit the image of those around us bidding fond farewells. We do not fit the stereotype, the mold of parting lovers. Perhaps that's the trouble. We don't fit anywhere.

Since Jim arrived home from the university two weeks ago, my life has been turned topsy-turvy. Neither he nor I suspected what a difference my faith would make in our relationship. He came home for the sole purpose of presenting me with a diamond, urging me to marry him at once. My head was full of visions of a fantastic wedding following his graduation from college next June. But he told me then that there would be no graduation in June. His reserve unit was being called up. Jim was heading for the Gulf—without God. He loves me. He wants me to marry him.

But for two weeks now we have existed in a stalemate.

Our lives hang suspended. We are beating the air. How can I convince him I am not the person he loved when he went away? How can I give my life, my love, to someone who doesn't love Christ as I do?

For two weeks we have talked about this. We have argued, even bickered. But neither of us has won over the other. One must win, one must lose. Not lose exactly—give in. But if I give in, how much will I lose?

Now it is time for Jim to leave, to don his uniform, and we have not really settled anything between us. I refused Jim's ring, but he will not accept my refusal. Over and over he has tried to convince me that he would never prevent me from attending church, from worshiping as I please. He says he would respect my beliefs. But he also says he would expect the same freedom for himself—to live as he pleases. He would not go to church. He would not *believe.* Again and again he says he sees no problem for us. He says we can make things work.

But how? I ask. How?

Suddenly my mind springs alive as a voice over the loudspeaker announces Jim's flight. It is time for him to pass the security checkpoint alone, board the plane. In a burst of emotion, Jim sweeps me into his arms and kisses me soundly. I surrender to his embrace, my senses dazzled by his warmth, his touch, the heady fragrance of his after-shave. I am so at home in his arms.

Then he releases me and clasps both my hands in his, squeezing so hard I nearly wince. "Just tell me this, Beth. Do you love me?"

"Yes, but—"

"Then you keep this." Fumbling in his pocket, he produces the engagement ring and presses it into my hand.

"But, Jim, I—"

"Stifle yourself, woman," he quips. "You love me, so wear my ring. Let yourself get used to it and you'll never take it off, believe me."

I stare at him, too dumbfounded to speak. He brushes my lips with a farewell kiss, flashes a triumphant grin, then turns and strides away. I watch him go, my fingers folded over the tiny eternal circle of his ring.

Then, from deep within me the sound wrenches itself loose and escapes in a sudden, emphatic, "Nooo!"

I run after Jim, catch his arm and push the ring back into his hand. In a voice light with wonder, I cry, "I love you, but I love Christ more!"

The warmth in his eyes turns cold. "No second chances, my darling," he warns me. "I might not come back."

My own words are all used up. I can only watch mutely as Jim pivots in anger and stalks away, without looking back.

For several long minutes my feet seem riveted to the floor. I cannot move. I can scarcely breathe. I watch the lines dwindle as people are absorbed into the steel belly of the plane. I stand motionless until the plane is loaded, the doors closed. At last the engines roar, and the sleek silver hulk begins to move.

As if hypnotized, I watch the great gleaming airliner taxi onto the runway, gradually sever itself from the earth, and slowly, gracefully climb into the luminous heavens.

Jim is gone. The thought stuns me. It is like a woeful echo ringing over and over in my mind. Automatically I turn and begin to walk. Slowly at first, as if in a daze. Then more quickly, with the hint of purpose in my steps.

I am on my way out of the terminal. My heels clack sharply on the tile as I walk. I stride quickly, growing breathless. My mind begins to whirl with new thoughts.

Now I am nearly running. My mind races with me. I realize it will take time, perhaps a long time, for the wound I feel inside to heal; time for me to forget about Jim. Will I ever forget? Will I completely recover? Only God knows! Will Jim ever believe? I do not know.

But of one thing I am certain: My life no longer hangs suspended. I am not beating the air. I know now what I am and what I am not.

I am not a spineless Raggedy Ann doll. I am not a beautiful fairy princess. But my heart swells with praises. I am a child of God! I know where I'm going. I know who's going with me!

This Marriage Thing

What does a woman do when her husband wants a stay-at-home wife and mother?

Marion pressed the spatula down vigorously on the hamburger patties, so that hot beads of grease spattered mercilessly on the enameled surface of her copper-toned stove. "This stuff is all fat," she said, letting irritation color her voice.

"Then buy the extra-lean stuff," said her husband. He looked like a young Johnny Carson, and he had Carson's dryness without the wit. He was too sober, scowling even now as he tore the cellophane off a package of buns.

"Extra-lean costs more, Jack, you know that."

He shrugged. "I said we could pick up some burgers out, but you said no."

She flipped the patties over and pressed them again. "They cost more out, and mine are better."

"Speaking of better, you could stand a better diet," he said, cagily easing the remark into the conversation.

"What's that supposed to mean?" She knew, but let him say it.

"You know."

"Right, I know. I hear it all the time. The girls at work, even my boss. You all sound alike."

"You want a healthy baby, don't you?"

She put her hands on what was left of her hips. She knew she looked like a cross between Lucille Ball and a beach ball, with her flame-red hair and watermelon tummy. It wasn't a pretty combination. "Really, Jack," she protested, "what kind of question is that? Do I want a healthy baby? No, I want a Tootsie Pop. Are you trying to make me feel guilty or something?"

He ignored her question and took the defensive. "So now you're condemning me because I want our baby to be healthy."

She took the hamburger buns out of his hands. "Believe it or not, Jack, it's what I want too. I gave up hot fudge sundaes, sausage pizza and Coke. I don't even eat rare meat since I read that article in that health magazine. And you know how I hate well-done steak."

"I'm not criticizing you, Marion," Jack replied. "I don't even know how on earth we got into this. I just want our baby to be—"

"Then let's forget it," she said curtly, scooping the hamburgers onto the buns. "The doctor says the baby's fine."

Jack retrieved jars of catsup, mustard and pickles from the refrigerator and followed his wife to the table. "How was your day?" he asked, settling on a safe, neutral topic.

She played along. "All right. Mr. Parker will be leaving for London next week. We have a lot of work to finish before then."

"I suppose Mr. Parker feels he can't get along without

you," Jack mused as he unscrewed the catsup cap and generously doused his burger.

Marion sat down across from him and eyed him quizzically. "Is there a deeper meaning in that remark?"

"No. It's just a comment. An observation." He bit into the hamburger.

"You're forgetting something, Jack."

"Oh, yeah," he said, swallowing his mouthful. Bowing his head, he prayed perfunctorily for God's blessing on the food. Then he glanced at Marion, who said nothing. "I suppose you're thinking I didn't sound very earnest, right?"

"I wasn't going to mention it. You know what they say about people living in glass houses not casting stones." Marion held a wedge of dill pickle between her fingertips. The juice was beginning to trickle down her fingers.

"I guess neither one of us has been much good at praying lately." Jack reached for a paper napkin from the container on the table and handed it to her. Under his breath, he added, "And it's not going to get any better until we get things straightened out."

Marion set the pickle on her plate and wiped off her hands. "I hope you don't think it's all my fault."

He stared at her in surprise. "No. Is that what you think? I'm well aware you're not the only one to blame for the tension around here lately. It's just that I hate this uncertainty. We have to come to some decision."

"*Your* decision, you mean."

"No, I mean *our* decision. You're seven months pregnant. We have to decide something pretty soon."

Marion pushed back her chair and stood up. "I forgot something to drink," she said, changing the subject. "Milk all right?"

"Yeah, fine. Did you hear what I said?"

Marion went to the refrigerator and removed a carton of

milk. She filled two glasses. "I heard you, Jack, but I can't answer. I feel like you're pushing me into a corner, and I don't like it."

"I don't like what this whole thing is doing to our marriage," said Jack sullenly. "All we do is bicker—or hedge. We can't even relax and talk to each other anymore."

"It doesn't have to be that way," replied Marion, setting the milk glasses on the table. "Just accept how I feel, Jack. I don't want to quit my job. I don't want to give up my career for the baby. There's no reason I can't take a leave of absence and get a sitter a few months after the baby is born."

"That's exactly the problem—"

"No, Jack. There would be no problem if you weren't so—so old-fashioned in your ideas."

Jack shook his head in wonderment. "You know, Marion, I must be crazy. I had this idea that all I had to do was marry a Christian girl and my marriage would be perfect. There would be no real problems, no serious disagreements, because we'd always be of one mind in the Lord. But it hasn't worked out that way at all, has it? We're hardly ever of one mind about anything!"

"You want a servant, a slave," said Marion accusingly. "I don't believe God wants me to give up my life for you and the baby. He wants me to be a whole person too. If that's selfish, I can't help it."

"Really? Well, the Bible says you're to be subject to your own husband," countered Jack, "or have you conveniently forgotten that?" He drained his milk and thumped the empty glass noisily on the table as if to make his point perfectly clear.

Marion sat down and took a bite of her hamburger. After a moment she cleared her throat and said, quite calmly, "That same Bible tells husbands to love their wives as Christ loves the Church. He died for the Church, Jack, remember?"

"You want me to die for you, Marion? Be a martyr? Is that what it'll take to make you happy?"

"Just give me a little breathing room, Jack. Don't force all these dusty stereotypes on me—your idea of the perfect little, obedient Christian wife."

"Don't worry, Marion," he dripped sarcasm. "There's no chance I'd confuse you with an image like that."

She met his gaze with a flash of anger in her green eyes. "Jack, I don't need your insults. I worked hard for five years to become an executive assistant at Brockton and Company. I'm good at my job and I love my work. I don't want anything—not even a baby—to change that."

"That's terrific," exclaimed Jack, slamming his fist on the table. "Maybe you've been reading too many women's magazines and listening too often to the crazy dames you work with. You're starting to sound like one of those women's libbers from the '60s. Only trouble is, Marion, this is the '90s!"

"Listen to yourself, Jack. If you're any example, male chauvinism is thriving as much in this decade as it did in the '50s!"

Jack's expression hardened, but his voice remained amazingly steady. "You're acting like a spoiled little girl, Marion. When are you going to get it through your head that you're about to become a mother? And that means responsibility!"

"It's your baby, too," she countered without missing a beat. "Why don't you stay home and take care of it? Men are doing that all the time these days."

Jack frowned. "We're going in circles again, Marion. Some men might be cut out to be Mr. Mom, but not me."

There was a long moment of silence before she said quietly, "But what if I'm not cut out to be *Mrs.* Mom?"

He eyed her curiously. "What are you saying, Marion—that you're scared of being a mother? Is that it?"

"I didn't say that."

"No, but you act like you don't want any part of this baby." He ran his fingers through his straw-blond hair. "I know we didn't plan on starting a family this soon. Maybe neither one of us is ready yet."

She twisted the corner of her napkin. "Are you saying we should have opted for—an abortion?"

"Of course not," he flared. "That was never an option for either of us. Certainly not for me!"

"For me neither," she said quickly. "If you know me at all, you know that, Jack."

He nodded, then said softly, "I guess that's one thing we agree on, Marion. God gave us this baby, to be born at this time. And He chose us to be its parents. I don't know why. But I know it's so."

Marion got up from the table and went into the living room. Jack followed her with a question. "You aren't through eating, are you?"

"Yes." She took a light jacket from the hall closet and slipped it over her shoulders, then picked up her handbag.

"Where are you going?" he asked.

"Out."

"Out? What kind of answer is that?"

She paused to look at him. "I'm going to Baskin-Robbins down the block. For an ice cream cone. Three scoops."

"I thought you swore off ice cream."

"Only hot fudge sundaes."

He followed her to the door. "Marion, wait. What's wrong? You act like—like you're running away from something."

She hovered in the doorway, one foot in, one foot out. Her eyes glistened as she answered, "I *am* running away, Jack. You guessed right. You're always right. You should be the Answer Man on TV."

"What are you talking about?"

"The baby. You said I'm scared of the baby."

"That was just idle talk. It didn't mean anything."

"Oh, but it did, Jack." Her shoulders sagged and she rocked back and forth a little, her arms crossed on her bountiful middle. "Don't you get it? I am afraid of the baby. A little itty-bitty baby I haven't even seen yet, unless you count those weird, floating patterns on the ultrasound screen."

He stared at her incredulously. "You're afraid—?"

"Yes! Of the baby! Of having it. Of taking care of it. Some prize I am, huh? Terrified of my own unborn child?"

Jack moved toward her, reaching out for her, ready to offer an embrace, but Marion slipped through the doorway and padded down the hall. "I need some fresh air," she called back. "Good night, Jack."

She moved as swiftly as her swollen body would carry her down the old stairway from their third-floor apartment to the street. The air was moist and cool; it looked as if it might rain at any moment. She slipped her arms into the sleeves of her jacket and walked down the tree-lined sidewalk toward Baskin-Robbins.

In a moment she heard Jack's footsteps behind her.

"Want some company?" he said, still several steps behind.

"It doesn't matter," she answered sharply.

He caught up with her and reached for her hand. "A lady shouldn't be out alone," he said lightly. "Besides, it looks like rain. A nasty night to be out."

"A lovely night," she argued. "Don't you smell the lilacs? It's a beautiful night."

"Yes, yes, that's just what I said. A wonderful night." Gently Jack pulled Marion to a stop. "Do you really want ice cream?"

"Yes. A triple-scoop heavenly hash."

"I'll ask again. Want some company?"

"I don't care. As long as I can keep walking. I don't ever want to stop."

"Wait, Marion." Jack held her fast. "Listen, hon, I didn't know—"

She turned away, lowering her gaze.

He persisted. "I didn't know you were afraid, you know, about the baby. I only said it to hurt you. I shouldn't have. I'm sorry. I had no idea you were really afraid."

"It doesn't matter," she said coolly.

"Yes, yes, of course it matters. Because—don't you see?—the truth is, I'm scared too, Marion. Parenthood is a whole new ball game for me too. I don't know the ground rules. I don't know if I'm going to be any good at it or if I'm going to botch the job. So much is at stake. Our baby's whole future!"

She met his gaze. "That's just how I feel, Jack. And when I think of having to face it all alone—"

He stared at her in surprise. "You're not alone, hon. We're in this together, all the way."

She shook her head slowly. "But I feel all alone, Jack. Like the baby's all my responsibility. Don't you understand? Until now, we've each had our jobs plus our life together, and everything fit. It was comfortable, predictable. But now my role is changing, and I don't know if I can handle it. I'm not sure I can adapt. I don't know who I'm supposed to be anymore."

Jack drew her into his arms and pressed her head against his shoulder. "It's okay, Marion. We're going to face this together. And if worse comes to worse, we'll be scared together." He chuckled under his breath. "Sure, we'll make mistakes with our kid. All parents do. Some humdingers, in fact. But we'll have the Lord to help us."

She turned her face toward his and breathed in the spicy fragrance of his cologne. "I guess that's something we've forgotten, haven't we, Jack?"

He nodded solemnly. "Yeah, we've really left God out of

things lately. And you can see what happens when we're left to our own devices."

"It's not a pretty sight," she smiled grimly. "Like me."

"You're a beautiful sight," he said, patting her round tummy. "I love you just the way you are."

She laughed. "You do not."

"But I want to. It's the unconditional love you mentioned earlier. Christ's love for the Church." He kissed her hair, her ear. "I want to be more loving, Marion. Help me."

"Let's help each other," she whispered.

He kissed the tip of her nose. "We have the Lord to help us."

"That's right. But He doesn't just erase all our problems."

"No, but He's the biggest plus a marriage can have."

"As long as we accept His help."

"Okay, so we both need to work on that."

She nodded. "Boy, do we ever!"

They walked along together arm in arm. "You still hungry for ice cream?" he asked.

She looked up and smiled. "What I really want is a hot fudge sundae."

"Sounds like a winner." He grinned. "But could we skip Baskin-Robbins and go home instead? I want to make for my wife the biggest hot fudge sundae ever."

"But the baby—?"

"Maybe our baby likes ice cream too."

They turned and walked back toward the timeworn apartment building. The night air was already cooler, heavy with moisture. Marion inhaled. She could almost taste the gathering rain.

"Jack, we still have some decisions to make," she ventured as they reached the stairway. "Like, what am I going to tell my boss in a few weeks?"

"I don't have the answer, Marion," he said, leading her up

the stairs. "It's something we'll have to pray about. I can't change my feelings overnight."

"I know. Same here. But maybe I could work at home, you know, for a few months after the baby comes, and then go back to Brockton part-time until—"

"Until the baby starts kindergarten?" he suggested.

"I don't know. I'm not promising anything, Jack. It's just a thought."

They reached their door, and he jabbed the key into the lock and turned it. "Who knows? Maybe I could even arrange my schedule to take care of the baby one or two days a week."

She looked wide-eyed at him. "Would you want to, Jack? And would your boss let you?"

"Probably not, but it's something to look into. I honestly never gave it a thought before, but anything's possible." He opened the door and reached inside for the light switch. "All I can say for sure, Marion, is that it's going to take the two of us working together to get through this whole thing."

"Give and take all the way, right? It's a tall order."

"Yeah, it is. But I believe God has good things planned for both of—I mean, all *three* of us, if we'll just let Him show us the way."

"You know, He's got His work cut out for Him," Marion teased. "He's dealing with two very mulish, pigheaded, intractable, opinionated—"

Jack leaned down and silenced her with a kiss, then whispered, "He already knows, Marion. God knows how stubborn we are—and He loves us anyway!" They both chuckled. Then tenderly he guided his very pregnant wife inside and shut the door.

Stranger in My Home

What does a woman do when she suddenly finds herself the mother of someone else's child?

The child sat looking out at the rain, her fingers pressed eagerly against the window, as if they would break through the glass and discover another world, something magnificent, a wonderland. She stared at the rain with wide, astonished eyes, saying nothing. Just watching.

"Janee, keep your hands off the glass," Barbara prodded gently. "We don't want smudge marks, do we?"

Obediently the child removed her hands. A flicker of shame crossed the four-year-old's face, but her eyes remained unblinking. Janee said nothing; it was an accusing silence. To break the awkward stillness, Barbara said, "Would you like some bread and butter?"

A quick shake of the head.

"No? Well, Mark and Becky and Anne will be home from school soon. Won't that be nice? You'll have someone to play with..." Barbara let her words drift off; Janee wasn't listening.

Already she had pressed her face back to the window, to the soft pattering rain.

The room was dark, moving with soft shadows. Janee sat framed by the curtains. The shallow light that penetrated the window effused a dusky halo around Janee's wheat-colored hair.

Barbara sat across the room on the sofa, sewing a button on one of Dale's shirts. She felt vaguely guilty now, and a little angry. The child's lack of response perplexed her. Why couldn't Janee blow up now and then, cry or throw a tantrum, like Mark and Becky and Anne did occasionally? What kind of child was she that she never said anything, never showed any feelings at all? Glancing at Janee, Barbara saw that she was biting her lower lip and her fingers fidgeted nervously with the hem of her dress. *Something's going on in that head of yours,* thought Barbara ruefully.

She nodded hopefully toward the TV set. "Do you want to watch 'Muppet Babies'?"

Janee looked around, moving her head with a deliberate slowness; her mouth froze into a pout. "No, I don't like 'Muppet Babies,'" she said.

Barbara tossed her husband's shirt on the couch and went to the kitchen to check the pot roast. Lifting the lid so that quick curls of steam escaped, Barbara noticed that her hand trembled. She let the lid fall back into place with a clatter and stared at her hands.

Janee's doing this to me, she thought dismally. *She's like a stranger in my house—taking over. My life isn't my own anymore; everything's tilted out of joint. It's simply not working out. She can't stay here any longer!*

Barbara glanced at the wall calendar. Janee had been with them more than a month now—since New Year's Day. That dreadful day she and Dale received the call from the family attorney in San Francisco. Dale had answered the phone, and she watched as his features froze. Looking dazed, he handed Barbara the phone, and she listened to the terrible news: Dale's sister Nancy and her husband, driving home from San Mateo, had been struck and killed by a drunken driver. Their daughter Janee, left home with a baby-sitter, was safe. Then came the request (a request made long ago by Janee's parents): Would Barbara and Dale fly up from Los Angeles to pick up Janee? Would they come immediately? Would they take her home with them?

Of course!

But now Barbara reflected that there was a difference between offering help in time of need and finding oneself suddenly the permanent mother of someone else's child. How far was one expected to go in bearing another's burden? she wondered.

After all, it wasn't as if Barbara hadn't tried to reach Janee. During those first few days she had tried very hard to make the child feel as if she were her own. She was determined to be a mother to her, to make up somehow for the child's terrible loss.

But Janee refused every offer of affection. She did not want to be tucked into bed at night; she turned her face to the wall when Barbara leaned down to kiss her good night. She gave no indication of desiring or needing Barbara's attention.

The worst moment had come toward the end of that first week. Janee had been playing in the backyard, riding the neighbor's tricycle. Barbara heard a scream and rushed outside to find the tricycle overturned and Janee crumpled on the ground, sobbing, her knee badly skinned. Impulsively Barbara took Janee into her arms and held her, murmuring as she would to her own child, "There, there, baby."

Fiercely Janee had pulled away from Barbara's embrace, crying, "I'm not your baby. You're not my mommy. I hate you!"

Barbara had watched, stricken and numb, as the child ran into the house. After that incident, she made it a point to do nothing to invite Janee's rebuke. Janee had not cried or shown any real emotion since that afternoon. An uneasy truce had settled over the household, but Barbara wasn't sure she could endure the oppressive atmosphere much longer.

"Dear God, how much am I supposed to take?" she said aloud, adjusting the flame under the roast.

Barbara's husband, Dale, was home on time for dinner this evening. Often he was away on short business trips—two or three days at a time—and not home for dinner at all. But tonight he was there, and Barbara knew they would have to talk.

Dale was a tall, big-boned man, fleshy and full-faced, with wispy, rust-colored hair and a generous grin; a man who relished his food, who pored over a meal, concentrating, savoring everything he ate. He refused to discuss anything at the table, but that was all right with Barbara. She would wait until the children were in bed before bringing up the problem of Janee.

"What do you mean you want to talk about Janee?" he said when she broached the subject later that evening. He was stretched out on the couch, nearly asleep. He shook his head, as if to diffuse his weariness. "What's there to say about Janee?"

"She can't stay here any longer, Dale."

Her husband sat up startled and stared at her, his eyes narrowing. "What are you talking about? She's here. There's no question now."

Barbara sat down beside him on the couch. "Yes, there is," she insisted. "You aren't home enough to know how it's been. You don't know."

"All right. Tell me what's the matter." There was an intensity in his eyes as he spoke.

"She has nothing to do with me. She avoids me. She's been here a month and she's still a stranger."

Dale shook his head ponderously. "Barby, Barby, you have to give her time. She just lost her parents. She's a baby. What do you want?"

Leaning forward slightly, Barbara pressed her fingertips against her temples as if she might alleviate something swelling within her skull, a pressure, a nagging irritation, growing. "I'm being a shrew about this, I know I am," she said shakily. "I shouldn't be this way, but I can't help myself. Dale, our own children are in school now. We had a routine. Now I'm tied down again. With no time for outside activities or my friends. I missed the luncheon with the girls yesterday...I didn't think I'd ever feel this way."

Dale lowered his head a little, looking her full in the face, and asked, "Just how do you feel?"

"I feel caught, trapped, a prisoner in my own house. I can't be myself. She watches me. She hates me. I feel it."

Dale slapped his knee angrily. "That's ridiculous! She's a little girl. She doesn't hate."

"I knew you'd think I was crazy," sighed Barbara, slumping back defeatedly. "I think it myself."

Dale reached over and put his arm around his wife. "No, honey, I don't think that. We'll figure something out."

Barbara pulled away gently, turning her shoulders slightly to face her husband. "Dale, why couldn't she stay with your sister Pam? She and Benny don't have any children."

Grunting audibly, he scowled and fixed his gaze on the fireplace across the room. At last he cleared his throat and said accusingly, "You know why Janee is with us and not with Pam."

"Because Nancy wanted it that way," Barbara replied simply.

"Because if anything ever happened to them, Nancy wanted Janee in a Christian home. That's why she's here."

"But we already have three children. Pam and Benny—"

"Pam and Benny would never take Janee to church," countered Dale, his voice rising precariously. "They have no interest in God. They don't have room in their lives for Janee; they don't have room for anyone but themselves."

Barbara sat forward stiffly. She clasped her hands together so that the bones of her knuckles stood out white under the thin flesh of her fingers. "Dale, what you've got to understand is that I'm no good for Janee either. I can't reach her. I can't give up my life to a child I can't reach. It would be better for her to leave now, before she's settled."

Dale stood up and walked across the room. He put his hand on the mantle of the fireplace and leaned heavily, as if he were not sure his legs would support his bulk. Quietly, so that Barbara had to strain to hear, he said, "I felt God wanted Janee here, Barby. You pray and search your heart; you pray for God to show you. Next week, Monday and Tuesday, I have to be away. But Tuesday night I'll be home and we'll make a decision then about Janee. We'll do whatever you think best."

Barbara went to her husband and received his embrace. "I don't want to send Janee away," he told her. "But you're my wife, Barby. I love you. I have to consider you first."

Later, as Barbara circled the coming Tuesday on her calendar, she realized that setting a specific date for their decision gave her a curious sense of relief. She was no longer facing an interminable road with Janee. Barbara had only to give the word and the child would be out of her life. Then everything would be as it had been. Barbara could once again devote herself to her own three children, and certainly Pam would be happy to have a child to raise. Pam needed someone like Janee. And wouldn't Pam be willing to see that the child went to church? Wouldn't she do that much?

Early Monday morning Dale left for San Diego. He promised to try to be back in Los Angeles in time for dinner Tuesday evening. Barbara said nothing about the decision they would make at that time, but privately she stole a relieved glance at the special date circled on her calendar.

Monday evening seemed marked by a surprising aura of quietness. Serenity. The children did their homework without being prodded; there were no arguments or fights; even Janee sat quietly after dinner coloring with large wax crayons in a Donald Duck coloring book. For the first time in weeks, Barbara felt contentment inside. Perhaps her home was finally righting itself.

Perhaps we will survive after all, she thought as she gathered the pajama-clad children together in Becky and Anne's room for family devotions. Loudly and energetically, they sang familiar choruses and then listened with a minimum of restlessness as Barbara read them a Bible story.

Spurred on by her evident success, Barbara smiled at Janee and asked if she would like to pray tonight. Janee's eyes shot wide open and she drew back as if she had been slapped. Vigorously she shook her head.

"All right then, Mark, would you pray tonight please?"

As Mark prayed, Barbara listened with dismay to the light scurrying sounds and the pattering of feet as Janee scampered off Becky's bed and ran out of the room. Moments later, Barbara found Janee in the small sewing room at the end of the hall that had been made over into a bedroom for the child. Janee had pulled the Raggedy Ann doll off the toy shelf and sat huddled in a corner, clutching the doll in her arms. The stuffed arms and legs of the doll stuck out crazily in several directions, the orange yarn hair was askew, and the painted face seemed to grin mockingly at Barbara.

Swiftly she picked up the child, put her in bed, tucking in the blankets with quick, efficient movements, then walked out of the room, flicking off the light switch with a decisiveness that left her trembling.

Later, in her own room, lying in bed, Barbara prayed impatiently, "Dear God, what else can I do? I simply can't help her!" Then, as the trembling subsided, Barbara reflected sadly that it was much easier to love people en masse—the homeless, the brave, the unsaved, all the people of the world whom one could clump together and tie with labels. But to love persons on a one-to-one basis was something else, an ability that seemed to elude Barbara completely.

"How do you love a child who doesn't invite love? How do you love her?" she said aloud, but her voice drifted off like a fine wisp of smoke in the night; her words were muffled by restless, troubled sleep and endless tossing.

Early Tuesday morning, while it was still dark, Barbara felt herself jerked out of bed. Stumbling blindly to her feet, she was aware of an incredible trembling around her—the bed, the furniture, the walls. The floor itself shook violently with quick spasmodic jerks. In the same instant, she heard a low insistent rumbling, an obscure sound, guttural, threatening.

Barbara ran immediately to Becky and Anne's room, screaming at them to get out of bed. Clumsily the girls scrambled to their feet and followed her into the hall, where her son Mark was already waiting, breathless.

"Earthquake!" he cried, his face chalky with fear.

"Stay in the hallway, here, in the doorway," Barbara gasped, pulling the children toward her, against her body. Nothing can hit us here."

There was a sudden crash from another room—a drawer

shooting out of a dresser perhaps; then another noise, and another. Barbara could imagine it: knickknacks sliding off tables, a lamp falling somewhere, paintings rattling against walls, books cascading off shelves.

Like a fiercely protective mother hen, Barbara embraced her children, praying for the quake to cease, moving her lips silently as if observing a ritual. For terrifying seconds, the children remained motionless, hushed in her arms, swallowed up as she was by the greater motion—the writhing of the earth beneath their feet, the jolting, jarring quiver of walls around them.

After a moment, Barbara was aware that the convulsive jolts had subsided to a smooth rocking motion. The walls and ceiling emitted unearthly sounds—rhythmic creaking noises, low muffled groanings, insistent clatterings from deep within the house.

The temblor seemed eternal—waves of an ocean going on and on, pervasive, ubiquitous. But gradually—actually within moments—the tremors ceased; the house was still.

Barbara released her children and straightened her body. Her muscles ached; she felt stiff. She marveled that everything had happened and was over in a minute. She could not comprehend it. A minute, and yet forever had passed through that minute, absorbed it, absorbed everything, her strength, her senses. Her thoughts were out of focus, blurred. She couldn't think. And then, abruptly, with a shudder, she remembered Janee.

"Janee! Where's Janee?" she demanded of her children, who looked at her blankly.

Barbara ran down the hall to the sewing room, Janee's room, and shoved open the door. Janee stood at the far wall, pressed fiercely against it, her expression wild, vivid with alarm. She looked unreal somehow, the gesture of her body seemingly frozen in a moment of time, as if she were a delicate piece of sculpture, not quite complete and terribly vulnerable.

On the floor lay Janee's Raggedy Ann, crumpled beneath the spilled-out contents of a dresser drawer. Toys had fallen off the shelf—a teddy bear, a Barbie doll, several storybooks. But the child was apparently untouched.

"Are you all right?" cried Barbara.

The child began to scream.

Impulsively Barbara gathered Janee into her arms, kissing the tears, the mussed hair, feeling the warmth and anguish of Janee's small frantic body. She was stricken that in those few seconds, she had forgotten Janee. In that moment, as the child's anguish became her own, Barbara pleaded, "Janee, darling, forgive me. I didn't mean to leave you alone. How can I help you? How!"

Something stirred inside Barbara as she held the child close. A seed of understanding not quite realized, but growing, becoming—what? An awareness of her own human limits, her selfishness? Of the need within her for Christ's love, unconditional love, that gives to others and demands nothing in return? The insight was still unclear, its implications uncertain, but it was a beginning, a wedge in her soul for the flowering of Christ's Spirit, His love. One thing was certain: with the insight came hope, genuine, unmistakable.

"We have so much to learn about love, Janee," Barbara whispered into the child's hair, while she muffled her sobs against her breast. "I love you, Janee. I know that you are frightened and lonely. But we want you to stay with us. It'll take time for you to be happy here, but we have lots of time Both of us. Time to learn. Time to love."

Waiting

What does a woman do when her family's future lies in the hands of her job-seeking husband?

The baby cries all the time, always crying. He is in a new place, a new bed. The people he sees are strange. He does not remember them. He has not seen these people, his grandparents, since he was a few months old. That was Christmas, almost a year ago, when we drove the 600 miles to my parents' home so they could share Christmas with their two grandchildren.

It was cold and biting then—snow everywhere, making a common denominator of the world: shacks and mansions alike clothed in dazzling white. Now it is sultry hot, dead air hanging over everything, the earth scorched, everything parched dry.

My husband, Jim, suggested we come here. I was glad it was his idea, not mine. Whatever happens, I'm glad Jim began it. Whatever happens, he will take it better knowing it started with him, his idea.

This is a good time, he told me. As good a time as any. They're laying off guys all the time, he said, what with the downturn of the economy, signs of a recession, higher inflation threatening. If I get a better job now, I'll beat them all to the punch.

It is Jim's idea that we are here, that he is looking for a better job, going for interviews, submitting his resume to agencies that might hold the gold key to that special position we hope is out there for him.

We have prayed about this, Jim and I. About his dissatisfaction with his present job, the gnawing possibility of being laid off, the constant lack of money forcing us to stretch every dollar to provide for the four of us.

Debbie is not yet four; Brian, a year this month. In five years of marriage we have gone from two to four, doubled. The Lord has always provided; we have lacked no necessities. God has been good.

Jim and I sense that we stand on the verge of something. At the periphery of—what? A valley? A mountaintop? A great high, a great low? God knows. We have prayed and felt the shudder of God on our lives. We sense His moving, the subtle beginnings of movement. His stirring. He is doing something with us. He has begun something, and we have no idea of it. It is still beyond us, a feeling, an awareness. He has not made His will for us tangible yet.

When Jim heard there were several job opportunities in the city where my parents live, he said, "What do you think? Would you like to live near your family? They could see more of Debbie and Brian."

I smiled, not daring yet to answer.

There are no people that I love in the city where I live—no family, no close friends, no one outside of Jim and my children. I am fond of people—people in our church, neighbors who come occasionally for coffee, random acquaintances. But Jim and I seem to drift above them, beyond them, not tied to them, not tied strongly to anyone there.

Were we to live in my parents' city, we would have relatives, old friends, familiar faces that mean something. We could let the ties go deep, enjoying people who care as deeply for us.

This is something I have not admitted before—that I want deep ties. I want more for Jim and me than we have known. I try to keep such desires flexible, pliable in God's hands. Home, job, ties, love—as God wishes, please; as God wills. There is more that He wants for us, things I have no knowledge of. More for us to learn. We are beginning, starting to learn.

While Jim keeps appointments and goes for interviews, I remain with our children in my mother's house. While my father works and Jim is gone, my mother and I talk and watch the children.

It is morning now, and my daughter moves around us like a breeze we scarcely notice, coming and going with her doll, with her plastic dishes, making the kitchen her magic castle, Brian's high chair her private fort.

She goes to my mother who is feeding Brian and asks for a Popsicle. She leans against my mother's leg and begins to whine in a high soft voice. Please, please, Grandma. She goes to my mother too often since we came here, always asking my mother for things, hoping to get her way.

I tell my daughter no, not now—yes, after lunch, if she is good; and she returns reluctantly to her private fort. My mother and I go on talking, picking up where we left off. We bring up old times and laugh a lot, recalling secrets and jokes and bits of ancient gossip. It is strange and pleasant to be a daughter again, to remember how it used to be. She is still lovely, my mother; I still see her as gentle and fine and very wise.

She too hopes that Jim will find a job, that we will be able to move to this city. There are so many things we could do together, so much we could do, she tells me. She is feeding Brian, giving him scrambled eggs and apple juice, aiming the tiny silver spoon into his open mouth. He is quiet with her, responds to her gentleness. I am pleased.

Whenever we leave him, when he is alone, he cries. His cries are long and relentless; they do not stop. He does not know this place, this home that is so familiar to me. He cries until we go to him, soothing him with whispers and kisses.

My mother washes Brian's hands and face and scoops him from the rented high chair. She rocks him against her shoulder, but she is watching me. She has been watching me all morning. While we sorted recipes from old magazines, when I bathed Brian and she buttoned up Debbie and tied her laces, she watched, saying nothing, just watching. She is too wise.

This morning, Jim told me he will have his final interview today. This is the most promising, he said. He has had three others in this city, but nothing worked out. Something wrong in each case. But he hopes this one will turn out. It would be work he enjoys, a good salary, a good future. Surely the Lord wants this for us. Wouldn't it mean more money for the Lord's work too? More money to tithe? This morning Jim agreed when I mentioned this. But then he frowned. "Are we rationalizing?" he asked. "Are we trying to bribe God?" No, that is not in our hearts.

This morning Jim told me that if he does not get this job, we will go home. We will have to assume that the Lord wants us where we are, in the city we have lived in since our marriage. We will have to go on from there, waiting on the Lord. Be of good courage. Wait on the Lord.

My heart sank at his words, and I was stunned to realize I did not want to give up and go home.

My mother in her wisdom realizes that something is going

on in my head, in my heart. As she rocks Brian, muffling his sleepy songs against her shoulder, she watches me, knowing I have steeled my will, my feelings.

"I want this for you," she says. "The job for Jim, all of you moving here, being able to share your lives. I want it."

"So do I."

"Too much?"

"I don't know. Maybe. Do you think so?"

My mother's eyes are reading the wall of my brain. She is gentle. Her eyes are full of understanding. "What if you have to go back? What if there is nothing here for you?"

I answer, but the words shoot upward, tightening my throat. "We will have to go home, is all. What else can we do?"

"But are you willing to let it go at that?"

I am not able to be as calm and objective as my mother. My feelings come too fast, too quickly—they rush at me, knocking my senses down. At this moment I can't face my mother any longer, can't have her watching, reading me. I take Brian from her, pull him awkwardly into my arms; his drowsy body is limp and I can scarcely hold him. I explain that it is time for his nap; I will put him to bed. I leave my mother watching, saying nothing.

For a moment, the cubicle that is Brian's room will be my oasis, a secret corner. I need—must have—time alone. I cannot face myself unless I am alone. I put Brian in bed and he flops onto his stomach and closes his eyes. His fists move in small sudden jerks and his eyelids flutter once or twice. Then his body seems to relax, and I know he sleeps.

In my body there is a steel will that does not relax. My muscles are tied to it, my nerves strung on it. My will is strong, going through me like wire, like perfectly balanced circuits, miniature cables.

In an hour or two Jim will come home, driving up. I will hear his car, my heart hammering at the sound of his car. I will watch him come through the doorway, watch his expression, and I will know instantly, before he speaks, what happened.

It will be almost too much to bear—the instant before knowledge like an explosion cut short, throttled, suspended in time like a photograph; and then the instant of comprehension, knowing which way it went, and either the gushing sweep of relief or the sudden dead-thud of disappointment inside me.

I dread the pain, the love-labor, of reading my husband, of knowing so swiftly—from a single glance—the direction of our lives. It is too much to take at once.

I sit, pondering, watching my baby, watching Brian. When he is awake, in control of his small, chubby frame, he moves constantly, quickly, like an animal. He cries deep heavy sobs for things I cannot comprehend. I cannot always reach him. I can only offer blind comfort, and love.

But he sleeps now, his body relaxed, his skin rosy, his fingers open. There are no tears, no spasms of anger or fear arching his frame. He is at peace, content, his face full of gentle dreams.

I know by noon my husband will arrive and give me news. If it is good, we will rejoice. If not, what then? What will I do?

If only I could relax. Rest and let God work. Wait on the Lord. Be of good courage. Wait, I say.

I cover Brian, watching his face, his open hands. God, open my hands, my mind. Help me surrender my will. Give peace.

I sit down in the chair beside Brian's bed, pressing my hands out flat on my lap. I let the wires of bone and muscle go loose, easing up, smoothing out. I give up my will, feel the steel flex, crumble, dissolve, spin out, away.

I have perhaps an hour before Jim comes home.

An hour to pray.

Patterns

What does a woman do when she has suffered a miscarriage and her pregnant neighbor needs her help?

Julie Spencer stood at the foot of the stairs staring up at the dark, her hand holding—her fingers white with gripping—the railing, which was old and brown like the walls, old like the whole apartment house with its faded paint peeling off in thin hard strips.

Julie wanted to climb the stairs—yet didn't want to climb the stairs. That is, she knew God was telling her to go up, but more than anything in the world, she wanted to stay down.

In her own apartment that morning, while she served coffee and toast to her husband, while she rose to get him whatever he asked, he asked again if she would go upstairs. "I don't know," she answered. She really didn't know what she would do.

Mr. Stevens, the manager of their apartment house, heard the girl again, her husband told her. Heard her sobbing through the thin apartment walls. "He told me about it," her husband went on, "because he thought maybe you could do something. Help her. Talk to her."

Julie did not really know the girl who lived upstairs, had seen her only occasionally as they passed going in or out, exchanging polite murmurs and quick stranger's glances as they went their own way. She remembered thinking that the girl was terribly young, too young to be married and about to become a mother.

Standing now at the foot of the stairs, Julie wondered how she allowed herself to be talked into things, things she wanted no part of. Mr. Stevens was too nosy for his own good; it was none of his business that the girl cried, none of his business that the girl's husband worked nights, leaving her alone to cry. It was none of Julie's business either.

But her husband thought it was. "You go talk to her," he said. "You're a Christian, aren't you? It's time for you to get out of yourself. See if she needs help. Talk to her."

All right, all right. She was going. Not because Mr. Stevens said so. Not even because her husband said so. God said so. He said it as if He were using real words telling her she had to do this. So she would.

Before climbing the stairs, she closed her eyes once tightly, as if she were pulling the shades to keep out something she didn't want to see. She had to think. What would she say? What was she going to say to this girl who was about to have a baby?

And then it hit her again the way it hit her so many times when she wasn't on her guard; the thought stole her breath with its suddenness: not long ago she had been like the girl upstairs, only not so far along—and her baby, her baby—

But there was no baby.

Her thoughts had carried her upstairs; she was already at the girl's door, knocking, waiting. The girl appeared, showing her face around the door like a timid, curious bird.

"Mrs. Spencer," she breathed.

"Hello, Mrs. Crumpton. I—I don't want to interfere, but I thought perhaps we could talk."

"My name's Cassie. Please come in." Was the girl already drawing a mask of blankness over her face? Shutting her out before she began? "Please sit down," the girl invited. "I'll make tea—"

The apartment was a miniature of Julie's place, drab and somehow stale with years of use, years of sheltering families, storing their countless words and myriad doings inside slender walls. The furniture was sparse, worn, standing awkward and apologetic against papered walls or pushed clumsily into corners. It was all somehow terribly vulnerable, thought Julie, like the girl would have been, too, if she were not covering her needs with the blankness.

Julie felt increasingly ill at ease. It was as if she had run into the street to rescue someone, only to find that her help was unwanted, perhaps not even needed. This was no sobbing child; this was a composed young woman, reserved perhaps, but efficient even as she lumbered slowly to her kitchen for tea things and served them on the stubby coffee table.

Cassie gave Julie tea and thin cookies on ancient china—cups and saucers with faded pink flowers and fine scattered cracks making delicate patterns. Their talk fell into patterns too—worn, safe, predictable patterns. The weather. Apartment living. Their husbands' jobs. Where the best sales could be found.

Almost an hour of it. Enough. Julie, wondering why she had ever come, had to get away. She set down her empty cup, trying desperately not to notice the little jolts, the baby's kicks in the girl's abdomen.

"It's been so good to meet you finally," she said, beginning to rise. "Perhaps we can get together again sometime—" It was futile, utterly futile, to think she could do anything here. She had been a fool—

"Yes, we'll have to do this again. Perhaps after my baby comes."

Julie struggled for composure. "When is it due?"

"Any time now."

"How nice."

The girl's voice was tentative. "I know you were expecting last year—"

"Yes, well, I had a miscarriage," Julie answered crisply.

"I know. I'm so sorry."

"Yes, well, that was over six months ago—" As if that made a difference, Julie thought, a fresh wave of pain surging over her.

"That must have been terrible," the girl sympathized.

"Yes. Yes," she repeated lamely. What was there to say?

"I think I would die. I'd just die." The girl seemed to be talking to herself now.

"No, you wouldn't," Julie assured her, knowing she herself was still dying inside.

The surface of the girl's blank face brightened. "Of course you're right," she agreed, too quickly.

The girl opened the door for Julie, but it was no good. Julie couldn't leave yet. Not till she said what she had come to say. What had she come to say?

She knew. She would speak and be gone. She sighed deeply, closing her eyes, gathering the words. "I can't go yet, Cassie," she began, not looking directly at the girl. "I know this will sound absurd to you, but God told me to come here to talk to you."

The girl looked as if she had been struck. The mask of blankness fell away, leaving her face glistening. Were there tears too? Julie wondered.

"I know how it sounds," Julie continued quickly. "But Mr. Stevens heard you crying. And he asked me to come. And my husband—" she faltered. "I haven't handled my own problems very well so I refused until God nudged me—"

The girl did not rebuke her, so she plunged ahead. "I don't even know what God wants me to tell you," she said, laughing a little, "except that the Lord Jesus loves you and will help you with—well, with whatever problems you have." She paused, wondering how the girl would respond. "Whatever makes you cry—"

Cassie said nothing. She crossed the room, her gaze flitting from one object to another, as if she might find among her own familiar things the words she wanted to use. Finally, she sat down on the couch, giving Julie her gaze, and—something else. Her confidence?

The girl explained: "I never left home until I married Danny. We have no family here. No one. When I knew the baby was coming, I got scared to death. I had all kinds of crazy ideas. I couldn't tell Danny; he wouldn't understand, and he's gone so much anyway. I'm not a religious person, Julie; I don't know anything about God, but I've been praying—begging Him—to send someone to me."

It was Julie's turn to be stunned. She went back into the room and sat down beside the girl.

"Most people don't want to talk about anything real," Cassie continued. "They don't want to be involved in other people's lives."

"I was that way," Julie replied, embarrassed. "God had to push me—"

The girl looked puzzled. "How do you know Him well enough to know He's pushing?"

Julie smiled. Here was her opportunity to share her faith in Christ. In spite of her weakness and reluctance, the Lord was using her. She felt suddenly invigorated; as if in giving of herself to someone else she could feel a healing of the ache within her.

Julie was aware of her voice penetrating the quiet, suddenly confessing to Cassie her sin of shutting God out after losing the baby; she heard herself explaining how she had nursed the ache, refusing to let God heal it, how not until she had looked beyond herself—back to God; back to serving Him by reaching others—not until this moment, in fact, had she caught hold again of Christ's love and power. The same power that Cassie could know, to see her through her own fears and loneliness.

As Julie watched hope bloom on the young girl's face, she caught hold of something else—an insight, a very clear, lovely revelation, the realization that God had His own pattern for things, that giving and receiving, losing and finding, were part of that pattern.

Cassie's needs, Julie's own need, losing the baby, struggling to find her way back, giving to another and finding healing—it all fit together; somehow it was all part of His plan. Julie couldn't understand it, but having caught a glimpse of His working, she could accept it—just as perhaps now she could begin to claim fully whatever pattern God had for her life. She poured these thoughts out in words, offering them to Cassie, her own deep pain easing as she did so.

Tears glistened in Cassie's eyes. "I'm sorry about your baby, Julie—but I'm glad that God nudged you my way."

Julie nodded. "Me too. And I'll be back if you want me to come."

"Oh, yes," Cassie exclaimed. "I'll make tea—tomorrow, if you can come. Maybe you can tell me more about God then."

"I'll be back. And I'll bring some crumpets to go with your tea." She paused, swallowing the lump that was still in her throat. "And, Cassie, I had a small layette that I was saving—some tiny little shirts and nightgowns. I'm going to bring those for your baby."

"Tomorrow then," Cassie whispered.

"Yes, tomorrow."

The Healing of Annie Warner

What does a woman do when the death of her child is about to destroy her marriage?

Annie Warner's eyes were closed. She stood at the meat counter clutching her purse strap as if she were holding the steel handlebar during a plunging, dizzying roller coaster ride. Her knuckles were white, rigid.

I will be all right, she told herself once, twice, three times. It was not enough. When she opened her eyes, the walls and signs and jars of pickled pigs' feet and sausages still swayed, blurred, and finally shot back as sharp as slivered glass. She reached out her hand and felt the cold glass of the meat counter against her palm.

"You okay, Mrs. Warner?"

She raised her eyes, and her vision whipped up the whimsical, solicitous figure of Mr. Appleton. Always ready to help. He had worked behind the meat counter at Larry's Market since she and Reece had moved to Center City nine years ago. She was convinced that if anyone looked like Pinocchio's old father, Geppetto, it must certainly be Mr. Appleton.

The fairy tale was suddenly fresh in her mind. Only the details were vague. Was he, Geppetto—like Pinocchio—swallowed by the whale? Was he swallowed? It occurred to her that she was being swallowed, but not by a whale. Who, what was the culprit?

"Can I get you a glass of water or something?" Mr. Appleton was leaning over the counter, peering at her, his tiny spectacles halfway down his nose.

"No—no, thank you. I'm okay, fine."

"You look white, like you're gonna be sick. I could get you some water."

Leave me alone, she thought. *Don't ask! I might just die right here. Die as quickly, as easily, as Bobby. Just stop breathing, trying, aching—and let go. Right here with the acrid smells of meat and blood—!* "I am fine," she said.

"Well, then, what would you like today?" Geppetto again.

"I just want—I'll take some of the ground round. Two pounds." But the thought pushed in on her, *I just want Bobby back and Reece and Bobby and me a family again, and I wouldn't bug Reece. I wouldn't cut him off from Bobby and me just because he doesn't believe—*

She wouldn't cut him off with her old refrain, "Bobby, Bobby, I don't care what your father said. I've told you before; I'll tell you again. You're not going fishing with him on Sunday. You belong in church. Just because your father doesn't go is no reason for you to—Bobby, I'm talking to you. Are you listening?"

He's not listening. He's not anything. He's not here.

"Here you are, Mrs. Warner. Will there be anything else?"

"No, nothing else. Thank you."

Annie Warner paid for the ground round and left the store.

Four blocks to walk to Danby Street. Not far when the weather was nice. A pleasant walk past muted, respectful houses—all holding their warmth inside. Looking gray outside. Sober. Holding the laughter in, muffling it with curtains and doors. So that she would forget that houses could hold laughter and talk and warm feelings. She would like to forget. Maybe she had. There was none of it in her house now. It was swept clean—gone with the toys and clothes and pictures of Bobby. Gone with the remnants of feeling she and Reece had kept for each other so that Bobby would have a family, think that he had a happy family. Now she didn't even have to pretend that.

Six months ago, just after the accident, Pastor Sheehan told her that Bobby's death could bring Reece and her back together. But she didn't care now—really didn't care—because now she knew, and Reece knew, too, that it was all her fault. Her doing. She would carry the guilt for Bobby for the rest of her life.

She plodded on. One block. Two blocks. She shifted her grocery bag, her focus blurring. She blinked. Wasn't that Bobby walking just ahead of her, wearing a green jacket and patched jeans, carrying a sack of groceries? Sauntering his independent eight-year-old walk. The breeze lifting his straight black hair, rippling through his open jacket. She ran along the sidewalk after him, hurrying to catch up, catching the wind too quickly in her throat. *Can't you wait up—can't you wait up for your mother?* She caught the sleeve of his jacket. He stopped and spun around. He was not Bobby.

"You want something, lady?"

Her hand shot back as if it had been burned. The face was someone else's. A stranger's. Nothing familiar in the eyes. But he saw something in hers. He stared, waiting. His mouth moved up and down accusingly, chewing gum. The gum bulged in his cheek.

"I'm sorry. I thought you were someone I knew. Excuse me." The boy frowned so that she could see his teeth and gums. Then he shifted the groceries in his arms and turned away, shuffling down the street. "Excuse me," she repeated, to nobody. She thought of the humorous comeback: *There is no excuse for you.* And it was true. She was without excuse.

Annie walked on, holding the package of meat to her chest, feeling the cold of it against her. She hated this thing inside her that made her see her son in every child, made her assess, compare, remember, ache, and resent. True, she had shut God out and would not let Him heal the wound. She nursed her bitterness, her guilt. Yet she continued to hold on to a facade, a sham of her life before. The lovely core of her relationship with Christ had withered, but she clung fast to the brittle shell of surface actions. She still attended every service at the church—always there in the pew, alone, not hearing, not listening, except to the guilt sounds inside her grinding out accusations.

Going to church gave her something to do. It gave life a thread of continuity, like building a wall of toothpicks to keep out wind or darkness. Maybe it accomplished nothing, but it was something to occupy her time.

The houses on Danby Street sat in a neat row, spaced evenly, barricaded against her bitterness. Only the windows belied the austere frames; the muffled patches of light coming like velvet through curtains and glass revealed the real warmth inside. It was dark now. How quickly it came. She had to get home—to the collection of empty rooms where Bobby used to live, where nothing lived now in the cells of the silent house.

Reece was already home. He let her in before she found her key. He took her package and set it on the counter while she put her coat away. He moved cumbrously, silent, saying nothing at all, as if he were hardly aware of her, as if he were listening to something within himself. He frowned a lot lately, she noticed. Not at her, at nothing in particular—just dark frowns over his coffee in the morning, frowns as he watched television, while he dressed and undressed or shaved. She left him with his frowns, never probing, never questioning. She had enough pain of her own. *Better to leave him to work out his own way,* she thought.

Reece returned to his newspaper while she began dinner.

"We're just having spaghetti," she told him apologetically, as they sat down at the table a few minutes later. "But it's a quick dinner to fix, and you always say you like it. There's still custard from last night, too."

He helped himself to the spaghetti. "This is fine," he said. "You going to church tonight?"

"I guess so. Unless you're too tired to take me." Since the accident, there was an understanding between them that Annie would not drive the car. Only Reece drove now. It had become routine for him to take her to church, then go off some place and pick her up afterward. She claimed that she would never get behind the wheel again.

"I'm tired, but I can drive you," he said.

"All right." Guilt nudged her. She knew Reece was having trouble at work. He was manager of a trucking firm, and some of the guys were rough and gave him a hard time. Reece could take care of himself, she knew that. But he wasn't young anymore, and lately, the job left him more tired than he ought to be. *But at least he gets out,* she thought. *He doesn't have to face the long days at home alone.*

"Why you scowling?" he asked.

"I didn't know I was," she replied distractedly.

She was recalling that it was Bobby who had brought her to God. When he was only five, Annie sent him to a neighborhood Bible club. It gave her a couple hours to shop or relax, and Bobby loved the stories and songs and playing with other children. After all, he was an only child; it was summertime and he was lonesome. He needed the experience of getting out on his own and meeting children his own age—to help prepare him for school in the fall.

She hadn't counted on him becoming a little home missionary. He was bubbling over with enthusiasm the day he accepted Christ as his own personal Savior. He told Annie; he told his dad. He wanted to start going to church every Sunday. He wanted his parents to know Jesus too. Reece laughed it off and left it to Annie to find a church for Bobby. So she and Bobby found one they liked and began to attend regularly. That's where she found Christ.

But her life was a struggle. She was so new in Christ, had so much to learn, and Reece resented his family's new interest. He launched a campaign to win Bobby back, to get him away from going to church, get him interested in fishing on Sunday. Anything.

She hadn't handled it right. In her ignorance, she had alienated Reece. He felt that she and Bobby were against him somehow. It wasn't true. They just wanted him to believe too.

Now, however, she didn't care. Her feelings about God—about everything—were numb. She only knew that if she hadn't insisted on going to prayer meeting that Wednesday night, Bobby would still be alive.

"How about some of that custard now?"

Annie looked up, startled. She had nearly forgotten Reece was in the room with her. "Yes," she said. "Yes, I'll get you some."

If it were up to her, they would never drive over the same street where it happened. But Reece was driving, and he never mentioned it, so neither did she. But she lived it over again each time. A tenseness would rise in her, increasing until they reached the intersection where the green Pontiac ran the red light and came crashing into Bobby's side of the car. There had been no opportunity to brake or speed ahead. There had been no time to reach out for Bobby, to shield him. She had told him earlier to fasten his seat belt, but he hadn't bothered. Why hadn't she insisted? One minute he was talking, telling her something. She had never been able to remember what he was telling her.

One minute he was talking. Then the green Pontiac. One minute Bobby, then the sound of crashing and everything going everywhere. Bobby was telling her something. Then there was the green Pontiac on them and she couldn't even remember now what Bobby said.

The intersection where it happened was quiet now. Every time they crossed it, there was no hint that anything tragic had ever happened there. It was like every other street. It was nothing special. Except in her head. In her head were the sirens, sounding thin like wires, off somewhere else. Except not somewhere else. There with her and the crumpled green Pontiac. There where the strangers came, doing things, keeping her quiet. Telling her she would be all right. Comforting her while they took Bobby from the car and put him in their ambulance and carried him off forever away from her.

In order to get to the church they had to drive through the intersection. Didn't have to. They could go out of their way. But Reece always drove it, silent, his jaw slack, resigned, never reminding her in words of what she had done.

Annie stared through the window, realizing that they were at this moment passing over the spot. Reece said something. The sound was guttural, broken. She looked at him, not wanting to look at him. For the first time she was aware of the intensity of his pain.

"Why did it happen?" he said.

She fixed her eyes on passing street signs—No Loading Zone, Speed Limit 25—Children Crossing. "It just happened is all," she answered. "Don't you believe that's all?"

"No. No. I know that's not all. There was a reason. I've always known, and I can't live with it anymore. I can't, Annie."

Here it is, she thought. *All the hatred and guilt built up between us. Now we have to look at it and inspect it like a laboratory specimen. I can't.*

"I can't, Reece. I can't think about it now," she said.

"I know you don't love me, Annie. Not anymore, anyway."

"Love you? I don't know—" It had been so long since they had talked about anything together, especially love. She no longer knew how to respond to him. His awkwardness, his pain—it was as if he were some sort of clumsy dentist probing a very sensitive cavity. She wanted him to stop. "We're almost at the church, Reece. Maybe we can talk tonight—later."

"If you want, Annie, I'll go home now and pack. I'll still pick you up at nine, but I won't go back to the house."

"You want to leave?"

He pulled up to the curb and turned off the engine. She gathered her Bible and purse off the seat, thinking that finally her religion and what she did to Bobby had driven Reece away. It surprised her to feel a new emptiness in the vacuum that was already within her.

Annie noticed that the church door was open and people were going inside. It seemed to her now that they were all strangers walking somewhere else. Not here. Not where the pain was—in Reece, in her, in this car, all so exposed, so vulnerable. She couldn't have them see the pain.

"You say you're going to leave," she repeated levelly.

Reece's arms lay across the steering wheel like lifeless weights. He hunched forward, letting his forehead rest on the back of his hands. "You and Bobby wanted me to go with you to church," he said. "I used to hear Bobby in his prayers at night praying for me. For old Dad. Why couldn't Dad go to church too, he'd say, so we'd all be a happy family—close, sitting together, singing, things like that? I thought it was cute, that's all. A cute little kid thing." He paused and drew in a breath as if there were not enough air to support the heaviness within him. He coughed. "You, Annie, you I just shut out."

"I know."

"I shouldn't have."

"I didn't go about it right," she said. "I shut you out too. I built a wall, trying to make you believe like I did. I was fighting against you. I should have tried to win you with love, not nagging."

"I will always see Bobby hopping out of the car and running up the church steps two at a time—"

"If I had stayed home that Wednesday night," she interrupted, "Bobby never would have been killed."

Reece stopped talking and stared at her, his lips still pursed, his jaw contorted. It was an odd expression, she thought. What did he see?

"Is that what you think? Is it?"

"It's true, Reece. Don't put it into words anymore, please." She opened the car door and set one foot on the curb.

"It wasn't you, Annie. It wasn't! I did it by my unbelief. God could have taken me, Annie, but He didn't. He took Bobby. And He took you. I don't have you anymore, either."

Annie pulled her foot back into the automobile and shut the door. She moved across the seat into her husband's arms. "God doesn't work that way, Reece," she whispered. "I don't know much about Him lately, but I do know that. It wasn't you. I guess it wasn't even me. It just happened. I don't know why, and I'll never forget it." She drew in a breath, her voice broken and gravelly. "I thought we were both gone, too, swallowed up, dead to each other, dead to God. But for the first time since Bobby died, I don't want it to be that way."

"Annie," he said, holding her hand, rubbing her slender fingers with his thumb. "Annie, maybe we can still get through this together."

"What do you mean?"

"I mean, we can find each other again. Can't we? I want to listen to you, Annie. I want to hear about the fears and guilt, and about what you've found in God. I'm ready to listen, Annie."

"I want to listen, too, Reece."

"We both have a lot to talk about, Annie. Maybe a lot to pray about, too." He nodded toward the church. "I'm going in with you. I don't know much about it, but I'm going in. And afterward, we'll go home and talk. Somehow we'll work things out. We'll stay up all night talking, if we have to."

Annie pressed her husband's hand against her cheek. "I think I'd like that, Reece," she said with a little smile.

It was the first time in half a year that she actually felt like smiling.

Clancy's Choice

What does a woman do when she realizes abortion was the wrong choice?

Clancy McKinnon slept in late that Tuesday morning, waking at 11:00 only because her telephone jangled beside her bed (a wrong number!), splitting her muggy dreams wide apart. In the cold glare of her bathroom mirror her long, tangled red hair seemed to jump in odd little bunches from the top and sides of her head. She ran her hand over it to smooth it, but the gesture was wasted. She splashed cold water on her face, patted it dry with a towel, and reached for the small plastic bottle of pain pills the doctor had given her.

Actually, there wasn't much pain. Not physically. She might have welcomed pain, might have considered it her just dues. Retribution, perhaps. Or was that just a fanciful thought? In fact, there was another pain (not pain really but something else, worse) and it was for this that she swallowed the pills now, double the dose the doctor had prescribed.

She went from her bathroom to her kitchen, glancing for an instant out the living room window of her first-floor apartment.

She saw immediately that the day was a blank—no sun, no real weather to speak of. A plain, rather dreary sky. Nothing.

She flipped on the light switch in her kitchen, although she could see well enough without it. She hoped somehow for a warm glow, but the light was merely something extra that did nothing to cheer her, so she turned it off. For no reason that she could think of, the room chilled her.

Clancy would have the rest of the week to recover. She didn't have to be back at work until next Monday. Who would ever have thought that she would use one of her precious weeks of vacation for this? For this!

She had expected to feel ill. She had even entertained the idea—remotely—that she might not survive. That idea was ludicrous, of course. An unreasonable fear that lingered from the scare stories of the past. From the days when such things were not spoken of in public. But these days everyone talked about it. Abortion. The newspapers and television were full of it—abortion rights activists, clinic bombings, picketers, states challenging Roe vs. Wade. Even Supreme Court nominees were praised or condemned because of their stand on this one issue. Everyone had an opinion on abortion.

Abortion. For Clancy, the word had jumped from the blatant headlines of newspapers and magazine covers into the tight recesses of her own skull. And there the word lodged, with new shades of meaning, something personal hushed in her senses, forever part of herself. The word had undergone a transformation. It was no longer the word women carelessly bandied back and forth in beauty parlors ("Did you know Anne had an abortion last week?" "No, I hadn't heard!"), or the subject of glib conversation among her friends or the girls at the office ("Why shouldn't we be able to have an abortion if we want one? It's our body. We have a right to privacy."). The word would never be neutral for her again. It was as much a part of her now as her own face, her hands.

Clancy turned on the stove and boiled water for coffee. She considered fixing a slice of toast but quickly dismissed the idea. She was not hungry.

At the counseling session on Saturday, a pleasant-faced, middle-aged woman who reminded her slightly of her own mother, told Clancy that she must know her mind, her real feelings. It was important that she be sure of her attitudes, so that there would be no guilt feelings later. The thought stole across Clancy's mind, Wasn't she doing something she *should* feel guilty about? But to the counselor whose smile was every bit as kind as her mother's, she said, "Yes, I understand." But what had she understood? Only that it would be wrong to feel guilty.

All right, she had no guilt feelings. At least it seemed that what she felt was not guilt. It was something else, which she had not yet thought out completely. Regret? Not really. What else could she have done? Matt wanted nothing to do with marriage or a baby—and now he seemed to want nothing to do with her either.

"You're pretty stupid to let something like this happen," he had told her, the anger rising in his voice. "I thought you were a big girl. I thought you could take care of things."

And then when she had begun to cry—stupidly, like a child reprimanded for some unthinkable misdeed—Matt had softened his tone, saying, "It's all right, Clancy. The damage can be undone. There's no problem."

At first she had been naive enough to wince at his words. Her baby—mere damage to be undone? Was it possible? And from that point, from that conversation, she had had to rethink all of her basic concepts about life. What did she really believe? What was truth? And what responsibility—if any—did truth place upon her?

From every side she heard the arguments. "It's your right to have control over your own body, to say whether or not you will bear a child." Matt said that. The law of the land said that. Women's Libbers had been saying it since Clancy was a child. Even some religious magazines said so. Could they all be wrong?

Mechanically Clancy had begun to adjust her ideas. She told herself that it was not really a child inside her body; it was simply tissue, protoplasm. Forget that doctors had demonstrated that an unborn child is unique and potentially independent of its mother's body. Remember only that much of society now says abortion is not an unreasonable choice for a woman to make. She had heard that, yes. She was not being *unreasonable!*

Like a lesson to be learned, she had recited these new ideas over and over in her mind until they sounded familiar and unsurprising, until she could call forth these predictable responses at will, casually, easily. A snow job on her mind, that's what it was. But it worked.

Yesterday morning, before the operation, she felt very little trepidation. She even managed some pleasant conversation with the doctor who assured her that since she was so prompt in terminating her pregnancy, it would be a relatively simple and painless procedure. "Some girls wait too long," he told her as he studied his instrument tray, "and then it can be risky. You were wise not to wait too long."

Clancy said nothing. She waited, steeling herself. And then, with a terrible, sickening *whoosh*, her baby was sucked away. Gone. Like that. Only not like that. There was pain—and a stabbing sensation that something precious, some part of her innermost self was being ripped out of her. It was like a rape, like she imagined rape would be, a violation of her most private parts, the destruction of something cherished that could never be recovered.

Even now, as Clancy drained her second cup of black coffee, she knew that she had been betrayed. By the system.

By the slogans. By the media. By the plastic smile of her counselor and the breezy manner of her physician. By all the arguments that sounded so reasonable in principle but shattered with the reality of a child she was already starting to mourn. Her child. The fragile filigrees of a dream that had died stillborn.

Clancy looked over at the clock and was startled to realize that it was already past noon. She ought to quit brooding and go get dressed or at least comb her hair. Of course, the doctor had said to take it easy for a couple of days. "There will probably be some cramping," he said. How kind he had sounded, how solicitous everyone was. How intent they all were that she should not feel bad about ending her baby's life. Hadn't they implied that she should take her abortion in stride, even look upon it as a positive act? After all, she was exercising her right of free choice. Wasn't that something to take pride in, the way some actresses on TV spoke of their abortions as if they were badges of courage?

But what Clancy wanted to know now was, Why had they all lied to her? Why hadn't someone told her she needed an answer she could live with for the rest of her life, not just today? Why hadn't they told her what it was really like—the horror, the sense of desecration and humiliation, the awful emptiness and loss? Why hadn't they warned her how she would really feel? And where were they now to reassure her, convince her she had done the right thing? Where was anyone now? All right, she had exercised control over her own body, but why did she feel so out of control now? She had played God. So why did God seem so far away?

It was strange. She hadn't thought much about God lately. Not for a long time, in fact. Once, several years ago, she had attended an evangelistic service at a nearby church. She had even gone forward to accept Jesus Christ as her Savior. Even now she could remember the ecstasy of it, of feeling that she was important, actually important, to God. "Give God control of your life," the minister had said. For weeks after that it seemed God walked with her, was her personal friend. It was a rare thing, a beautiful time.

And then gradually, without quite realizing that she had done it, she dismissed God from her life. She ignored Him. Forgot Him. Lost touch. Forgetting had not been deliberate, simply careless. She had been merely—neglectful.

It struck her suddenly that her life thus far had been a series of losses: God. Matt. Her baby. Herself.

Yes, it was true. Even herself. Her hold on life seemed tenuous at best. Somehow, in attempting to exercise control over her own life, her body, she had irrevocably lost control. She realized that now. Pouring herself another cup of coffee, which she didn't want and knew she wouldn't drink, she wondered what she should do now.

She ought to set goals, make plans, organize her life in some direction. But these were words that meant nothing to her. Still, it seemed necessary to go through the motions of planning a future—the next hour, the next week, the next year. She must find some basis for living or she would not survive.

Then, another thought occurred to Clancy. It was already too late. She had not survived. She had gone too far, destroyed too much. It was horribly ironic, she admitted reluctantly. Every action she had taken had been to ensure her own survival, to assert her own rights and proclaim her freedom. Yet those very deeds had condemned her. And now there wasn't a chance for survival.

Or was there? The Bible talked about hope. She remembered that. Somewhere it said the truth shall make you free. What did that mean? Hadn't the truth already condemned her? What truth could possibly free her now?

From a crevice of her mind came the words, "And you are

Christ's, and Christ is God's." A fascinating thought, but what did it mean? If there was still hope, it was too elusive to claim today.

In fact, it was all too much to think about now. Once she might have made an effort, but at this moment her mind felt sluggish, too confused to wrestle with such lofty concepts. Perhaps one day she would come out of this, break through the oppressive lethargy of this day, this particular hour. At the moment she could only believe that she had not survived, but she could be wrong even about that. Wearily dismissing the matter from her mind, she sipped her coffee, which was as cold as the room, as cold as her senses.

A Burst of Yellow Sun

What does a woman do when she fears her brand-new marriage is a mistake?

A crisp snap of yellow sun touches fire to the morning, toasting my neck and arms beaver brown. I tie a red scarf around my hair and kick off my sandals, letting my toes wiggle free in the grass. Almost, almost I feel that yellow sun bursting free inside me again like it did a long time ago, as it used to do when I was free—before decisions were made and courses set firm. Before the sun inside me popped like a balloon.

I am hanging up clothes in the backyard. It is terribly warm, and it is terribly absurd for me, a bride of seven months, to be analyzing like this again. I pull the scarf off my head, release it, and watch it waft to the grass. I sit down in the grass beside the clothespin bag and close my eyes, feeling that familiar pressure in my head. It's hurting again. Let the clothes hang themselves!

Dear Lord, dear Lord, has it all been a mistake? Is that

what's wrong with me? I am analyzing again, I know it. But I can't help it. There has to be an answer.

"Darling—?"

I open my eyes and stare upward. "Jeffrey."

"Linda, what are you doing in the grass?" He smiles tolerantly like a parent who has caught his child in fanciful play.

"I just sat down a moment—the sun was so warm."

"Hon, I've got several calls to make. Mrs. Ramsey is sick again, so I'll be stopping by the hospital."

"What about lunch?"

"Not today. I'll grab a hamburger or something."

Jeffrey is very tall and, at the moment, from my vantage point in the grass, he appears to be a magnificent tower. That's the bride talking! I scurry to my feet and kiss his lips, and we walk together arm in arm to the car.

"I need a clean shirt for tonight."

"Okay."

"And be ready, Linda. Last Wednesday night we were almost late for prayer meeting. After all, I *am* the minister."

His words prick me. Why does he make me feel like a scolded child? "Don't worry," I assure him, "I'll fix something fast for dinner."

"No more hash—"

"Nope." I want to say more. I want to tell him what he's doing to me, but I have no words for it. Only this feeling of hurt and disappointment.

Jeffrey leaves, and I return to my clothesline and my thoughts. I remember the lovely, cold December when I became Mrs. Jeffrey Daniels. We were the perfect couple, like the smiling twosome on top of the snowy-white wedding cake. In his father's church we marched, vowed, and kissed, and everyone said it was a perfect wedding.

It was, too, except that Jeff's father, the minister, was unable to perform the ceremony. A week before the wedding he suffered a stroke. Jeff was so devastated, he even considered postponing our wedding, but his mom insisted we go ahead. Still, it wasn't the same for Jeff. He was disappointed that a stranger married us and preoccupied about his dad throughout our honeymoon. I had a feeling Jeff was starting our marriage with a chip on his shoulder because things weren't going the way he expected. It was almost as if I and our marriage were somehow to blame for his dad's stroke. But when his dad made a full recovery, I hoped Jeff and I could begin our perfect marriage as well.

And they lived happily ever after. Isn't that what everyone says? Isn't that what we're taught to expect? But that's the part I choke on now. I don't think I ask for perfection, only a little happiness in my marriage. But I'm not happy, and—Lord, I know it—Jeffrey's not happy either. There, I've admitted it, haven't I!

But what went wrong? Why can't I figure it out?

Right from the start Jeffrey and I considered ourselves right for each other—both of us Christians, both eager to live for the Lord. Jeff was beginning his last year of seminary when we met, so I knew he planned to be a minister. And he learned soon enough that I had always envisioned myself as a minister's wife. So weren't we perfect for each other? Wasn't it the Lord's will that we fall in love and marry?

Funny how my dreams of being a minister's wife always had me sitting serenely in the first pew, wearing a stylish dress, my hair freshly permed, my makeup impeccable, while I listened proudly to every word of wisdom from my very own pastor-husband. Surely as a minister and a man of God, Jeff would make the perfect husband. Spiritual, compassionate, understanding, supportive.

How is it I never saw myself in his old shirt and a red scarf hanging up his socks on a backyard clothesline, and all the while feeling somehow misunderstood, unloved and unappreciated. As if I've failed him somehow. Failed to live up to his expectations. But then, hasn't he failed to live up to mine as well?

But maybe I'm being too picky. I knew reality would be different from the dreams. I was prepared for that. What I wasn't prepared for was—what? What is it that's wrong? Why are we making each other unhappy?

I know this much: Something is gone from our lives that once was there. It doesn't make sense. Jeffrey has his own church now, and we are doing the Lord's work together. Yet, we're not really together, not in spirit. We are each revolving in our own little circle, and the circles never touch. In fact, the circles seem to be spinning farther and farther away from each other. I wonder if Jeffrey thinks I am hindering him somehow? Is that why he resents me? Does he think I am somehow spoiling his relationship with God? The idea is preposterous, but still—

I hear the phone. I drop Jeffrey's shirt back in the basket and let the clothespins fall. I bound up the back steps, dash through the kitchen to the hall, catching the phone on the third ring before the answering machine trips on. I am out of breath, my mind whirling, but I hear Jeff's mother clearly. She is crying. Jeffrey's father is in the hospital again. Another stroke, more severe.

"What hospital?" I ask, but I can't understand her through her sobs. "Which hospital did they take him to?" I repeat. "Jeffrey's visiting now at Northside. What? Townsend General? All right, I'll try to reach Jeffrey. We'll be there as soon as we can."

I hang up the receiver, find the number for Northside, dial—who was it Jeffrey was going to visit? Rhoads? No, Ramsey.

"Mrs. Ramsey's room, please. Yes, is the Reverend Daniels there, please?"

When he comes on the line, I tell Jeff that his father has been taken to Townsend. No, I don't know how bad it is. I can already hear the shock and dismay in Jeff's voice as he says, "I'll meet you at the hospital."

As I hang up the receiver, I feel a knot of anguish growing in my throat, spreading through my frame. I grab my purse and car keys and run, not even locking the parsonage door behind me. Fighting back tears, I drive blindly, pushing the speed limit—all the time I wonder, *How will we survive this time?*

Fifteen minutes later I rush into the hospital. Jeff is in the main lobby, his features drawn, his eyes searching mine for answers. I reach out to hug him but he turns away. I feel so unprepared to face a crisis now. I wish I could be home again in the backyard with nothing more demanding than hanging Jeff's clothes on the line. I look down at my clothes. I am still in Jeff's old shirt, looking like a poor washer-woman, hardly someone who can give Jeff the support he needs. I start to apologize. He does not hear me.

We meet Jeff's mother in the cardiac care waiting room. Her face is gray and strained, as if a plaster mask had been pasted over her usual vital expression. She tells us a staff doctor is with Dad, but Dad's doctor will be here shortly.

Sitting in a hospital is like waiting for a bus you have a feeling will never come. You wait forever because there's nothing else you can do, but the waiting is bitter agony.

Jeffrey phones the church to tell them he won't be there for prayer meeting. His tone is professional, controlled. He asks the head deacon to take over, and I hear him request prayer for his dad. Then he sits by his mother, but they don't talk nor touch, and after awhile I go get all of us some coffee.

When I return with the coffee, Jeff is standing by a window. His face is partially covered by one hand, but I can see his jaw is set, and I know he is praying. I sit down by Mrs.

Daniels, and we drink our coffee. I think a prayer in my head, but it drifts away before it's complete, and I let it go, knowing I can't pray well when I'm with someone.

Finally I go down the hall to dispose of the Styrofoam cups, and I keep going until I am in the ladies' rest room—alone. I let myself cry now and talk out loud to God. Prayer is best for me when I can talk out loud. But I find myself praying not only for Jeff's dad but for Jeff and me as well. I want to help Jeff, to reach him and meet his need, but I don't know how. I don't know what to do.

When I return to the waiting room, I find the staff doctor talking to Jeff and his mother. He is saying there is little he can tell us now, but that we will get a complete report from Dad's physician, who is presently examining him. He adds that it may be some time before there is any definite word.

There is nothing we can do, so we go to the cafeteria for a bite of dinner, but we don't eat. Again, we wait. Jeffrey is so quiet that I am afraid even to hold his hand. I know how close he has always been to his dad. He couldn't live without his dad. *Dear Lord, what am I thinking? What if his dad dies?*

We stay at the hospital until long past midnight. At last Dad's doctor comes to us, tells us that this has been a bad one. He can make no promises. We must wait, perhaps a day or two.

I am frightened. The worry lines on Jeff's face deepen, but I see a strange look of peace on his mother's face. We hug one another and weep and she whispers a prayer of thanks to God that Dad is still alive. Then the doctor permits us a few minutes in Dad's room. We enter cautiously, not sure what we'll find. We hear the beep of the monitor, watch its uneven patterns. Dad is ashen, one corner of his mouth drooping. But he is asleep, his relaxed features belying the ordeal of the last 12 hours. We gather around his bed and pray again for God's complete healing. Jeff's voice breaks but his mother's lifts in praise to God for answered prayer.

Now it is time to go home. We are all terribly tired. We leave my car at the hospital. Jeff and I drive his mother home, assuring her we will pick her up and go see Dad first thing in the morning. She smiles and tells us that she will be all right alone—she insists on it.

Then Jeffrey and I go home. I know we are both desperately worn and empty. We go to bed, each of us silent, our thoughts locked far apart. In bed, Jeffrey turns his back to me. He is forgetting or purposely ignoring our nightly prayer. I am too drained inside to cry. I want to reach out to him, but even after all the events of this night, we are apart. I wonder, *How will the Lord ever bring us back now?*

Before sleep engulfs me, I am brought back to awareness by a sound. I listen, and it is a sob. I am startled to realize it is Jeffrey. I turn over and touch his shoulder, but he is still.

"Jeff—Jeffrey? I love you."

Suddenly he turns to me and I am in his arms. He holds me so tightly that I can scarcely breathe. I have never known Jeff to cry before, but he is sobbing now, his chest heaving with anguish, and I am frightened. I remain still until he finishes; I am quiet, knowing it is for him to speak.

"Linda, I'm sorry. I'm so sorry."

"Jeff, what is it? I don't understand."

We sit on the edge of the bed, side by side in the dark, holding each other close. After a long while, Jeffrey speaks. "Linda, I saw something tonight I didn't like at all."

My heart stirs with alarm as I whisper, "Something I did?"

"No, darling. Something in me."

"What, Jeff?"

He steadies his voice, his face a perfect silhouette. "Linda, I've worked so hard these past six months to be a good minister."

"I know, Jeff. You've done wonderfully."

"But I did it for my dad, Linda. I wanted to please him, more than anything in the world. I saw that tonight."

"He is pleased, Jeff. He's very proud of you."

"That's not the point, hon."

I study his features in the shadows. "Tell me, Jeff. I don't understand."

His voice breaks. "Linda, I've lost my joy. I was trying to please Dad rather than God."

"But you've been doing the Lord's work—"

"For all the wrong reasons. Christ wants me to serve Him because I love Him, not because I want to show my dad I can be as good a minister as he is."

"But why are you apologizing to me, Jeff?"

He turns my face toward his. "You really don't know, Linda?"

In a small voice, I reply, "I know you haven't been happy with me as your wife. And you've been disappointed in our marriage."

"Oh, Linda, is that how I've made you feel? I'm so sorry. It's true, I've been blaming you for my dissatisfaction. I thought somehow our marriage had been a mistake. I guess I wanted it to be your fault. But it wasn't you; it was me!"

A sense of relief spreads through me. "Oh, Jeff, I knew something was wrong. I wanted to reach out and help you, but I didn't know how."

"How could you know, sweetheart? I was being hard on you because I was angry with myself. And I was using my dad as a measuring stick instead of the Lord." He holds me tighter, pressing my cheek against his collarbone. "But tonight, it was like the Lord held a mirror up showing me what I was doing. When I knew Dad might not make it—that I might still lose him, I realized that was the area of my life I had never committed."

"Then it wasn't me?" I ask, needing to know for sure. "You're not sorry you married me?"

"Are you serious? You're the woman I've waited for all my life."

Tears spill from my eyes. "Oh, Jeff, when you were so critical, so quick to find fault, I thought you didn't love me anymore."

"Forgive me, darling. I do love you, Linda. Listen, we're going to get through this, and we're going to pray that Dad pulls through. I promise, we'll be stronger than before." He kisses the top of my head. "Pray with me now. Help me get this straightened out. I need your prayers."

Jeffrey and I kneel by the bed. The floor is cold and hard on my knees, so different from the plush warm grass I walked in this morning. How long ago was the morning! Nevertheless, I am bursting inside with yellow sun, thanking God that this—a dark room and cold floor and two persons praying together for God's will—is the reality of life...and part of my place as a minister's wife.

A Gift of Loneliness

What does a woman do when she finds herself alone and lonely in a strange place at Christmastime?

Today is Christmas Eve. The calendar says so. Shopping malls and department stores strung with reams and streams of red and green yuletide decorations say so. And radio and television spewing "Jingle Bells" and "Jolly Old St. Nicholas" heartily agree: December 24 is here.

This morning I peered out my front window and noticed an artificial wreath on the door of the apartment adjoining mine. It surprised me that Randy Tate, a swinging bachelor computer analyst, would have the Christmas spirit. But my spark of appreciation died swiftly as my gaze absorbed the patio area of our "Polynesian Winds" apartment complex. Bright sunlight gleamed on the fanning leaves of palm trees and shimmered in the egg-blue water of the oval swimming pool. *California Christmas,* I mused with a cynicism that was rare for me. What was I, a true-blue, loyal Ohio girl, doing in a place like this?

In desperation I put on my cardigan sweater and walked the four blocks to the Plaza Shopping Center, where "Silent Night" floated out over the loudspeaker, mingling with the buzz of shoppers' voices and the noise of traffic.

The joy of Christmas had totally eluded me this year, and I had simply dismissed my plight—until now. Now Christmas was almost here, and I couldn't ignore it—or my feelings—any longer. I dearly wanted to capture some small portion of the Christmas spirit to carry me through the next 24 hours.

Meandering through a toy shop, I tried to assume an air of purposefulness, as if I might actually purchase a Nintendo game, a stuffed green Teenage Mutant Ninja Turtle, or a bug-eyed Bart Simpson doll. I smiled merrily at clerks who asked if they could help me as I replied in my cheeriest voice, "No, thank you, I'm just looking."

True. Just looking. Looking for something to pull me out of my doldrums, this blue mood I was in. The clerks couldn't help me with that. In fact, zigzagging through crowds of bustling last-minute shoppers wasn't the answer either. No way.

I found the closest Big Boy's, sat down at the lunch counter and ordered a bowl of chili and a hot fudge sundae. Julie Andrews was singing "I'll Be Home for Christmas," but the speaker system wasn't turned up loud enough for me to hear the words above the restaurant din.

But the words were in my head anyway. I watched graceful spirals of steam escape from my chili and thought of smoke curling out of chimneys back home. I pictured snow—thick, luscious landscapes of white, brilliant under the winter sun. And snowy nights, blue and glistening with magic. Ohio winter. It would pass by without me this year.

There is a certain sense of release that comes from indulging in self-pity. A sort of bittersweet pain fills up the empty spots inside you. Momentarily, at least. So I indulged. I nursed a spoonful of hot fudge and reminisced.

I thought about my graduation last spring from the small Christian college in my hometown and how excited I was about the prospects of the coming year. I had applied to teach at several Christian elementary schools across the country, including one in my own hometown. Somehow I never really expected to go anywhere else, that is, not until a Los Angeles school accepted my application.

"California!" cried my mother when I showed her the acceptance letter. "That's so far. Surely you could get a job somewhere closer."

"Good teaching positions aren't easy to find these days, Mom," I told her with an authority in my voice I hardly felt. "Besides, I prayed about it, and this is the school that needs me."

In August I left for California. An urgent sense of having a mission to accomplish carried me through the wearisome, often chaotic days of apartment hunting, finding a church home, and adjusting to the routines and responsibilities of teaching a class of 30 zestful, energetic fourth graders. I made friends with several of the teachers and found a pleasant social niche in the career class at a nearby church. I was managing rather well, I thought—considering.

Considering that for the first time my family was not the focal point of my life, and my activities no longer revolved around Mom and Dad, brothers and sisters, and assorted other relatives. I had lived at home even while attending college, so I had never really experienced a gradual "breaking away" process from my family. Instead, all at once, I had uprooted myself from all that was familiar to face a totally new life. And in a sense, it was a shock to my system.

I realized that, for better or worse, I was carving out my own future apart from family, friends, and old ties. Security blankets were packed away with high school annuals, old snapshots, and notebooks crammed with college lecture notes. I saw for the first time that I was building my own home now, and whether that home eventually included a husband and children or whether I would remain the sole member, it was nevertheless something new and special and separate from my parents' home. Listen, that was an awesome realization.

Still, I could have handled everything if it hadn't been for Christmas. I mean, I was coping all right until I realized I would be spending my first Christmas away from home—alone. My reserves of stoicism and bravery promptly melted, and I had to admit that I had succumbed to that old bugaboo—homesickness.

Recollections of past Christmases flooded back over me. I wanted once again to see children stuffed into snowsuits, tree branches heavy with snow, and lovely curlicue etchings of frost on windowpanes. I wanted to smell the pies and cookies Mom would be baking. And feel the warmth of the fire Dad would build in the fireplace. I wanted to have a snowball fight with my brothers and go ice-skating on Wren's Pond with my sisters. What I wanted was Christmas as I had always known it!

I considered flying home for the holidays. My spirit was willing, but my bank account was weak, almost empty, in fact. I couldn't squeeze a one-way trip to Palm Springs into my budget, let alone a round-trip airline ticket to Ohio. Especially since I still had my student loan to pay off.

So, unfortunately, I had nothing in common with Miss Julie Andrews, who would be home for Christmas (so she sang), while I would remain—alas!—right where I was. However, Julie was no longer singing. Instead, Bing Crosby was well into "White Christmas" and my chili was cold and my sundae a globby pool of milky white and dark chocolate swirls. Feeling somehow embarrassed, I paid my check and escaped into the bright afternoon sunshine and congested preholiday traffic.

Before returning to my apartment, I stopped at a K Mart and browsed among their Christmas decorations. I remembered the small artificial tree on my dresser strung with paper ornaments my students had made me. But it needed something more. On impulse I bought a package of candy canes, some tinsel, and a plastic star. It was another inept attempt to prompt some nuance of holiday spirit—and was ultimately ineffectual. Walking home with my meager package, I felt even more depressed.

As I approached my door, I heard the rhythmic beat of soft rock music coming from the apartment next door. Randy Tate must be having another of his many rollicking parties. I almost envied his steady stream of friends who came and went with such regularity, but I detested the late hours they kept and the noise they made. Twice I had reported Randy to the landlord. Reluctantly, of course, since Randy is single and quite a hunk, and I didn't want to alienate him entirely. In fact, right now I just wished I had a party to go to myself, and special people to celebrate with.

As I entered my apartment, I was painfully aware of the sharp contrast to the noisy, bustling, celebrating world outside. My rooms were silent and void of any indication that Christmas was only hours away. I removed a turkey TV dinner from the freezer and put it in the oven. Then I sat down and tried to decide how to spend the evening.

Not that there was much choice. Most of my friends had gone to visit relatives. In the weeks preceding Christmas vacation the teachers' lounge had been a buzz of conversation as everyone discussed holiday plans, including visits to San Francisco, Santa Barbara, and San Diego. Certainly with a hint or two I could have wangled an invitation, so that at least I could have shared Christmas with someone's family. But since hinting seemed so inappropriate, I merely evaded the issue when asked about my holiday plans.

Now, however, my bravado was waning. I was ready to accept practically any invitation. I stared expectantly at the telephone. Nothing. But the timer on the stove was buzzing.

I went to the kitchen, took my TV dinner from the oven, and gingerly removed the aluminum foil. I stared at the steaming contents and imagined a case of indigestion already poised for attack. I really wasn't hungry.

But I was ready to make every effort to salvage what remained of Christmas Eve. Somewhere in the city there had to be someone as lonely and available as I. Eagerly I flipped through the pages of my address book and began to dial numbers. Janice Smith hadn't mentioned any special plans, and she wasn't married, so maybe—no answer. Well then, Ruthie Davis had family in North Dakota, but she never mentioned going there for the holidays—no answer there either.

Undaunted I flipped on. How about Phyllis Carr from church—didn't we work on a committee together last month? She was always so friendly. I dialed. This time—an answer!

"Hello, Phyllis," I said, trying not to sound too eager. "Guess who! What? No—but you're close. Yes, from church. That's right. I just thought I'd—well, wish you Merry Christmas. What? Am I going where? Oh, yes, with the career class to Big Bear for the winter retreat. Next weekend—right! Yes, I'm going. Are you? Great. But I was really wondering about—tonight. Are you doing anything special? Oh, on your way to Glendale—just going out the door? Well, I won't keep you. Have a good time now. Good-bye."

In a state of abject depression I replaced the receiver and slunk to the kitchen to consume my TV dinner. Apparently I would just have to write off Christmas this year. Sleep through it or something.

Then an even more depressing thought occurred to me. In my last letter home I had promised my mother I would call her on Christmas Eve. But in my present frame of mind, how could I possibly talk to her? She would sense immediately that something was wrong, that I felt miserable. Knowing that, she might try to persuade me to give my notice for second semester and come home to substitute teach or something. In my weakness I might even yield, and such a commitment to Mom would be difficult to wriggle out of later. The temptation to pack up and go home loomed over me like a thundercloud.

But whatever my feelings, I had to call Mom tonight. And with the time difference, it was much later in Ohio. I would have to call soon. After all, I promised. I would simply have to trust the Lord to keep Mom from guessing how unhappy I was.

As I reached for the phone, the doorbell rang. *Ah, saved by the bell,* I thought. *Maybe this is my answer—someone to spend Christmas with!* I rushed to the door, opened it eagerly and looked up into the smiling face of—Randy Tate. He stood there in his overcoat with a bag of groceries in his arms. "Merry Christmas, kiddo," he greeted.

"Merry Christmas," I stammered back. Randy was even more handsome up close. Suddenly I felt tongue-tied and self-conscious.

"I had to run out for some holiday spirits," he chuckled, "if you know what I mean. I saw your light and figured maybe you were alone on Christmas Eve."

"Well, it just so happens—"

"We're having a big bash at my place, and you're welcome to come on over. I guarantee you'll have a blast."

I stared up dumbfounded at Randy. He was actually asking me to one of his parties? It was a startling idea. "I—I heard the music playing—" I said, imagining myself one of Randy's guests.

He pulled a bottle of whiskey from his sack and winked at me. "Come on over, Babe. We're gonna celebrate good. We may not come up for air until New Year's."

Suddenly, reality struck and any thought of attending Randy's party evaporated like smoke. "Thanks, but I really can't make it."

He shrugged. "Okay. Just hope we don't keep you awake tonight."

I smiled grimly. "Same here."

He nodded toward the apartment on the other side of his. "You know the Medinas? The old couple in 211? Real grouches. Always complaining about my parties. All alone in the world, so they got nothing to do but complain, you know? They even got me in trouble with the landlord."

I felt my pulse quicken. "They did?"

"Sure. I figure it was them. They're such sourpusses. Forgotten how it feels to be young. Not like us, right?"

"Well, actually, I should explain—"

"Listen, I gotta run, but if you change your mind, just come on over. Always room for one more." He was still grinning as he turned away, waved, and called back, "One thing's for sure, Randy Tate knows how to celebrate Christmas!"

As I closed the door on Randy, my spirits sank lower than ever. I knew there was no way I'd feel comfortable at his party, and yet his music reverberating through my walls reminded me that everyone else was celebrating and having a good time. Except me. And worst of all, I still hadn't called my mother. How could I possibly put on a good front for her when she knew me so well?

I slouched in the corner of the sofa, my hand on the phone, bawling, tears making a mess of my makeup. "Oh, God, I'm lonely," I cried. "How can I call my mom?" I wanted to *feel* better so that I would *sound* better over the phone. "What good is Christmas? What—" It struck me then. Christmas. Christmas was Christ. I'd been weighed down by the tinsel, worried about me, drenched in self-pity. Suddenly my self-pity was turning into prayer.

As I prayed I began to feel the presence of the Lord—a warm, comforting presence. I poured out my heart, telling Him just how I felt, how lonely and depressed I was. The Lord began showing me I didn't have to feel that way, that I was choosing to feel despondent when I could choose to be happy in Him. I began to rejoice, to be thankful for my present circumstances, even the fact that I had to spend Christmas alone.

It didn't make sense to me, but I wanted to be obedient. I recalled two verses from Psalm 63 and said them aloud: "Because thy lovingkindness is better than life, my lips shall praise thee. Thus will I bless thee while I live: I will lift up my hands in thy name." Then I thanked Him that I was alone and that it was Christmas Eve. I thanked Him for putting me on my own away from family and friends. I praised God for giving me no one to rely on but Him. It was then I realized—Christ was all I needed. No matter what life held for me, I could rejoice because I would always have Him!

In the silence of my room and over the muted beat of the rock music next door, I began to sing, "He's all I need, He's all I need. Jesus is all I need." For several minutes I sat there like that, singing. Then I picked up the phone and called Mom. Just as I expected, she sounded a little sad and lonely. The rest of the family was off skating at Wren's Pond, she said, but she was waiting by the phone, waiting for my call. She was anxious to know how I was doing—and she missed me.

"I miss you, too, Mom," I told her. "More than I can say. But I'm fine. I really am. My plans for tomorrow? Well, I'm not sure. I think I'll bake some cookies and take them over to an older couple two doors from me. The Medinas. No, I don't know them, but I hear they're all alone, and I think we have a lot in common."

I paused, drawing in a breath and working to control the emotion in my voice. "I guess there are lots of lonely, forgotten people in the world who need a friend, Mom, but I've been too involved in my own life to notice them. Maybe the Lord wants me to start looking around a little more for others in need."

And then, smiling because for the first time in a long time it was true, I said, "Mom, I'm learning that no matter where you are or what your circumstances, if you have the Lord, that's enough. You don't really need anything else. Other people might think they know how to celebrate Christmas, but I'm celebrating with the *One* that Christmas is all about. And, Mom, that's the best Christmas gift anyone can have!"

The Engagement Party

What does a woman do when she realizes God may want her to remain single for the rest of her life?

All afternoon I scout department stores in the mall, looking for just the right gift to give my younger sister Sara, a proper present for Sara and Stan when my parents honor them tonight with an engagement party. I consider Austrian crystal, Hummel figurines, a silk flower arrangement, even a pocket color TV, but nothing seems quite right for the "perfect couple."

In desperation I even consider something as mundane as a coffeepot, until I remember that Stan, when I went with him, never drank coffee. Finally, around 4:30, I give up and settle for a chef salad and diet drink at Big Boy's.

I don't want any part of it, I reflect solemnly, imagining how tonight will be. *I don't want any part of an engagement party! Why didn't I just tell my parents I was busy tonight? A prior engagement with good ol' neighbor Larry Heath, the Tom Cruise of Centerville!*

Two preteen boys in Levi's and neon T-shirts sit in the booth across from me. I watch them play with a plastic catsup container. The larger boy—he is chubby and soft-looking, not muscular—aims and hits the other boy with a fat red squirt along his cheek and neck, so that the red stuff oozes like blood onto his shirt. A waitress comes over, glaring as she wipes her hands on a towel, and grabs the container out of the boy's hand.

"Hey, I need that for my fries," he protests, grabbing it back. She frowns, starts to say something, then shrugs and shuffles off.

"I'm wounded!" exclaims the smaller boy with the tomato-streaked face, clutching his cheek so that the catsup runs gruesomely down his fingers. Like something from a Stephen King horror flick.

Irritated, I look toward another table where a middle-aged man in a suit is eating fried shrimp. When I look back, I notice the large boy watching me with narrow, scrutinizing eyes. He is still holding the catsup container. *Don't you dare!* I warn silently, glancing down at my new white velour sweater. It bothers me—that look in his eyes. Who does he think he is? He keeps staring. I stare back, wanting to call out and say, *Hey, get a life, kid! Mind your own business! Who do you think I am?*

But the question echoes tauntingly in my mind: *Who do you think I am?*

I'm Margie Sawyer, a dedicated Christian who gave her life for the Lord's service a year ago July. I'm committed...but I don't want to go to Sara's engagement party. I don't want any part of it. There it is again, this feeling of rebellion, of resentment.

I'm not in love with Stan. I never was. We dated a lot. I

liked him, he liked me. But nothing clicked romantically. It doesn't bother me that he loves Sara now—Sara, two years younger and about to become a wife.

The smaller boy has spotted his chubby friend watching me. He lets out a great whoop so that the man eating shrimp looks up startled. "Hey, you got a girlfriend," I hear the boy squeal, shoving an elbow into his buddy's ribs.

I summon my most menacing glare and aim it at the boy with catsup on his face. He grins, showing uneven teeth. I even consider getting up and walking out, but I'm not through eating. Besides, the boys are preparing to go.

"You ain't gonna leave your girlfriend all alone, are you?" Catsup-face drawls as they swagger past me. I stare into my plate, concentrating on my salad.

There is no reason I should feel humiliated or bothered by the playfulness of youngsters, I tell myself. *Just because they called me "girlfriend." I'm no one's girlfriend. I used to be Stan's. I didn't love him, but it was good to have him to depend on. When there's no one—like now, no one at all—you get scared sometimes wondering if there will ever be anyone.*

A tomato wedge sticks in my throat. I wash down the lump with my diet drink. I'm not hungry anymore—if I ever was hungry.

I am fighting a feeling of abject depression—self-pity. I push the feeling away, but it bumps back harder; I feel strapped, bound, as if my emotions are shrouded by heavy canvas.

Most of the time such feelings are remote. I am too busy with my studies, preparing to teach—perhaps on the mission field or in a Christian school. A year ago July I committed everything to Christ, whatever I am, for His service. Most of the time I rejoice in His will, knowing He has a wonderful plan for me. Most of the time I am fine.

But sometimes—like now—I am reminded of what might be the Lord's will for me—a life alone, unmarried. No husband. No babies. No family of my own.

I am 22 years old and a college senior this year. Senior panic—someone mentioned it once, laughing like it was really a big joke. No one gets senior panic anymore, they say; women are too liberated these days, too independent to need a man. I agreed and laughed too. Then.

Sara just turned 20 and probably won't finish college. She will likely work a year or so until Stan gets his master's degree; then I figure she'll quit and have a baby. I will be an aunt. Someone's maiden aunt.

I don't want anyone to know about these thoughts and feelings. I keep them to myself. People might say I don't have enough faith. They might question my dedication.

Sometimes I wonder, *What dedication?*

As I leave Big Boy's and go out into the crisp late-afternoon air, I think again about my neighbor Larry Heath. I could go with him to a party tonight. Yes, with Larry Heath. Larry, who considers himself heaven's gift to women. Larry, whom I've ignored most of my life. He's 25, single, and still living at home. He dabbles in real estate and insurance and obscure investments. Looks like a poor man's Dustin Hoffman. He's not so bad, just not so good either. He's not a Christian. He's cynical. Likes to party. And he thinks he's totally cool.

Last night he telephoned—one of the many calls I've received from him lately. "You can't blame a guy for trying," he answered when I said no to his invitation. "You know, Babe, you've always been special to me, and now that Stan is out of the picture...Anyway, if you change your mind, the party's at Joe Danby's on Seventh Street. Believe me, it'll be...radical."

Suddenly, I can't get Larry's call out of my mind. If nothing more, his invitation offers the escape route I've been looking for all along. An excuse to avoid the festivities with Sara and Stan.

Seventh Street. I know where that is. I could take the downtown bus. It goes right by Seventh. I could be there before seven. I could skip the engagement party. Why not do something daring, impulsive? Sure, Mother might be hurt, but she'll be involved with Sara and Stan, and Father will just have to understand that I have my own life to lead.

I am excited now. I am practically skipping along the sidewalk like a schoolgirl. The depression has been swept clean from my mind. I am convinced that this party is just what I need. It'll be great having a real date and forgetting my silly anxieties. I need someone tonight. I need to feel that I belong to someone, even if it's just a few brief hours at somebody's party.

The bench at the bus stop is occupied, but the woman, seeing me approach, gathers her packages so that I can sit down. She is a big woman with full shoulders, thick arms and smooth skin. She is wearing a faded housedress and a brown cardigan sweater. There is a quality of weariness about her, making her appear older than the smoothness of her face would suggest. She smiles. I smile back, studying her without looking directly at her. She sits surrounded by her packages, knitting something.

"This here is for my grandchild. My daughter's baby," she tells me as if I had asked.

"Oh, really?" I reply politely. "How old is the baby?"

"Actually, he—or she's—not born yet. It's due early November. I'll have the sweater done by then."

"It's a lovely color," I say. "Sort of chartreuse, isn't it?"

She nods. "I figure that's better than pink or blue, seeing as how I don't know whether it's a boy or girl."

"Smart thinking," I agree. "Are you taking the bus to visit your daughter?"

"No, I just got off work. I'm a cleaning lady at the Beverly Lane Apartments just down the block. I ride the bus every day." She eyes me quizzically. "I don't recall seeing you at this stop before."

"Right. I don't usually take the bus. I live with my folks a couple blocks from here. But I'm going to a party over on Seventh Street."

"Seventh Street? Goodness. That's quite a ways from here."

"I know. I hadn't planned to go, but it sort of came up unexpectedly." I watch her fingers lovingly knit that sweater and find myself wondering if I'll ever have babies to knit for. "Is this your first grandchild?"

"Yes, it sure is." Her voice grows wistful. "I just wish George was here to see that baby. He'd be so proud."

"George?"

"He was my husband. Been gone nearly five years now."

"I'm sorry."

"It's okay, honey. I figure God gives and God takes away. The good Lord knows what He's doing, don't you think so?"

I am caught off guard. A stranger voicing my own thoughts. *God gave Stan...God took away Stan...God knows what He's doing. Doesn't He?* "You sound like you're a Christian," I note cautiously.

The woman heaves a sigh. "Oh, I suppose. Isn't everybody? I don't get to church much though, working such long hours." She meets my gaze. "Are you?"

"A Christian? Yes, I am." I feel like I should say more, but the words evaporate in my mind.

Both of us are silent for a moment. Then she asks, "So, you got a nice young man in your life?"

I shake my head, feeling the warmth rush to my face. Even

a stranger manages to bring me back to my current quandary—single and alone with no prospects for the future.

She reaches over and pats my hand. "Well, someone nice will come along, you'll see."

I smile, wondering if I should tell this nice lady that I've given my life to God and He may not have a nice young man in my future. But even as I think it, I realize how cynical I sound. I never meant it to be this way. I only wanted to do God's will. Why does my commitment suddenly feel like a millstone around my neck? "I'm not sure a husband is in God's plan," I manage at last.

"What? Not in God's plan?" Her bushy brows rise indignantly. "I don't know much about God, but I know He does right by us. There'll be someone to love you. You wait and see."

I try to find the words to tell this woman of my commitment, my resolve to serve God wherever He wants me to go. "I've promised Him my life, don't you see? I really want to serve Him. And He may send me to some foreign country. Or He may want me to remain single. I just don't know yet what He wants."

The woman stares at me with eyes of amazement. "You talk of Him—God—like you know Him so well—"

I feel suddenly humbled. "I do know Him. Jesus—His Spirit—lives in my heart—"

The woman shakes her head slowly. "I don't know Him like that. I hope He's there somewhere watching over me. I believe it, but I don't know Him..."

"You can, you know," I say quickly.

"What?"

"Know Him. God. You can know Him personally."

"Really? No, I don't think so. He wouldn't have time for me—"

"Yes, He does. He has all the time in the world for you—

and for me. His love is greater than anything we can imagine."

"It sounds very nice," she says wistfully. "I wish I had your faith."

Suddenly I find myself pouring out the feelings I've bottled up for so long—how I committed my life to God and yearn to serve and know Him better, and yet how anxious I feel wondering what that commitment might cost me. "Jesus is the best thing that ever happened to me," I conclude softly. "He's my closest friend. I don't want to disappoint Him, but I don't know if I can measure up either."

The woman smiles. "If God's love is as big as you say, it don't matter, does it?"

I return her smile. "You're right. We're saved by grace. Kept by grace. Sometimes I forget that."

She reaches over and clasps my hand. "Anyone who has God for a friend is going to be okay. I just wish He was my friend like that."

"He can be. Would you like me to tell you how?"

She looks down the street. "Our bus is coming. Maybe we can sit together and chat."

"I'd like that." But, suddenly, the thought of going with Larry Heath to Joe Danby's wild party leaves a knot in my stomach and a sour taste in my mouth.

I watch uncertainly as the huge shuddering vehicle pulls up to the curb, spewing dust and fumes and making a great swooshing sound as it wheezes to a stop. The door creaks open. I catch a glimpse of the driver's face as he looks our way.

For an instant I don't know which way to turn. Then, swiftly, I help the woman with her packages and follow her onto the bus. "I can't ride as far as I'd planned," I tell her as we sit down together in the narrow seat. "I'll be getting off after we've had a chance to talk."

She looks surprised. "Really, dear? I thought you were going all the way to Seventh Street. A party, you said."

I smile, and I actually feel good as I say the words: "I've changed my mind. You see, my sister is announcing her engagement tonight, and I don't want to miss the celebration."

Petals in the Storm

What does a woman do when the love-ties to her mother and daughter threaten to break?

All right, here I am. I am sitting in a hospital waiting room and have nothing to do but to wait. I will sit here until the doctor comes to me and says, Mrs. Sawyer, Liz Sawyer, your mother is...Will he say she is dead? Will he say, We opened her up and she is full of cancer, rotten with cancer? He will say she is going to die—dying! And I will say I already know.

In this waiting room someone has hung paintings, outrageous paintings of fruit and bowls that fall right off the canvas; stiff flat little apples floating above a crude table, because the artist couldn't make them sit down, couldn't make them real enough to sit on the table like they should. I would like to take a black crayon and scribble on those canvases and scratch out the apples. They are not real; they cannot pretend to be real. They have no right to be there.

I am here, but I am also somewhere else. If I were only

here, I could not stand it, could not stand to be closed up, waiting to hear. So I am somewhere else, except when Bonnie, my fifteen-year-old daughter, interrupts to show me a picture in the magazine she is reading. I try not to look at her, try not to encourage her interruptions. I am happier somewhere else.

In my mind I am standing with my mother and my daughter, and we are holding hands, forming a chain, an arc, an open circle. I am in the middle. Between them. Each of them has one empty hand. But not I. My hands are full. I am mother and daughter. Daughter of my mother. Mother of my daughter. In my mind, thinking this, I am closed in—but it is good (not like this waiting room), and I am very warm and secure.

When I was a child my mother had a garden; she gathered flowers from the garden; she made bouquets for the house, and the rooms smelled of lilacs and roses. One rainy day she took the petals of a rose and strung them on pink thread. "Here is a necklace for you," she told me, putting the petals around my neck. In my joy I ran out into the rainstorm and watched the glistening raindrops falling on my precious petals. I wore the necklace to bed and cried when the petals bruised and finally turned crisp and brown and crackled apart.

When I asked my mother for another necklace, she said something that I remember as: "Life is your petal chain, Liz. You will discover that all of the attachments between people—parents and children, husbands and wives, brothers and sisters, friends with friends, all relationships—are love chains for you to enjoy. But they must be treasured, because they are fragile things and cannot last forever." I recall that I smiled, understanding nothing my mother said.

When I realize that I have not thought of that petal chain

for nearly 20 years, I am aware how far my mind has wandered. I am getting downright saccharine—a softy. But no one can accuse me of that. I am not like my mother. I am nothing like my mother. People walk on her. Hurt her. She says nothing. She smiles too much, is too kind. Even to me. To me, her unkind daughter.

Sitting here with nothing to do, I make an attempt to put together the features of my mother's face—her eyes, nose, mouth. The way her hair curls softly around her ears. Her neck. Shoulders. But I cannot remember what my mother looks like. I cannot see her. What is wrong with me? Where am I? Where am I really? I see a face—it is pastel, vague—like the soft, flimsy doll faces on some of those mawkish drugstore greeting cards. But it is not my mother's face. I cannot reach her.

I tried. Wasn't I trying? When I sat by her bed before the operation, didn't I say the right things? I chose my words carefully. She never knew I thought she might die, was afraid she would die. My voice didn't crack or break; I showed no emotion. I smiled. Talking about Bonnie. Bonnie's going away to school next year. Bonnie's grades. Bonnie's father coming home from London in two weeks. His business trip wrapped up, successful. All good things, all pleasant things. I never once slipped, never once let her know I thought I might never see her again. There are things one does not talk about. There are things about which there is nothing to say.

Basically I am happy. I am not worried. My life has not changed drastically in 20 years. In the circle of my existence stand my mother and my daughter. There is my husband, too, but he is not often there, and therefore not often needed.

I stand in the middle, in the open circle, touched on each side by someone else. There is room to move, but I do not choose to move far. It is better than being here.

I am rather independent. I have always depended on my mother—in some ways—but I am a person in my own right too. I came from her, out of her, always to be a part of her. But I am myself too. I am nothing like my mother, even though I am part of her, though we are part of each other. She is too good, too quiet in her ways. She walks through life on tiptoe, never disturbing anything, leaving everything neatly in its place. She is beautiful but quiet and will leave a silent mark when she is gone.

I am loud and large and bump things when I move. I am not beautiful. I am not quiet. I bump things, knocking them down. My noises are worse than my mother's silences—but they are mine. My own sounds. Something of me. Something to remain when she is gone. These things I cannot talk of, these things have no words—and if they did, I could not speak them. I am better off somewhere else, away from this. I am better off not here.

When I was a girl I heard my mother, listened to her silences, watched her ways, always watching, observing. She let me hurt her more than once, more than once, saying nothing. I had to hurt her, didn't want to—had to. It took a long time, a long growing-up time, to stop seeing only her, to start to see someone else emerging—to see myself becoming something separate, apart from her. It was hard going. It was a heavy plodding task, building up the sounds and noises of myself out of her silences. It was a long time before I could start to see myself, build my own face in my mind without looking in a mirror.

She never said whether I went too far the other way. I wonder if she thought so, if she thought I was trying to break the love chain, trying to smash the circle with my bumping? If I went too far, it was to keep from hating her, to keep from being sucked up by her. I feel guilty, thinking I went too far, thinking I could have done more and didn't. I feel guilty, but it is better than being snuffed out. Feeling guilty is better than feeling resentment for the other way it might have been.

My daughter interrupts, saying something about going to the hospital cafeteria, and my mind, like a rubber band, snaps back from somewhere else to here. I look at her, thinking she looks like a stranger—someone I don't know, someone I don't want to talk to now. She must see my coldness, because she backs down.

"The cafeteria was a bad idea," she says. "Forget it."

No. We will go to the cafeteria. We haven't eaten since last night when we checked into the hotel at seven; a marvelous hotel (they advertised) with cable TV, king-size beds and air-conditioning—in November—and even porcelain bathtubs. Not to mention Howard Johnson's restaurant next door. But best of all, a five-minute drive from the hospital. Five minutes. You can't beat that.

Bonnie is slipping out of her chair, smoothing her short skirt, collecting her coat and purse, walking ahead of me down the corridor to the cafeteria. She is graceful like her grandmother and full of silences I do not understand.

We get into line. We stand in line with the nurses and doctors and perhaps half a dozen other people like ourselves, who are waiting to hear the outcome of someone's operation. We move along, selecting napkins and silverware, a salad, a plate of something, a slice of cake, a glass of water. I pay the cashier for our food and we grapple with our trays until we find a vacant table. The dishes clatter as we set them on the table, as we arrange things so that everything will fit nicely. Bonnie's chili and cheese sandwich. My mashed potatoes and—whatever. Silverware clattering. Chairs scuffing the floor as we get into them. Bonnie's face is pink, as if she might be embarrassed, as if she might be afraid that people are watching us sit down and get settled.

It does not bother me. It bothers her—my noises and my bumping bother her. It occurs to me that she too is struggling to emerge, struggling to be born, as I struggled to be separate from my mother. Do people have to spend their entire lives struggling to become complete, whole in themselves? It is too terrible to think of. I suddenly pity Bonnie. Her face is smooth, untouched—nearly blank. She has so far to go.

We eat our food. It is tasteless and as antiseptic as the smell that permeates the hospital rooms. The smell is everywhere. In our mouths, in our stomachs. We cannot eat much. If we could only get away from the smell, we'd feel better.

We stop at the main desk on our way back from the cafeteria, but there is still no word from the doctor. We go back to the waiting room, back to where the walls are cluttered with badly done oil paintings wearing worn "For Sale" signs. Back to the faltering fruit, to the poor imitation of life on canvas. But then, what is real? Who am I to say what is real? Who am I to judge?

Yet why shouldn't I judge? I have gone through a great deal to have the right to my own opinions. I have struggled to come through, to find my place, to be myself. That is saying a lot. Perhaps that is saying something I have been afraid to say before. It is a confusing idea, something that is not yet clear in my mind. I am still not entirely here.

Bonnie and I sit down, saying little. It is difficult to talk to Bonnie, to know what to say. My sounds say so little. Perhaps her silences say something, but I do not understand them. We talk often but never say anything; we are careful about that.

I mention the oil paintings—how poorly done they are, what a mockery of reality they actually are. Bonnie nods; she has my artistic sense, that much I know.

Bonnie has a need to talk. I see the need naked in her eyes. I have not seen it like this before, not in Bonnie.

"You can tell me, Bonnie. What's the matter? What's wrong with you?"

Her words are like a gasp, hardly a sound at all. "It's Grandma. I just know she's going to die!"

"No!" I shout. "How dare you say that?" My hand like a strap swings toward her face; I feel the softness of her cheek against my palm. Impact, sting. Then horror—worse than the nakedness—in her eyes!

"Dear God," I hear myself cry. I pull Bonnie into my arms and hold her. For an instant our bodies rock together. The sounds that come forth seem to come from somewhere else, from another person. But they are coming from me, and I have never heard such sounds before. It is as if something were breaking apart, as if someone were screaming through the wretched process of birth, willing herself to be born. The noises are my own. I am screaming, "Not my mother, dear God! Not my mother, please!"

As quickly as the sounds began, they are gone. I am empty. Bonnie soothes me with her silence. I feel her strength growing, blooming. The room is full of her silence.

I am silent too, thinking again of the arc, the love chains, the open circle. Somehow I realize how terribly important this moment is. I must be more to Bonnie than I have been; I must be more. I recognize, too, that I cannot keep the circle from changing. The time will come when I must open my hand and let go. Let my mother go. Someday, Bonnie's child will join us in the circle, and Bonnie will be in the middle. She will be both mother and daughter. And in time—it is a mystery—the circle will revolve again. Bonnie too will have to open her hand, releasing me.

The Secret of Martha Tidings

What does a woman do when she suspects her neighbor of child abuse?

Martha Tidings, sitting gray-faced and sullen in her faded flannel bathrobe, fidgeted with the handle of a stained coffee mug. "You come here regular as the milkman," she told Trudy, who stood just inside the doorway. "Sit down if you like. Have some coffee. It don't matter to me."

Trudy hesitated only a moment, then removed a pile of newspapers from a nearby chair and sat down. "I just wondered how you were doing," she replied, glancing at the soiled table and deciding against coffee.

"I do all right. It's a wonder, no man in the house and four kids to raise. But I manage."

"I'm glad everything's all right," said Trudy. "My son, Timmy, hasn't seen Ryan in school for a couple of days. Is he ill?"

Martha glanced up, her eyes narrowing, her face older

than her 35 years. "Ryan? Naw, he's—he's all right. He fell down the back porch steps and got bumped up. But he'll be back in school tomorrow."

"I'm glad he's okay," said Trudy, glancing around the small, cluttered kitchen. A year-old calendar hung askew on one wall. The stove was black with grease, the cupboards grimy, and the drain board stacked with dishes.

"Does that mean Ryan can go with us to church this Sunday?" asked Trudy, returning her gaze to the stony face of her neighbor.

"He does what he pleases," the woman answered bluntly. She drained her coffee cup and wiped her mouth with her hand. "But don't think just because that church of yours gave us a handout that I'm going to show up at services."

Trudy shook her head emphatically. "There's no obligation for the food, Mrs. Tidings. We just wanted you to know we care about you and your children."

The woman broke into sudden laughter, hard and bawdy and disdainful, which she as quickly stifled with one large hand. Nevertheless, Trudy felt put down, ridiculed. Already she was aware of the small stirrings of resentment that always came when she confronted Mrs. Tidings.

"I suppose I should be going," said Trudy, rising.

"Don't take no offense, Mrs. Carr. I just can't figure what you and your church crowd want from me. First you come around friendly-like and get my boy goin' to church with your boy. Then you bring boxes of food over from your church people, and now here you are again—paying a *social* call. I just gotta ask, what is it you want?"

Trudy groped for words. "Like I said, we care about your family, Mrs. Tidings. And we just want to help meet your needs."

The woman absently flicked toast crumbs off the table. "The way I figure it, lady, nobody gets nothin' for nothin'.

And, if you ask me, you got some nerve thinking my needs are any of your business. Not that I'm fool enough to turn down charity, mind you."

Trudy drew back involuntarily. "I'm sorry, Mrs. Tidings, that you feel I'm intruding on your privacy. It was a mistake for me to come here."

Turning sharply on her heel, Trudy walked out of the house, letting the door slam behind her. Not until she had walked the block back to her own home was she aware of the weakness in her legs. Reaching for the doorknob, her hand trembled with anger.

That evening, Trudy shared her negative feelings with her husband. "I can't help it, Mark," she told him after Timmy had gone to bed. "I want to like that woman, but she makes me so angry. She's so—so haughty. She doesn't appreciate anything we try to do for her."

"How do you think she should act?"

Trudy shrugged. "I don't know. Appreciative, I suppose. Instead, she makes me feel—uncomfortable. As if I'm imposing or something."

"Maybe you are."

"Mark! Ever since Timmy brought Ryan home from school to play, I've tried to reach that family for Christ. We've taken Ryan with us to church and the church has provided food for Mrs. Tidings when I know she didn't have more than a crust of bread in the house. How could that be imposing?"

"Well, you've had enough psychology in your nurse's training to know that people aren't predictable," offered Mark. "Hon, no matter what their poverty level, people have their pride." He spread open the newspaper on his lap but his eyes remained on Trudy. "I wonder, hon," he added thoughtfully, "are you doing these things for this woman out of a sense of love or just because you feel it's your Christian duty?"

Trudy thought a moment, then smiled weakly. "I've already answered that one, haven't I? How can I love someone I don't even like?"

"That's one you're going to have to settle between you and the Lord," replied Mark. He jostled his paper and Trudy knew instinctively that Mark had said all he intended on the subject.

In her personal devotions that evening Trudy was convicted of one thing in particular: She ought to apologize to Mrs. Tidings for the way she had stalked out of her house that morning. She would begin with that and trust the Lord for the rest.

The next afternoon Martha Tidings promptly dismissed Trudy's apology with a bit of her own philosophy. "We all get in a huff one time or another," she said, nervously wiping out a coffee cup with a stained dish towel. "Take me now. When I get mad I can't see straight. That's the truth. I see red, like a bull or something."

Trudy smiled politely, but her eyes were on a chubby jam-smeared toddler scudding along under the table. With a single swoop, Mrs. Tidings leaned over, gathered up the child, and hoisted him onto the tabletop where he perched bird-like, mouth open and hands waving gleefully. His mother opened a jar of baby food and methodically pushed spoonfuls of thick, dark stuff into the child's eager mouth.

"How old is he?" asked Trudy as the red-faced youngster noisily clacked his two front teeth against the spoon.

"Just over a year. His pa left when he found out I was expecting this one. He said three was too many, and four—well, there was no way he could take four kids. So he just up and left."

"I'm so sorry, Mrs. Tidings. I didn't realize—"

"Yeah, well, I suppose I coulda got one of them abortions,

but I figured the kid was probably worth ten of his old man, the ol' good for nothin'."

"You've had to cope with an awful lot, Mrs. Tidings—"

"Just plain Martha, okay, Mrs. Carr? Just Martha."

Trudy nodded. "Of course. And I'm just Trudy."

"Yeah, okay. Trudy. Here, hold this youngun' while I get a cloth to clean him up."

Several times in the next month Trudy stopped by to visit with Martha. Sometimes she brought a sackful of groceries or some items of clothing Timmy had outgrown that would likely fit the smaller Tidings children. Occasionally Trudy came with cookies she had just baked. Whatever she brought, she had learned to stir as little fanfare as possible.

While Trudy could not claim a close friendship with Martha, she was aware of a certain love, not from herself but generated by Christ, which gradually pervaded her attitude toward the woman. She was still irritated by Martha's coarseness and carelessness, but a greater sense of tolerance and concern made the irritations seem less significant. Trudy began to believe that it was only a matter of time before she would be able to introduce Martha to Christ.

One afternoon Martha lamented the aches and pains that caring for her children brought her. "I get so I want to pack them all off somewhere," she complained, pulling a shirt over the head of her squalling toddler. "The baby cries and the older ones fight. Ryan, he's only eight, but he's so pigheaded sometimes!"

"I guess it's easier for me, having only one child, but even Timmy is a handful at times," conceded Trudy. "But I've found I can always trust God to help me," she added gently.

Martha shook her head vigorously. "No," she said. "No, I don't want you to talk about that. God doesn't care nothin' for me."

"That's not so, Martha," insisted Trudy. "God loves you. I know He does. You see—"

"No, no more. I don't want to hear no more. It's impossible, I tell you!"

Trudy returned home that day feeling discouraged about ever reaching Martha. What more could she do when her neighbor was so adamant? How could she reach someone who refused to listen? More to the point, how could God reach someone whose heart seemed so hardened?

Trudy kept her neighbor in her prayers for the rest of the day. Then, unexpectedly, late that evening Trudy was catapulted harshly back into the center of Martha's problems.

Shortly before midnight, the telephone rang. It was Martha, her voice strained and edged with—what? Terror? Dismay?

"You're a nurse, aren't you?"

"What?" asked Trudy, still groggy.

"A nurse. Your boy told mine you were a nurse."

"Yes," answered Trudy blankly.

"You have to come. You're the only one. Please come right away."

"What? Come over? What's wrong, Martha?"

"It's Ryan. Hurry!" The line went dead.

"Who's that? What's the matter?" Mark mumbled, rising sleepily on one elbow.

"Martha Tidings says she needs a nurse at once. I'll go, but you stay with Timmy. If I can't come back soon, I'll call you."

"You be careful, Trudy, you hear? It's late. If there's trouble, let me know and I'll be right there."

"I'm sure it's something I can handle," said Trudy, slipping on her slacks and blouse. "If it was an emergency, she would have called 9-1-1, wouldn't she?" Without waiting for an answer, Trudy grabbed her coat from the closet and hurried out the door.

Martha was waiting in her open doorway, her face contorted with alarm and despair. She lamented over and over, "I didn't know what to do, Trudy. I just didn't know."

"What's wrong, Martha? You said Ryan..."

"Yeah, he's in here." She led Trudy into a cluttered bedroom where Ryan was apparently asleep. But as Trudy approached the bedside, she drew back stunned. "Martha, what on earth—? This child—his face—he's been severely beaten!"

"You tell me," cried Martha urgently, "you tell me if he's still alive. Tell me he'll be all right."

"Who did this?" uttered Trudy as she felt for a pulse.

"Will he be all right?" persisted Martha, her voice rising shrilly.

"I don't know, I don't know!" Trudy shook her head, attempting to clear a terrible confusion billowing in her brain. "Call 9-1-1," she told Martha. "Tell them to get an ambulance over here fast."

"No ambulance! I can't."

"You must," demanded Trudy, blotting the rivulet of blood that oozed from the child's mouth. "Ryan needs medical attention. He's having trouble breathing." Gently, she cleared his airway, praying.

"No, no doctors. No hospitals. You help him."

Trudy pivoted sharply, facing Martha. "Don't you understand? Without proper care Ryan might die!" She lunged for the phone, her hands trembling as she dialed 9-1-1, but her voice was calm. She heard herself give the name, address, heard herself whisper, "Hurry."

Martha buried her face in her huge hands. "They'll know. The doctors—everyone will know."

"Know what?" exclaimed Trudy. Comprehension swept over her. "What are you afraid of, Martha?"

Martha wiped at the tears on her broad face and sniffed loudly. "They'll know—"

"What? That you did this?" cried Trudy? "Is that what you're saying? You did this to Ryan?"

"They'll know I beat my son," sobbed Martha. "I beat my own boy."

Trudy closed her eyes for a moment and fought for a prayer. But she had no words, nothing.

Martha bent over her son and whimpered softly. "I'm sorry, Ryan, baby. I didn't mean to hurt you. You made me so mad, I just couldn't stop. I couldn't."

Looking up as Trudy returned to the bedside, Martha implored, "You understand, don't you, Trudy? I can't help myself. Ryan pushes me. He drives me to this. I begin spankin' him and I can't stop. I try, but I can't. I wish to God I could stop!"

Trudy recoiled. How could she comfort a woman who beat her own child? "You could have gotten help, Martha. There are organizations all set up to help—"

"People like me? Is that what you was gonna say? You must think I'm some kind of monster."

"No, it's just that I—I don't know what to say—"

Martha eyed her mournfully. "They'll call the police, won't they? They'll question me. They'll take my kids away. I won't have nothin' left, Trudy."

"You don't know that, Martha. Right now we've got to concentrate on Ryan, on getting him help."

"Will you come along, Trudy? To the hospital? There's no one else I can ask."

Trudy thought of Mark at home in bed, and her own son sleeping soundly in his bed. "Yes, I'll come. Just let me call my husband."

"And if the police come—will you stay? Stay with me?"

Trudy nodded. It was going to be a long, dark night. She wondered silently what this night would hold for all of them before daybreak. Did she have the strength to endure it? The wisdom? The compassion? Only with God's help.

Outside a siren wailed, growing closer. The two women sat by the bed waiting, mutely watching the boy in the pale bedroom light.

"You see now why God couldn't love me," Martha groaned, pushing damp strands of hair back from her face. "God must hate me for what I done—just like I hate myself."

"No, Martha, that's not so." Fighting the shock and weariness in her bones, Trudy reached out and placed her hand on Martha's shoulder. She groped for the right words. "What's so special about God is that He loves us—you and me—no matter what we've done. And if we're truly sorry, He'll forgive us and help us do what's right."

"Naw, it can't be. God would forgive me? Even for what I did to Ryan? Why should He?"

"Because He loves you, Martha. But you need to let Him help you. And let others help you."

As the paramedics burst into the room, Martha rubbed her temples distractedly. "I don't know how."

"I'll help you," Trudy whispered. "Start with that, Martha. Hold on to that." She watched as one medic leaned down and gently turned Ryan's head so that he could breathe easier. *Help Ryan, God,* she prayed silently. *And Martha too.*

As they lifted him on the stretcher, Ryan stirred slightly. Life was strange, Trudy reflected silently. She didn't know why, but God had chosen her to show His love to this woman and her family. It wasn't something Trudy could do by herself, but even now she could feel His love reaching out to Martha, reaching out to Ryan, and it warmed her, even in this moment of horror.

Somewhere within herself Trudy knew the darkness of this hour would pass and that God would turn night into morning, heartbreak into blessing.

The Day the Dog Attacked

What does a woman do when depression hits and she yearns to be free of her family?

At the time of the scream, Ruth was on her hands and knees on the kitchen floor wiping up the spills around Benny's high chair. Glancing up, she noticed an irregular glob of grape jelly on the wall, an annoying reminder of her clash with the children that morning.

Four-year-old Becky had helped herself to bread and jelly and was taking obvious pleasure in the fact that two-year-old Benny stood empty-handed, drooling, as his sister smugly spooned out an extra helping of the lush purple stuff.

"Bread, Mama. Bread," Benny whined.

She, their weary, exasperated mother, was busy cleaning the oven, her hands confined by skin-tight protective rubber gloves; she could not go to Benny's rescue now. Annoyed, she thought, *You'll have to solve your own problems, Benny!*

"Bread, Mama," he said again and, able to stand it no longer, he lunged for that bountiful spoon. His fist closed around the silver stem, but the precious contents shot out, splattering a violet bouquet on the bare white wall. He broke into a mournful howl while Becky screamed in protest over her interrupted feast.

That had been the end of the oven cleaning. Now, on her hands and knees, Ruth noticed the spot of jelly she had missed wiping up earlier, and all the irritations of the day assailed her afresh. How, she wondered fiercely, could she ever be free? And even as she entertained the thought, a pall of guilt slipped over her, like a shroud enveloping her mind.

I should be thankful, she told herself chidingly. ***The Lord has given me everything I asked for—a kind, loving husband, two beautiful children, a good home. What's the matter with me? Why can't I appreciate what I have?***

These questions were not new; they had bombarded her spirits before, following close upon other more ominous thoughts—doubts, depression, despair. She was always a little unnerved when the despair hit; there was no reason for it.

Yet, too often in the last couple of years, as she spent long hours alone with her babies, caring for them day and night, seeing them through colds and croup, feeding and bathing and clothing them, a wretched, uncontrollable feeling would overtake her, like a voluminous cloud, black and threatening.

The feeling would pass after a while, but never soon enough. She was always left a little weak and frightened, wondering how this could be happening to her. How could she, a Christian who deeply loved the Lord and her family, be so weak, so unappreciative? And sweeping quickly upon the tide of guilt was a bitter loneliness. Was she the only woman in the world who could not cope?

It was little comfort that her husband Richard seemed to cope so well with everything. Rarely did he complain of problems with his job. He found time to be a deacon in the church, to help with the boys' club on Friday nights, to drive the church bus on Sundays.

On the other hand, she seemed never able to finish her tasks; the children clung to her with demands; somehow, she had even allowed herself to lose touch with her friends. And, of course, there was no time to pursue old hobbies or to enjoy favorite pastimes.

But she had asked for this life, hadn't she? She had felt overjoyed when Richard agreed she could give up her secretarial job at Webber's Manufacturing to stay home and start a family. Now that she had what she had longed for all her life, why couldn't she enjoy it? And worst of all, lately her depression was affecting her marriage. Richard had started noticing how unhappy and irritated she was. But when he questioned her and asked how he could help, she shut him out, pushed him away. Yet, all too often she took her frustration out on him, blaming him somehow for not easing her pain, when she herself had no idea how to solve her dilemma.

But how could she tell Richard what was wrong when she couldn't even articulate for herself why she felt so depressed? Except that life was overwhelming her with its demands, and there seemed to be no end in sight. Sometimes she wished she could just close her eyes and forget everything in blissful sleep, until all her problems simply disappeared.

These had been her thoughts at the moment of the scream. The scream seemed to come from somewhere in her own mind—her own desperate inner protest, perhaps. It took a moment to realize that the horrifying sound was not part of her but something beyond her. It came from the front yard.

She sprang to her feet and ran to the front door, throwing it open to sunlight and gently inrushing air, sweet with the fragrance of freshly cut grass. She had let the children out in the yard only minutes ago. The older Baker youngsters had come asking if they could play, and she had been happy to have the children out from underfoot while she tackled the kitchen chores.

The scream. It was Benny's. She knew that. There was something about it that chilled her, left her palms moist and cold. Her eyes darted across the yard and focused swiftly upon a blur of movement—Benny in his blue sweater, his arms flaying the air, his face contorted in pain. And on top of him the neighbor's Doberman pinscher, his teeth snapping and gnashing at Benny's vulnerable face. With horror she saw a stream of red spurt from one smooth white cheek as Benny pushed helplessly at the dog.

"No, no, no, no!" she screamed, flying into the yard with the energy of a mad woman. In that sudden instant of flight toward her child, her thoughts raced even faster. It stunned her to realize that at the root of her consciousness a terrifying question had lain dormant since the time her children were no more than a pleasant expectation—*What if I lost a child?* Now the question lay open and exposed like a wound in her mind. How could she stand it?

Frantically she grabbed at the enraged animal, feeling beneath his smooth dark hair the intense power of his body. She clawed at the animal with a frenzy that amazed her, but it seemed that her child and the dog were joined in an incredible struggle, rolling together as one, a single terrible unit.

At first she hadn't noticed the other children milling about, so complete had her attention been on Benny and the dog. Now, however, she was aware of the older Baker boy joining her in her attempts to pull the animal off her son.

"It's Peterson's dog," he said breathlessly. "He gets mean sometimes."

She heard Becky's voice: "I watched Benny, Mama. I watched him like a good girl, but the doggy came." She began to whimper.

Behind Ruth, she heard someone running, a man's angry voice commanding, "Tiger, let go."

Mr. Peterson, the dog's owner was there, a strap in his hands. He gave a solid swat to the dog's hind quarters.

The Doberman pinscher released Benny, pulled back, his yellowed, blood-stained teeth bared, snarling. The owner seized the animal around the middle. The dog yipped furiously as his legs spun in the air; then he sprang from Peterson's arms and scampered back to his own yard with a protesting howl, the owner hot on his heels.

Ruth knelt down and cradled Benny in her arms. "Get someone," she cried.

"My ma's coming," said the Baker boy.

"I have to take Benny to the hospital," she told Mrs. Baker. "My husband has the car. Can you help me? I need help!"

"I'll drive you," said the woman.

At the hospital, Benny was promptly taken to the emergency room for treatment. Ruth tried to follow, but the nurse stopped her. "We'll take care of your son," she said.

Another nurse handed Ruth several forms to fill out and asked when Benny had his last tetanus shot. "We'll need to know about the dog too," she said. "He will have to be watched for rabies."

"It's our neighbor's dog," said Mrs. Baker. "I know he's had whatever shots dogs need. But he's temperamental and doesn't like small children."

Ruth, her mind dazed, sluggishly filled out the necessary forms. Then she realized that for the moment there was nothing else she could do. She and Mrs. Baker sat down in the waiting room and exchanged thin, weary smiles.

"He'll be all right, Mrs.—may I call you Ruth?"

"Of course, and you're—?"

"Janice."

"Yes, I remember now. You wouldn't believe we've lived in the same neighborhood for over a year, would you?"

"Well, neighbors aren't as close these days as they used to be."

"It seems like I'm so busy with the children that I don't see anyone," Ruth explained apologetically. "It seems like I only get out for shopping and church anymore."

"Yes, I remember when mine were small like that. They had me climbing the walls sometimes. I thought for sure I was going to go bonkers before I had them all in school."

"You mean you felt that way too? A little crazy?" asked Ruth, surprised.

"Oh, my yes. What young mother doesn't at times?"

Ruth nodded. "I guess I've been so isolated for so long, I forget that other mothers are going through the same trials."

Janice smiled. "Believe it or not, I reached the place with my kids where I thought something was wrong with me. I expected the little men in white coats to come looking for me with a net. In fact, I even considered getting some counseling."

Ruth studied her intently. "Did you do it?"

Janice shifted in her chair, settling back comfortably. "No, we couldn't afford it. Besides, I discovered what I really needed was to spend a little more time sharing my problems and needs with others."

"Others?"

"You know. My husband, my mother, my friends, even God. Not that I'm all that religious, of course. But I realized I was trying to do it all myself, carry all the burdens alone. Like I was afraid I'd look weak if I admitted I needed help."

Ruth nodded grimly. "I know just what you mean. Lately, I've even forgotten to tell God that I needed His help and strength. And I can't see myself dumping on everyone else. It's just not me."

Janice shrugged. "Well, it worked for me. My husband and I got closer than ever when he realized how much I needed him. He started watching the kids while I took a computer class on Tuesday nights. Now I do typing at home to earn a little extra money. And my mother enjoys spending time with her grandchildren while I get out once a week to see my friends."

"It sounds like you've found all the answers," said Ruth wistfully.

Janice laughed. "No. I still go crazy sometimes. But at least I know it's only temporary insanity. And when I need a break now and then, I'm not ashamed to admit it."

"I know what you're saying," said Ruth, "but I just hate to appear helpless and weak, although I suppose that's just what I am."

"You're no such thing," protested Janice. "Look at the way you rescued your boy and got help for him. I can tell, you're a strong woman and a good mother."

Ruth stared at her hands. "I don't know. I try, but I'm not sure what Richard thinks anymore." She sat forward suddenly. "I just remembered, I should call my husband. He doesn't even know what happened." As she tried to stand, she realized she was trembling. Her knees were like Jell-O. She sat back down with a sigh. "I guess I'm more stressed out than I thought."

Janice patted her arm. "Who wouldn't be at a time like this? Would you like me to check with the nurse about your son, so you'll have something definite to tell your husband?"

"Would you mind?" asked Ruth.

"Of course not. I'll just be a minute."

When she was alone, Ruth put her head in her hands and tried to pray for Benny. If she ever needed God's help, it was now. So much had happened in this past hour that her head was spinning, her thoughts reeling. What was God trying to teach her? What was He trying to do?

There was a message in all of this somewhere. Ruth sensed it. This had happened for a reason. Why? If she was to hold on to her sanity, she had to see the plan, the purpose. She couldn't bear to think that life assailed her randomly with its crises and tragedies.

God, help me, she pleaded silently. *Help me through this!*

As she focused her thoughts on God, she pictured a loving Christ reaching out His arms to enfold and console her. Whatever might happen, Jesus loved her and He loved Benny. That much she knew. He held them both in His gentle, protective hands. Of course. She could feel Him even now easing the tension, filling her senses with Himself. Her Savior was the eye of the hurricane—that small, safe place in the center of life's turbulence where there was peace and calm. Why was it she fled to that sheltering place so seldom, choosing instead to bear all her burdens alone?

Just as Janice said. Janice was right. No one should try to bear her burdens alone. But wasn't that just what Ruth had been trying to do? Hadn't she been holding on too tightly, trying too hard in her own strength? Was she willing to relax a little more, to let go and let God take charge?

It would mean accepting the challenge of surrendering her feelings and needs to God a dozen times a day. Turning to Christ every time the depression hit or the kids got her down. It would involve a constant, deliberate relinquishing of her will to the Holy Spirit.

And it would mean being honest with Richard about her needs. Admitting she needed his help. She wasn't Superwoman. She couldn't do it all. And when she couldn't cope, someone else would have to step in. Richard, or her mother, or maybe even Janice. Maybe they could spell each other now and then. Ruth's mind whirled with possibilities.

It surprised her to realize that she no longer felt crushed; she felt a sense of excitement and anticipation, an awareness of God moving directly in the circumstances of her life. Then something else occurred to her. If God could deliver her through the terrifying experience of this last hour, if He could give her peace even now when she didn't know how Benny would be, then certainly He could see her through the trying, commonplace hours of everyday life. She would survive. Perhaps she would even triumph!

"Ruth?"

Ruth glanced up and saw that Janice Baker was standing beside her, smiling.

"Benny?"

"The nurse said he will need quite a few stitches, but he's going to be all right."

"Thank God!" Ruth stood up uncertainly.

Janice put her hand on Ruth's arm to steady her. "The nurse said the doctor will be out in a few minutes to talk with you."

"All right, but I've got to call Richard and tell him."

Janice gestured toward the information desk. "There's a phone right there."

"Yes, good," said Ruth. Impulsively she turned and took her neighbor's hands. "Thank you, Janice. You've helped me more than I can say. I hope we can see more of each other now. I hope we can be good friends."

"I hope so too," said Janice, smiling.

With shaky fingers Ruth dialed her husband's number. When she heard the familiar voice on the line, a feeling of profound love wafted through her like a morning breeze, invigorating her.

"Richard," she said, and her voice barely trembled, "Richard, something has happened—to Benny. No, wait, let me explain. Benny's all right. In fact, thank God, for the first time in months I believe we're all going to be all right, darling!"

of the moving beast as the [illegible] something else [illegible] through the [illegible] would [illegible] ever [illegible] would be [illegible] [illegible]

[illegible]

Pete glanced up and saw [illegible]. [illegible] was [illegible] her [illegible]

[illegible]

[illegible]

"There [illegible]"

[illegible] put [illegible] and [illegible] ready [illegible] [illegible] you.

"All right, but [illegible]"

[illegible]

[illegible]

[illegible]

End of December

What does a woman do when she realizes it's too late to save her wayward child?

The first of October: He is a big boy now. I keep telling myself that. He is a big boy. A man. I should leave him alone, stop worrying. He says I nag him. Sometimes I do. I can see it in myself sometimes—the anxiety twisting my words into something bitter, something I don't mean.

I care. I care what happens to him—what he does, where he goes, who he sees. A mother has a right to care, doesn't she? I have prayed for Danny since his birth, prayed for a good life for him, prayed that he would love God, serve God. For 18 years I've prayed, just as his father prayed, until his death two years ago.

Tonight, when Danny got home from work, I said to him, "Danny, I fixed your favorite beef stew, with plenty of onions and garlic, like you like it."

He brushed by me, going straight to his room, saying

nothing. He is too quiet these days, too sullen. All his thoughts turn inward. I cannot reach him.

He came out of his room wearing old clothes—worn Levi's, his rumpled leather jacket—and blew a kiss my way. "Don't wait up," he called as he went out.

But I *am* waiting up. Sitting before the TV, my mind lulled by the bright, flashing images on the screen. I'm vaguely aware of a monotonous, droning conversation—a late-night talk show, I suppose. I do not watch; it does not interest me. The people on TV are distant, not connected to me. Unreal. Still, the television is like a companion, here with me but not intrusive. It eases my sense of aloneness.

My Bible is open on my lap. I read the same verses over and over, making them part of me, part of my thoughts. "And all things, whatsoever ye shall ask in prayer, believing, ye shall receive." *All things...All!*

The national anthem is playing now. I am surprised to see that the station is going off the air. I turn off the TV, watching the screen go dark.

Shortly the silence of the room is stunned by the opening of a door, the sound of movement, footsteps. Danny comes into the room, moving heavily, his expression unguarded, devastated. When he sees me watching, he glares at me as if I had just slapped him.

"What are you doing—spying?" he mutters.

"No, no, of course not," I cry, going to him. There is something about him tonight that I have not seen before and it chills me, terrifies me. "Danny, what is it? What's the matter?"

"Nothing." He shakes me off, eluding my touch. There is a terrible, astonished, dazed look in his eyes.

I grab his arms, shaking him. "What's the matter with you? Tell me!"

Awkwardly he pulls away, turning his back, escaping me.

"Leave me alone," he cries.

End of December

The middle of November: I am awakened out of sleep by the telephone. The sound cuts into my slumber. I try to absorb it into my dreams, but the noise is insistent, repeating itself again and again. A shrill, abrasive ringing. I shake myself awake, shattering the fragments of sleep that stubbornly clutch my senses. I make my way through the darkness to the phone, pick it up quickly and say hello.

"Mother?"

"Danny?"

"Yes, Mom."

"What's wrong? Where are you?"

"Uh, there's been some trouble, I'm afraid."

"Trouble? What kind of trouble?"

"Well, I was with Mickey, this friend of mine—"

"Mickey? I don't know any Mickey."

"No, I don't think you know him, Mother. Listen, he and I were, uh...arrested tonight. We're at the police station. Can you come down?"

"Arrested? Oh, Danny, no."

"It's okay, Mom. I just need you to come down here."

"All right. You hold on. I'll be there right away. As soon as I get dressed. I'll hurry, Danny."

"Uh, you'd better bring the money you keep in the bureau."

"What? The money? Our savings?"

"You'll have to post bond, Mom. You know, for my bail."

"Oh, Danny! Your bail? All right, if you say so."

"Thanks, Mother. I knew I could count on you."

"Danny? Danny, listen to me. What were you arrested for?"

"It's a bum rap, Mom, believe me."

"Just tell me, Danny. What are the charges?"

There is a long pause before he answers me.

"Possession of cocaine."

Two days later: It is a bright day for November. The sun beats on the cold ground, absorbing the earth's chill. I have gone from room to room opening the curtains vigorously, welcoming light and warmth.

Now I am in my kitchen on this lovely morning, frying thick strips of bacon and scrambling perfect golden eggs in sizzling butter. A feast for my son, who is home with me again.

He is out on bail. He is as shaken as I. This will not happen again, he says. I believe him. I love him. We will survive this. We pray that he will receive a suspended sentence, that he will be able to pick up his life and go on. He is so young, and this is his first offense. Certainly they will not be too hard on him.

Danny comes into the room wearing his best suit, straightening his tie with quick, nervous fingers. His face is strained and hopeful, his eyes gleaming with expectancy. He sits down at the table and pours himself a glass of orange juice.

"I don't want to be late this morning," he says eagerly, speaking of his job as a salesman at Gregory's Men's Shop downtown. He has worked there nearly two months, never missing a day until his arrest the other night. It is the best job he has had in over a year. "Things are going to be different now, Mother," he tells me. "You'll see. I've tried to go cold turkey before, but the guys always kept after me, messing me up. I won't let them bug me this time. That's a promise."

I nod my approval. "Danny, God can help you with this," I say, draining the bacon on sheets of paper towel. "God can give you the strength to resist Mickey and the others, to resist drugs."

"Sure, Mother," he says, smiling. He butters a slice of toast and breaks it apart unevenly. "You always did say that, Mom, even when I was a little kid crying over a dead bird or a broken toy. 'Trust God. He will help you,' you said. You never change, do you, Mother?"

"I suppose not," I reply.

"*Don't* ever change," he says, and I am startled by the strange throb in his voice. I stare at him, but he is eating his toast.

"But do you ever do it?" I ask him gently.

"Do what?"

"Trust God. Pray."

He frowns, his irritation obvious. His words are clipped. "I suppose I do sometimes. I don't know."

"When you were seven you accepted Christ as your Savior in a summer vacation Bible school. Do you remember?"

"Yes. No. I can't remember. That was a long time ago."

"You were so excited when you came home and told your father and me."

Danny clears his throat, a deliberate, disruptive cough. "Mother," he says impatiently, "is that bacon ready yet?"

The telephone rings and I go to answer it, motioning for Danny to help himself to the food on the stove. The voice on the phone belongs to Danny's boss, the manager at Gregory's Men's Shop. "It's Mr. Mason," I tell Danny, handing him the receiver.

Without wishing to, I hear Danny's side of the conversation. "Yes, Mr. Mason," he says respectfully. After a moment, his voice changes, growing thin and precarious. "But I don't understand. I thought you were pleased with my work. Yes, I see. No, I understand your position. Right. Good-bye, Mr. Mason."

There is an incredible hurt in Danny's eyes as he hangs up the receiver and turns to me, but any hint of vulnerability is quickly erased by his anger.

"They don't want a jailbird working for their precious store," he explodes, heading for the door.

"Is that what they said?"

"No, but that's what they meant."

"How did they know?"

"They just do, okay?"

"Where are you going, Danny?"

"Out! To find Mickey, someone. Anyone!"

"When will you be back?"

"Never!"

The end of December: This day is not real; it is not linked to any other day, to any other time. It stands alone, a freak among days. A terrible culmination to the six weeks that have passed since Danny left home in deep despair.

This day began with a phone call. An unfamiliar voice, frightening in its control, its smooth perfect enunciation. What did the man say? Where did he begin? His words crept insidiously into my mind, stunning me. I did not believe him. I thought he must be crazy.

He said, "We have your son. We *believe* we have your son. Can you come down here? Can you come?"

"Where?" I asked. "Who is this?"

A lengthy, embarrassed silence. "I'm sorry," he said awkwardly. "This is the County Morgue."

The morgue. A sterile, lifeless building with cold, somber, colorless walls. A fort, massive and forbidding. A place without personality. Without humanity. Its rooms are as untouched as tombs.

My eyes evade any objects that might define these rooms. I do not touch anything. I keep my arms pressed against my body, a useless, protective gesture. I stare at the floor, aware of the echoing sound of my heels on hard tile. I try not to listen; I try not to see. I do not want this to be real.

But it *is* real. A man with a grave, expressionless face shows me the body and waits without comment for my reply.

For a long time I cannot make myself look. I feel the man's eyes on me, this keeper of the dead. He's waiting. I am trapped. I cannot escape. I cannot run. I steel myself. I look. The horror mushrooms up like a deadly, paralyzing gas. "Yes," I say, nodding dazedly. "Yes, this is my son."

Moments later I learn the circumstances of Danny's death. He was found by police in a cheap rooming house on South Street. A "crack house," they called it. He had been dead more than 24 hours. Cause of death? Crack cocaine.

I wonder, was it an accident? Suicide? Even murder? I will never know.

Someone offers to drive me home, but I shake my head. I have my car. I need time alone to think.

I begin to drive, but I don't know where I'm heading. Over and over I tell myself this day will pass. I will survive. But how can I make sense of what has happened? I am numb. I am dying inside my heart.

On the screen of my mind I see images, pictures flipping past my mind's eye, memories like faded snapshots. Danny in his crib, smiling and bright-eyed, his chubby hands extended, begging me to pick him up. Danny learning to walk, tottering across the room, falling, skinning his knee, screaming until I gather him in my arms and kiss away his hurt. Danny leaving for school with his "Star Trek" lunch box, waving good-bye, one big, lonely tear glistening on his cheek.

My son.

My Danny.

Gone.

This I know: I loved my son. I would have molded his life myself if God had let me. But I could only reach so far. Danny lived his own life, made his own choices, died alone. I loved him, I prayed for him. I tried to guide him. What more could I do? What more can a mother do?

I am trembling, weeping. I pull my automobile over to the

curb and turn off the engine, my body racked with sobs—uncontrollable, agonizing sobs. It is too soon. Too soon to go on, to do even routine things like driving. I bury my face in my hands, groping for answers. But there are none. What's happening to me? I'm a Christian. I'm supposed to be strong. But I'm falling apart, devastated, crumbling. My son. My son.

A thought startles me: As long as the earth revolves there will be Christians like me who lose loved ones who don't know the Lord. They will grieve as I grieve. They will wonder what more they could have done. They will even feel guilty.

I know, I know. God forces no one to trust in Him. He bends nobody's will if that person chooses not to yield. Till Christ returns there will be those of us who pray and wait and finally come to this. The end of December. The day when the waiting is over and the prayers for our beloved must be put aside. The day when we can do nothing more than trust that God *still* is good and knows what's best for us.

"Dear God," I lament, "dear God, I had so many hopes for Danny. So many hopes for my boy!"

But for this moment—and for the rest of my life—I cling to one enduring hope—that on a summer morning in Bible school 11 years ago, Danny's decision then was real.

Letters Home

What does a young woman do when she believes the only way out is to run away?

August 14, 1991

Dear Father:

This letter surprises you, doesn't it? You didn't expect to hear from me again. I can imagine you hungrily reading these words, searching for clues. I can see your face, sober and intent, the lines of your face nearly menacing in their intensity. I see you as if you were here.

I am all right. Believe me. Jason is with me. You met him once but I don't think you remember him. You met him but showed no interest. He is not like you, nothing like you. He is with me and we are all right.

He has money. Not a lot, but enough. We will get along. This morning we had breakfast in a diner in—no, that's not important. We felt drugged and dazed from driving all night, being awake all night. We sat and drank coffee and talked nonsense, silly half-sentences with silences between that made us want to giggle.

We weren't sure yet what was happening, what we were doing. It wasn't clear in our minds what was going on. Jason kept saying, "Hey, Cindy, are you my girl?" Over and over. I laughed and changed the subject, because I could see the waitress watching us from the corner of her eye.

I don't love Jason, Daddy, but he's real and he's here. He's real and I don't have to think about him, wondering who he is and what his life means. I don't want to think about things like that anymore.

At lunchtime we stopped at a McDonald's, then bought stuff from a grocery store across the street—crackers, Coke and magazines to read in the car.

Is Mother okay? You must have talked to her by now. She must have told you I was gone. When she checked my room this morning, she must have seen that I didn't come home last night.

I wasn't going to leave a note—it seemed like a little-kid thing to do. Then at the last minute, before I left to meet Jason, I scribbled a note on the back of a grocery receipt and put it like a marker in Mother's Bible. I knew she would find it there. I said, "I'm leaving. Don't worry. Forget me. Love, Cindy." I wanted her to know my disappearance was voluntary. You must know all of this already. Mother must have called you by now.

Tonight Jason and I are staying at this little place off the main highway. It was so late by the time we stopped that the nicer places were already filled. We couldn't afford them anyway. Our room has dreary walls with dark, ugly stains. The carpet is dull and smooth from wear. There was a cockroach in the shower, perched there in the corner like a terrible little intruder. I screamed and Jason had to go kill it. He called me a baby afterward, and I pouted until he apologized. I think we both felt funny, not really knowing what we were going to do or why we were together like this. But we're all right now. We got through this first day.

Jason is asleep now and here I am, writing you on this crummy motel stationery. I've never tried to talk to you before, so why am I writing now when there's no possible way you can touch my life again?

I want to sleep, Father, but I'm afraid to. Where will my mind go? What will I dream? I want to stay in control. But I'm so tired; we have so many miles to cover tomorrow.

Maybe I should think only happy thoughts, remember the best of times. How about our first Christmas in the new house? When was it, 1980? That long ago? Yes. I will pour myself into the memory—the sounds, the smells, the tastes. I will step through the eyes, behind the faces of the people in that house—you, Daddy...and Mother, Jeannine, and myself. I will become part of that day again, the day itself, until I am no longer here, until at last I sleep.

Your daughter, Cindy

I sit with my daughter's letter in my hand, thinking back, reflecting on *Christmas Day, 1980:* Beautiful! It couldn't be more perfect. A man couldn't be more proud. The house dazzles like the snow gathering in drifts outside the windows. Everything is new. I take pleasure in seeing, in looking at everything. The rooms still smell of paint and varnish. The smells mix with the pungent fragrance of the freshly cut fir tree standing in the living room. Beyond these smells are the blending aromas of sizzling bacon and hot coffee.

I join Marian in the kitchen where she is fixing breakfast. She is in her blue velour robe and her hair hangs in soft curls, slightly tangled. I sit down and she brings me coffee, smiling.

Playfully she pops a piece of sweet roll into my mouth, then leans over and kisses the crumbs from my lips. I pull her down on my lap and nuzzle the top of her head.

In the other room I hear Jeannine and Cindy, their voices high and shrill—the voices of happy, excited children. Jeannine is ten, Cindy seven. I am warmed by their laughter and joy. They are lovely, marvelous creatures, and they are mine.

Jeannine, our firstborn—perhaps secretly my favorite—comes to me, her blue eyes sparkling, her hair flowing in soft blond waves around her face. "Daddy, do you want to play Monopoly?" she asks, holding out her new game.

Immediately Cindy, dark and wiry, clamors for my attention. "Love my baby, Daddy," she says, thrusting her new doll against my chest.

"Hold on," I cry, teasingly waving them off. To Cindy I say, "She's your doll, honey. *You* love her, okay?" To Jeannine, "Maybe we can play your new game tonight, baby."

"Not tonight," interrupts Marian.

"Why not?"

"We have church—a special Christmas program. The girls are in the children's choir, remember?"

I sip my coffee thoughtfully. "What do you think of the new church, Marian?"

She glances around at me. "I like it. Don't you?"

"Yes, I suppose so. The minister seems a little—extreme perhaps. He expects people to make such drastic commitments. Give your life to Christ, he says. What does he mean by that? Why is he so urgent? Does he think our lives will fall apart if we don't give ourselves to God?"

Marian shakes her head vaguely. "I don't know. I like the church. I like the pastor."

I am persistent. "Our other church—where we lived before—was more balanced. It wasn't an all-or-nothing matter. We gave God our Sunday morning. He gave us the rest of the week. Don't look at me like I'm being facetious, Marian. I'm being practical. How can anyone think about God all the time?"

"I think the pastor means that we should commit our lives and thoughts to Christ so that we can be the kind of people God wants us to—"

"Hold it, Marian," I say, lifting my hand in protest. "I'll go along with that, but only to an extent. I admit God should be recognized, but I'm not going to be narrow-minded about it. And I don't want anyone forcing the girls into a narrow, restricted mold either. I want them to have full, free lives. I want them to make their own choices, do you understand?"

August 19, 1991

Dear Daddy:

I've been traveling for ages. Only five days really, but it seems like forever. Every day I see different places, new towns, strange people. But it's funny. They all look the same now—the restaurants, the gas stations, the motels, even the people. They are all connected by endless chains of roads, like arteries stretching over a vast giant.

They tire me out. Everything has become so predictable. There is no suspense, nothing to look forward to, nothing to hope for.

Jason is remote. He seems to be propelled by some secret determination, a power of will that keeps him going. He has nothing to say. He lets me talk, do all the talking, and he listens with a sort of distracted smile, as if he is humoring me. It doesn't matter. He lets me talk. I have so much to say, but none of it is important, none of it makes any sense.

While Jason drives, I talk. I sit and study the intense profile of his face and let the words pour out of my mouth, as if I cannot help myself, as if there is so much to be said before we reach the next stop—a restaurant, motel, whatever.

It sounds crazy, I know. I don't want to be crazy, but sometimes I feel there is no other choice. I drive myself crazy. I do it to myself. Why? Do other people feel this way? Do you?

But yes, of course. I remember. The night Jeannine died. You were crazy with grief that night. I remember that more than I remember the accident. The accident isn't real anymore, but I remember afterward. I couldn't stop trembling. I thought I would shake to pieces.

I was 12, not a little girl anymore. But I crawled onto your lap like a baby. I sobbed in your arms. I will never forget. I sobbed and you said, "Jeannine, Jeannine!" Then you pushed me away and stumbled out of the room. I heard you tell Mother that no loving God would take Jeannine from us. You said there was no God. I remember that night. I lost Jeannine. I lost you. And I was never quite sure of God again.

I've rambled on too much. Forgive me, okay? We are camped in another of those crummy motel rooms and Jason has just come in with hamburgers and fries. We are eating in tonight.

Give Mother my love if you see her.

Love, Cindy

I stare blindly at Cindy's second letter. I am her father. But I think back to the night my other daughter died. *January 21, 1986:* It was a pleasant evening if I do say so myself. Mother was glad to see Marian and me and the girls, and, of course, Cindy and Jeannine adore their grandmother. She liked the gifts we gave her too—the VCR and our own homemade videos. Jumpy, amateur clips of Jeannine and Cindy laughing, acting like clowns, doing their campy routines and silly imitations. It's good to get together, to share birthdays and good times. Besides, Mother isn't getting any younger. The look on her face when Marian brought in that cake with all those candles! Hey, I should have videotaped it!

Sure, I think of it now, when we're on our way home. Oh well, next time. Right, if we ever make it home. Man, these roads! They're impossible tonight. The snow is still falling and the highways are a cake of ice. I suppose we should have stayed home, but it meant so much to Mother to have us come.

It looks like Marian is nearly asleep—or else hypnotized by the snow. The girls have been quiet for quite a while. I suppose they're asleep. I don't dare take my eyes off the road to glance into the back seat. I don't hear any snoring though. For a 12-year-old Cindy sure can snore. I pity her husband someday. Well, there's plenty of time before—

Hey, what's going on—Marian! We hit ice! The car—it's skimming the road sideways. I can't hold the wheel! Dear God, where are we going? Marian, hold on! We're off the road—it can't be—that house—no! Oh, please, no!

Marian?

Marian, are you all right? We hit this house. We're partway inside. People are coming. They look dazed and frightened, as if they cannot believe we are real. They were watching TV. They are coming to us through the splinters and glass and debris. They stare at us as if we are alien creatures invading their world. Yes, we are. We need help.

Are we all okay? Marian? Good, darling. Cindy, what about you? Good. Just sit back and relax, honey. And, Jeannine, how are you? Jeannine, baby, I said, are you all right? Did you hear me? Jeannine! Oh my God, no! Not Jeannine, please! Please, not my Jeannine!

August 26, 1991

Dear Father:

I really shouldn't keep writing you like this. After all, I ran away. But in my mind, somehow, I keep running back, don't I? I don't know why I do anything. Why did I run away?

Mother was good to me. She had so many things on her mind, but she still found time for me. Her new job exhausted her—did she tell you about the job? You hadn't been around lately, so maybe you didn't know.

And, of course, Mother was still very involved in the church, which I'm sure doesn't surprise you. She always told me that she was praying for us, for you and me. It still surprises me to think that she is praying for you, Father, after everything that happened. I would have thought she would hate you. But no. That's Mother for you—full of love and hope. How does she do it? She says her strength is in Christ. I don't understand that. But sometimes I envy her. She seems to live at peace with life. Although she lost Jeannine and you—and now me—she still has peace. I marvel at that. There is only chaos inside me.

I am tired of traveling. I am sick of cheap hamburgers and warm Cokes and dingy motel rooms. I am sick of staring out the window at roads and houses and other cars and lousy little towns with dumb names I've never heard before.

I'm bored, and what's worse, Jason is bored too. He doesn't listen anymore. When I talk he looks preoccupied and puts on one of his heavy metal tapes, drowning out my words. I bought some paperbacks but the car jounces too much to read. Now when he drives, I sit and think and keep my mouth shut.

The nights are even worse. After a cheap dinner—tacos or pizza or franks and beans—Jason parks me in some crummy motel room; then he goes out and drinks.

I never know when he's going to come back, and when he does, sometimes he's drunk. It frightens me when he gets drunk. I don't know him. He doesn't know himself.

I know now that a lot of things are going on in Jason's head. But I don't want to know what they are. I don't want to be concerned about Jason, about his problems.

Still, I don't want to lose Jason either. At night I sit and watch TV (if the room has one that's working). I sit and wonder if Jason will come back. That's what terrifies me—what if Jason goes away some night and never comes back?

Who would I have? What would I do then?

Cindy

I stuff Cindy's letter back in the envelope and put it on my desk with her other letters. Cindy is forcing me to remember *October 6, 1990:* She is standing in the doorway, holding her school books against her chest, staring at me. She looks uncomfortable. Shifting from one foot to the other, she says, "Mother said you wanted to see me, Father."

"Did she tell you why?" I ask, stalling.

Cindy shakes her head. Her voice is edged with something—anger, suspicion? "Why is Mother upset?"

I motion for Cindy to sit beside me on the couch. All the words that come to my mind sound flat and tasteless. I consider a dozen ways of beginning—

"I have homework, Daddy," Cindy says impatiently.

"This won't take long," I tell her. "I—I'm going away, Cindy."

Her eyes are cool, penetrating. "Where are you going?"

"I'm moving to an apartment. You're old enough for me to be honest with you. Cindy, your mother and I are getting a divorce."

I cannot tell whether Cindy is shocked. She sits very still, staring at her hands. She gently gnaws her lower lip, but she always does that when she's thinking seriously about something. I am anxious to finish this conversation, to escape this house and the people I'm hurting.

"Cindy?"

She looks at me. "Then we won't be a family anymore," she says matter-of-factly.

"You'll always be my daughter," I tell her, trying to soften the blow. "We'll get together, do things, go out to eat."

"You don't love Mother anymore?"

I shake my head soberly. "I'm afraid not."

For an instant she looks at me pleadingly. "Why do you have to leave? What are you going to do?"

I grasp at words but realize I have said nothing. Cindy watches me intently, demanding an answer.

"If you must know, there's someone else," I blurt out at last. This takes her off guard. She looks stricken. I rush on to explain. "She's a girl I met at work about a year ago. She's very nice, Cindy. She's a little younger than I am, but we get along very well."

"Do you love her?" asks Cindy, her voice barely audible.

I dodge the question. "We have a good—a very good relationship, Cindy."

"Oh," she says dully, "an affair."

"It's more than that, Cindy. I don't expect you to understand, but I hope we can still be friends."

She gives me a peculiar glance. "Friends?" she asks, as if the word is foreign to her.

Hurriedly I correct my blunder. "Well, we're more than friends, of course. You'll always be my little girl—"

Cindy stands up stiffly, formally, facing me like a soldier. Her face has locked out all emotion. She announces, "I must go now, Father. Mother may need me for something."

She turns to go and does not look back. Not once.

September 3, 1991

Father:

I am so lonely and scared. I don't know what's happening to me anymore. Sometimes I want so much to talk to Mother, but I'm afraid to contact her. It would only stir up more hurt and she would beg me to come home. It's easier writing you like this because you have your own life now and you can be more objective about me. Besides, you can't answer my letters; you can only read them.

A strange, ugly thing happened tonight, and my heart still races when I think of it. Jason and I had dinner at a little Italian restaurant. It was raining terribly hard afterward, and the car was parked nearly a block away, so Jason said he would go after the car and pick me up in front of the restaurant. This was fine with me since I've had the sniffles lately.

So there I was standing just outside the restaurant door under the canopy, watching the rain come down in torrents. I kept squinting through the rain, trying to see Jason's car, but there was nothing—just the rain beating on the canopy, noisy as a drum. As the minutes passed, I started feeling scared inside. What if Jason didn't come back? Maybe he saw this as a good opportunity to ditch me.

Finally I felt so panicky that I started walking toward the parking lot. I was so scared because I had no money. There was no one to help me and nowhere to go.

I walked faster through the rain toward the place where I knew the car was parked. I started to cry and my tears got mixed up with the rain drenching my face. I couldn't see anything, and my feet were soaked. It was all I could do to keep from slipping and falling down.

Suddenly I realized there was a car beside me. It stopped and I stopped too, thinking it was Jason. Someone reached over and opened the door for me, and I started to step inside. Then I saw that it wasn't Jason. Horrified, I stepped back, but the man grabbed hold of my wrist.

"Get in," he said.

"No," I cried. "Let go. You're hurting me!"

"Mind me and you won't get hurt," he said and tightened his hold.

I was too scared to scream. All I could think was, *God help me!*

"Get in," the man coaxed again, trying to pull me inside. "We're just going for a little ride, Babe."

In a burst of energy, I yanked my wrist free. I stumbled, trying to get away, but like lightning the man stretched across the seat and his hand, his nails, grazed my arm. I ran, screaming, nearly hysterical.

When Jason caught up with me moments later, I was still screaming. He tried to tell me that the car engine was wet and wouldn't start right away but that he had finally found me and I was all right now. He held me close and kept telling me I was all right, but I couldn't stop screaming. In my mind I am still screaming.

I keep hearing Jason's words: "You're all right now." But am I? Have I ever been all right? Will I ever be?

I can't stop shivering, Daddy. I feel the way I felt the night that Jeannine died. I understood that you loved Jeannine more, Daddy. I accept the fact that you no longer love my mother. I don't blame you for those things. Believe me. But I can't reach out to you either; do you understand? I can't reach out to anyone.

Tonight I tried to pray. I really did. I said the words the way I've heard Mother say them. But they weren't my words. They didn't mean anything. I couldn't make them work like Mother does.

I'm not Mother. I'm not like her. Once I could have been—

did you know that, Daddy? I could have gone Mother's way, loving God like she does. I don't know now why I didn't go her way. Why did I go your way instead of hers? Why did you let me choose? Why did you expect me to know then what I had no way of knowing until now?

Why, Daddy?

Death in the Family

What does a woman do when she returns home at the death of her father to face long-buried family conflicts?

From the road the house looked the same as ever—an aging, nondescript two-story with rambling porch and Gothic bric-a-brac trim. Bright forsythia bushes spread their branches in an effort to camouflage the shabbiness of peeling paint and weather-worn shutters. It looked just as I remembered. No one would guess that the hub of this place was missing. My father was gone. Dead.

I pulled into the driveway, turned off the engine of my rented Avis Oldsmobile and got out. I walked up the steps like I'd done a thousand times before. Everything was the same; everything was different. My insides were as icy as my hands, as stone cold as the stinging March air. I had come to this house of death to offer life, but I was dead inside. This was the first time I ever returned home that my father was not at the door to greet me!

But my mother rushed out to meet me before I even

reached the door. She embraced me, sobbing "Elizabeth" over and over into my hair. At last she looked at me and her face seemed disturbingly ajar. "Your father's gone," she moaned, as if to tell me something I did not know. "I can't believe it, Elizabeth. He can't be gone."

"I know, Mama. I'm so sorry." I clung to her as we both wept. Then I whispered, "Don't cry, Mama. I'm here now."

We went inside where familiar sights and smells stirred up painful, tantalizing bits and pieces of my childhood. I had grown up in this house, had known no other place until I went away to college and then to Illinois to teach. Did my parents ever get over their disappointment at my not staying home and teaching at Central High? But how could I have returned as a teacher to the dim, familiar halls and timeworn classrooms I had known as a student? Did my father ever understand my need to go elsewhere?

"Your sister Laura and her family are here," Mother announced as we went into the living room. Laura was feeding her baby—a plump, red-faced cherub more interested in the knickknacks on the table than in the bottle his mother kept poking into his mouth. Laura's husband, Alan, had taken possession of my father's chair; he sat there, leafing through a magazine. He looked as if he would rather be anywhere else but here. Steven, their four-year-old, had his nose plastered against the TV set, watching a rerun of "The Cosby Show."

My sister gave the baby to Alan, then approached me with eyes red from weeping. We hugged each other and cried some more.

Laura didn't realize that she aggravated the guilt I felt. She was never my father's favorite, but she had stayed at home, married a hometown boy, and given my parents grandchildren. I, their "wayward" daughter, insisted on an education, became what they considered a religious fanatic, and—

except for brief annual visits—moved out of their lives for good.

On those temporary excursions home, to their endless distress I came, not accompanied by the ideal husband and the promise of offspring, but with vague chatter about classroom projects, student behavioral problems, and the latest fads in teaching techniques. And, worst of all, I came with my new faith, wearing it like a medal, waving it like a flag or—did my parents think—like a weapon?

Everyone in my family made it immediately clear they were not interested in my "religious conversion." Nor would they consider trading their stained-glass church for the evangelistic chapel where I first heard the gospel.

"Have you eaten, dear?" Mother asked, jarring me from my reverie. She gave me her customary once-over that indicted me for being too skinny.

"I ate on the plane," I answered, hoping she wouldn't pursue the matter and discover that "dinner" was coffee and two finger-sandwiches.

"Well, you'll want to get comfortable, so run upstairs and change. Your room is just as you left it," she said, as if the idea of stepping back into my college days somehow appealed to me. I kissed her cheek briefly and ran upstairs propelled by the sudden threat of more tears.

In the closet I helped myself to '80s-style clothes I had placed there long ago and forgotten—items hardly fashionable now but still very comfortable. Old scrapbooks and mementos occupied dressers and shelves; favorite photos peered at me from the wall and framed the yellowing mirror, offering a kaleidoscope of instant memories. Father and I arm-in-arm at my high school graduation, his hair dark, his face not yet old. In those days I thought he would live forever.

Another photo showed Father and Mother with Laura and me at the lake. The year I was 10. We were all grinning at the camera, standing awkward and embarrassed, waiting for the countdown and, *Click!*

Looking at Father's face again, his cheerful, animated expression, I felt convinced that he was not dead—that if I skipped downstairs I would find him—not Alan—in his favorite chair reading the sports page, calling in his warm, scratchy voice, "Elizabeth, don't run in the house!"

No. He would not say that anymore. That was 20 years ago. That long? Yes. *That long.*

I tried to recall just how Father looked the last time I saw him, but his face eluded me. I forced myself to trace his features in my mind—the sparse white hair, the sagging jowls, the still-twinkling eyes. Even this recollection was stilted and incomplete, not fresh and spontaneous the way I longed to remember him. I decided to do what I feared I would not be brave enough to do—enter my parents' room where my father died.

I slipped down the hall and noiselessly opened the door. Entering, I was instantly confronted by the subtle, familiar smell of my father's things. I closed my eyes and breathed deeply, savoring that elusive scent, imagining his presence beside me. The air in the room was close; the shades were pulled and everything was neatly in its place, giving the room an odd, not-lived-in quality. Yet my father's billfold and some change lay on the dresser; his old slippers rested beside the bed. It was as if the room were waiting for my father's return, anticipating his arrival at any moment—just as I was waiting.

I sat down on the bed—the bed my father died in—and allowed quick, warm tears to spill out of my eyes again. I cried silently, watching as some of the tears made dark, round stains on the bedspread. I felt a loneliness that only my father could ease, an ache only he could erase. I longed for his comfort, but he was the source of my pain.

I wondered if there was something more I could have

done. How I had wanted my father to share my faith in Christ! I prayed for him, never really believing he would die and leave me torn with wondering. I tried to witness to him, to tell him of the joy he could know, if only he would believe and accept God's gift of salvation. I remember that it was a nervous, breathless speech, born of my burden but delivered with self-consciousness and a measure of fear. *Why,* I asked now, *is it so incredibly hard to witness to those you love most, those who know you best?*

When I had said all I could think of to say, I had blurted, "Well, Father, what do you think?" Without conviction he had murmured, "Elizabeth, dear, I already believe all that," as if it should have been obvious! Then he rattled his newspaper, and I knew I had been dismissed. I never had a chance to talk to my father again—at least not about things that really mattered.

Last Christmas I sent my parents a Bible—a lovely leather-bound edition. Neither Mother nor Father ever mentioned it, except for Mother's scribbled postscript, "Rec'd your gift. Lovely. Thanks. I put it by your father's chair."

Now, in the silence of my father's room, I whispered, "Dear God, if only I could be certain my father knew You!"

The baby's scream sliced rudely through my prayer, and I jumped up, recalling Laura and her family downstairs. Fresh guilt spurted inside me as I realized Mother was undoubtedly slaving away over the stove, cooking an elaborate meal for her family.

Nothing will ever sever my mother from her kitchen, I reflected as I hurried downstairs to that private domain where wonderful aromas attacked my senses. My culinary skills were zilch, but I insisted on lending a hand. Mother directed me to the buffet and suggested I set the table. Laura hovered nearby, wearily rocking her sobbing baby. Her face was white, expressionless, her eyes red from crying. We had never been especially close, but I wished now that I could offer something to ease her pain. Ironically, I recalled that I had already offered her the only hope I knew. But she wasn't interested.

The dinner table looked like a celebration. It seemed wrong that Father should miss such a meal. I wondered, *Is he experiencing a greater, heavenly celebration? Or, God forbid, is he mourning his missed opportunity?* I cut off such questions. They only tormented my mind, exhausting me.

"This was one of your father's favorite meals," my mother remarked, passing me the plate of fried chicken. "He loved the drumsticks. There was never a problem though, because I like the white meat best."

"Is everything set for tomorrow?" I asked cautiously.

"We made all the arrangements this morning," Laura replied.

"Of course, we already had our plot," Mother explained. "A lovely spot in the cemetery out by the lake. It's so much more private than that cemetery across from the new shopping mall."

"I suppose everyone in town will be pouring in here tomorrow after the funeral," remarked Laura.

"Oh, my, yes!" Mother replied with a firm nod. "The ladies from church are bringing in the entire dinner. They told me I wasn't to lift a finger." Mother's gaze dropped and she added reflectively, "Oh, if only your father could be here to see all his old friends he hasn't seen in ages...and, of course, his family."

I felt Mother's gaze drift over and rest on me, and the guilt surged afresh. I had not been home since last summer. I had seen so little of Father during the last years of his life. *I am guilty, guilty, guilty! Guilty of giving so little of my time and attention to the man I loved so dearly!*

I pushed my chair back from the table and ran blindly

upstairs to the sanctuary of my room. I buried my face in the pillow, muffling my sobs. I tried to pray, but the words were snatched away by a fit of coughing and hiccups. I had come here to my father's house hoping to be used of God; instead, I found myself feeling devastated by recriminations and guilt.

At last my sobs ran dry. I found the strength of will to sit up and pray, to share my need with the One who had become my dearest Friend. We talked together in the silence of my room and gradually, imperceptibly, I felt His healing. I slipped into the bathroom to wash my face, then with new determination returned downstairs.

I was surprised to find the table had already been cleared and the dishes washed. Mother was alone, carefully replacing the silver in the buffet.

"Where's Laura?" I asked.

"Oh, she went home," said Mother. "The children were so tired. They all stayed with me last night. I couldn't stand to be alone. But none of us slept. Tonight you're here, so I told them to go home and sleep in their own beds. They'll need their rest for tomorrow."

I was amazed at how practical and self-reliant my mother could be at such a time. I went over and put my arm around her. We walked together to the living room and sat down. I sensed a new, poignant closeness between us now that we were alone. I tried to think of something comforting to say, but my mind was blank. We sat for several minutes taking solace from the quietness that enveloped us.

"It's so hard to understand," my mother murmured softly. "Your father and I were saving for a cruise to Hawaii next summer. Did I ever write you that? Your father wanted to see Hawaii more than any place in the world. He was even reading the book by that author—what's his name?"

"James Michener."

"Yes, him. Your father had almost finished it. Only a few

chapters to go. I ask you, Elizabeth, why couldn't he have lived just one more year so we could go to Hawaii together?"

I had no answer. I could only give my mother's hand a sympathetic squeeze.

"Well, he enjoyed his dreams. That's something, I suppose," Mother reflected.

"Yes," I agreed, nodding.

"And he enjoyed that Bible you sent for Christmas, dear," Mother continued, her voice almost a melody.

My mind stood at attention. Unknowingly my mother had just broached vital territory. "You say he enjoyed it?" I repeated carefully.

"Oh, my, yes. Every evening he would sit in his chair and read it. Sat there for hours sometimes."

As my mother spoke, a thread of excitement shot through my veins. "Where is the Bible, Mother?" I asked.

"Right there," she said, pointing to the end table by his favorite chair. She crossed the room and picked up the book and handed it to me. Eagerly I leafed through the pages, praying urgently for a sign that my father had made a commitment to Christ. I scanned the pages hungrily, seeking clues—underlined verses, notations in the margins, anything!

Nothing. I could not find a single mark, not the slightest hint. Biting my lip to hide my disappointment, I handed the Bible back to my mother. The power of the Spirit that had filled me just minutes before seemed to be ebbing away, evaporating. I fought to hold on.

Now Mother glanced through the Bible, moving her fingers gently, tenderly. "This book meant so much to your father, I suppose I should record his death here where you list births and deaths." She held up the Bible for me to see. The page was decorated with an ornate, old-fashioned design of swirling pastel flowers and leaves. I looked away, somehow repulsed.

Mother shook her head slowly, looking baffled. "Your father must have been getting a little senile in his old age," she remarked. "Couldn't even remember his own birthday."

"What do you mean?" I asked.

Mother held out the Bible for me to see again. "Your father's birthday was August 25th, but look here, under 'Births.' In his own handwriting—his name and the date January 17th. If that doesn't beat all—forgetting his own birthday!"

As I took the open Bible in my hands and stared at my father's neat script, I noticed a Scripture reference following the date. John 3:7. I knew that verse by heart.

Marvel not that I said unto you, You must be born again.

My mother could not possibly understand my sudden explosion of joy. She could not begin to comprehend what I now realized: My father had recorded the date of his "new" birth! Christ had indeed become his personal Savior and Lord.

I was already resolving that my mother would know of his decision before my visit home was over. Just as Laura and Alan and the rest of my family would learn the reason for my joy. What a privilege it would be to share with those I loved the news of my father's glorious, eternal celebration!

The Velvet Clasp

What does a woman do when she must put her mother in a nursing home to die?

Saturday, September 23: The house is ancient. Worse than I expected. The rooms smell of illness and dying. The walls are like dark hands, holding the smells inside.

When I first entered the nursing home, I thought my own breath would be snatched away. *What am I thinking of?* I wanted to scream. *I can't leave my mother here. I can't leave her here to die!*

I know, I realize—the doctor has convinced me—that there is nothing more I can do for her at home. It is too much for me to try to care for her. I am not qualified. I don't have the strength. All right, I know all the arguments. I know this is the way it has to be. I only wish we could afford a nicer place, a place with pleasant windows to welcome the sun.

John and I brought her here this morning. We refused the ambulance. We brought her here ourselves. She didn't say anything during the drive. Later, she smiled wanly and kissed us good-bye and said she would be fine, her lips dry, colorless. She said the words she knew we wanted to hear, and with her smile, the unspoken words we hoped were true: *I understand. I don't blame you for bringing me here.*

We smiled, too—thin, difficult smiles—and drove home in silence. I felt like a part of my middle had been gouged out, leaving me with a terrible vulnerability to pain. Silently my mind stormed against the inequities of life—stormed a blank wall, however, for life owes no one an explanation. I could only think, at this moment, behind those walls some nurse is putting another ailing old woman to bed. What does she see? A broken body? Eyes going blank behind sagging lids? Just another terminal patient?

She is my mother, who bore me in her youth and spent her life on me. Before my world was, she was. She was my world. I was a child then, straining to attain her beauty, her wisdom, her velvet clasp on life. Now, of course, I have put her in this final house. I have declared her dead because she will die soon.

John hates me when I am like this. He calls me morbid. Morose. He is right. I should try to see things as he does—objectively. But then, it's not his mother, is it?

When we left today a group of young people were just arriving. The nurse said they come from a nearby college to sing and talk to the patients—to cheer them, I suppose. Do they really believe there is anything they can do? Anything anyone can do?

When John and I get home this evening I am going to fix him the best dinner he's had in a month. Something really flamboyant. *Veal Scaloppine* or *Filet Mignon.* I'll have to dig into my recipes. I have to get over this feeling that my hold on life is being torn from me. It's this thing about confronting death.

And it's the horror that someday my children will have to drive me somewhere and leave me too!

Saturday, October 14: I feel encouraged today. We drove out to see Mother. She is not failing as quickly as I had supposed. She is clinging to life, perhaps afraid to let go. She has made friends with the lady who shares her room. They talk about their grandchildren and knit and watch game shows on her portable TV. She says the food—the little she eats—is not too bad and she is in no real pain. But she complains that the nurses are too busy. Yet she enjoys the young people who come each Saturday. They are from that religious school, and so, of course, they sing hymns and read from the Bible. Still, Mother finds them entertaining.

In fact, John and I happened to be there when they arrived today, so we stayed and listened. I admit that the students certainly seemed sincere, and they were extremely kind. Before they left they stopped to talk with each of the patients, shaking hands, occasionally praying with someone.

But, thinking of it now, I find their solicitation terribly pathetic. I mean, how can these callow students, these mere children presume to know the answers to life and death? How can they be so confident and enthusiastic when they know these old people are sick and dying?

But then, we are all dying.

Saturday, November 4: I am terribly upset. John says I shouldn't write when I am upset. I should read a book or take a bath or scrub the kitchen floor. I may do all of those.

When we drove out to see Mother today, we found her spouting all those frazzled cliches about God and heaven that those religious students have been peddling. Her voice was frail—barely a whisper these days—but she was determined. I could hardly believe it—my own mother! I never thought her mind would fail like this, that she'd let herself be brainwashed by a lot of hollow promises.

John says I should be happy that she is no longer afraid.

For a while she was saying that no one took care of her, that no one came when she called. She is over that now. But now—this! I don't mind her having hope, but what happens when she finds out that her hopes are made of dreams and dust?

She actually told me that Jesus Christ is her "personal Savior" now and that dying will be simply "an entering into His presence." Nothing I said could shake her. She is absolutely unmoving in this ridiculous optimism. I know that such blind faith can lead only to disappointment. After all, what can it do for her when she actually has to face death?

But what can I do? My hands are tied. She won't listen to me. Well, enough of this for now. I can't think of it any longer.

John is calling me. My bath water is ready.

Thursday, November 16: It is over. They called us at seven this morning. They said we would have to hurry or we would be too late. John drove like a madman. Almost killed us both. But we got there in time to talk to her.

It was strange—so terribly unreal. It's still too soon to sort out my feelings. I don't know what really happened in that room this morning. I lost my mother—that was the surface of it. The facts. But there was more—a whole other thing going on. An undercurrent. A happening beyond description. There are no words for it. I cannot even attach thoughts to it. I am left only with feelings and impressions. They are more real to me than the facts.

The impressions first: My mother faced the ultimate horror, the antithesis of life, unafraid. The fear of death that we are born with was not in her. The wordless terror that is a part of us all, all of our lives, was not there. She had something, was aware—saw—something! It was good. Her velvet clasp on life was present even as she eased into death.

Now to try to express my feelings: I am convinced my mother did not die. Call me irrational, refusing to face reality—whatever. I am convinced. Somehow, that gentle woman slipped from life into life. I saw it on her face. I know her; I know what I saw.

I don't understand it, but I believe I touched the edge of a miracle today. There is more to it than I know, and I must discover it. That's why John is driving me to that college. I have the students' names on a slip of paper. I will find them and talk with them. John and I together will listen to what they have to say.

If there is an answer to death, they have found it.

Mother found it.

We must find it too.

Marcie

What does a young woman do when she discovers her best friend in college is hooked on cocaine?

Marcie. Marcie in my mind, in every corner, everywhere. Always, always Marcie. Her long hair yellow as sun and straight down her back like a summer waterfall. Someone said she ironed it to make it stay that way, but I never saw her do it, so I don't know.

Most clearly I remember her sitting at a desk by the library stacks. She worked at the library part-time to pay her tuition. She had a scholarship, she told me, but it didn't pay enough. Not when you had to buy art supplies all the time. I know too. We were both art majors, and last year was our freshman year at State.

I always think of that year as a beginning and ending. Really, a conglomerate of beginnings and endings. And Marcie—smooth, dear Marcie—strung out through it all, showing up in all the odds and ends of memory that still trip across my mind when I let my defenses down.

I remember Marcie always helping me—showing me how to keep mascara from bothering my contact lenses, lending me funky clothes she got at the little fashion boutique in the mall, driving me places in her little red Honda. Buying me pizza when I was broke. Sometimes we sat for hours at a back-corner table in some lovely dim pizza parlor, nursing Pepsis and reciting poems by Sylvia Plath or Anne Sexton. Dark, maudlin poems about death and dying.

Sometimes we talked in hushed tones about what death would be like, or what it must be like to be the loneliest person in the world. Marcie was that person, she told me once. But I said no, not anymore. I wouldn't let her be.

You know, it's hard to realize that I didn't like Marcie at first. Aloof, cool, beautiful Marcie, I thought. Snobbish. Unapproachable. She sat two rows behind me in history of civilization. Three seats over in English composition. And we were together in freshman drawing, too, where there were no assigned seats, where you just took whatever bench you chose and set up your drawing board and turned in your outside work. That was the procedure.

It got so that Marcie always chose the bench next to me, and we would talk and compare drawings. We found out we were in the same dorm, so we started meeting together in the study lounge. Second semester, Marcie helped me get a job in the library with her. I worked at the desk in periodicals.

It's funny how you can be friends with someone and see her all the time and yet still keep compartments of yourself sealed off. Like keeping all your thoughts and feelings about something in a strongbox. In a whole year, I never let Marcie know me—the whole me, and I guess I didn't really know her. If I had known her, maybe I would have tried harder to help her. Maybe I wouldn't have been such a cop-out. But I know how dumb it is to talk like that now, as if there were something I could do—or undo. What's done is done. I can't go back.

Back. Straight back into last year when we were freshmen together, when being together was routine, when talking was as easy as breathing. Frowning, tapping her 2B pencil on her sketch pad, she would say, "I get so sick of drawing boxes and cylinders and weird machines. I hate straight lines; I hate perspective. I may be another Modigliani, and he never worried about perspective." I agreed and mentioned Van Gogh, too. There was certainly more to art than perspective, I said.

Art problems were easy to share. We both had problems. We understood the problems. When we started gesture drawing and mine looked like a two-year-old's squiggles, Marcie spent her free time for days showing me that it involved more than making elaborate stick figures. And when we went on to contour drawing, I showed her how to keep her figures from looking crude and disjointed. I remember how pleased I was to help her for a change.

I remember thinking, too, that art was getting better for me, but somehow it was getting worse for Marcie. That should have meant something to me. It should have been some kind of sign. A warning. Flashing red light. Or at least, yellow caution.

I know now that I didn't notice danger signals because I was too busy enjoying my freedom. Freedom from home. From parents. From the reputation of being a committed Christian. Those words stick like peanut butter in my mouth, in my mind. Face it, girl. Going away to college gave me my first opportunity to be whatever I chose. No one knew me for carrying my Bible to class, for taking a stand on drinking and drugs. No one at college knew that I had given myself to the Person of Christ. Least of all, Marcie. And now she will never know.

One day in the spring of our year together, I almost told her, almost heard the words spilling out about the joys of the Christian life. But I stopped myself in mid-sentence, for the joys were not all that fresh for me anymore. But I did say I would pray for her. She was disconsolate over several *D*'s on recent drawings. When I said I would pray for her, she snorted and said, "Who do you think you're going to pray to?"

I didn't answer.

I find now that I can frown at the moon for hours, or pray in absolute contrition on my knees all night; I can do so many things, but I cannot go back and give Marcie an answer. I cannot add one word to all that I ever said to her.

I recall one other afternoon toward the end of second semester, while we sat in my room and sipped diet sodas, it occurred to me that I ought to tell Marcie about Christ being more than a Christmas story, about how He really is what life is all about. She was remarking that so many of the kids on campus get high on drugs, and I replied, "Yeah, but there are a lot of other things to get high on."

"Name one," she said.

I thought of saying Christ, but instead I said religion, which I knew would be an empty nothing-word for her. She pretended to choke on her soft drink, and we both had a good laugh. Forgive me, Marcie, for letting it go at that. Forgive my silence and my laughter.

I remember, too, that Marcie and I never really had many opportunities to talk after that afternoon. When I saw her at the library she was always busy, always looking downward at a book or something, her brows knitted in a frown. She didn't have time anymore for drives or pizza or poetry. We didn't compare drawings anymore, and I knew her grades were slipping rapidly.

I remember that I began to feel scared inside. I didn't want to think about what might be happening to Marcie. I had heard of kids at school who got hooked on drugs—coke, crack, ice, speed—and went crashing to the bottom. You heard all kinds of scare stories. Marcie once asked me if I ever tried pot or coke. I laughed and said, no, I never bothered. But I didn't turn the question around to her. I wonder, was she waiting for me to ask?

I never knew for sure that Marcie was taking cocaine until the last month of our freshman year. I recall that I was happy about it being May, and I was already working on a tan. I wanted Marcie to join me on the sun deck.

I should have knocked at her door, but impulsively I went on in. My first glimpse was of Marcie bent over her desk tapping white powder into little rows on her hand mirror. Then she held the mirror close to her nose and sniffed the particles into her nostrils, inhaling deeply.

Marcie, I should have said something. Maybe I could have stopped you. I should have tried. Dear God, maybe there was nothing in the world I could have done to stop her. I don't know. I don't know how it could have been. If I had said stop...if I mentioned Jesus...if I had started somewhere!

For all of my life I will carry a snapshot in my mind. Marcie at her desk...that one sudden scene...sunlight glinting on her hair...deadly white powder on her mirror...Marcie getting high on cocaine.

That's all there was to it. That's all I saw. Because then—with the slap of shock from seeing her like that—in the instant that I understood, I broke away from the doorway. Soundlessly I ran, escaping decision or responsibility, and found again my own room. I shut the door and got hold of my pillow and sobbed into it until it was time to go to dinner.

I saw Marcie once after that. In the library. She was going toward the stacks with an armload of books. She didn't see me, but I looked away anyway, busying myself with a *Newsweek* someone had just returned.

Two weeks later, when I heard of Marcie's death—when I learned she died of an overdose of cocaine—I felt dead inside. The raveling thread of communication between Christ and me nearly snapped. And would have if He hadn't kept hold of me.

This year—my sophomore year—I see things as they are. I know now I lost a year that could have been spent for Christ. I lost a friend. I lost myself. I can change nothing of that year. Yet, I will come through. I must.

Marcie lost more. All. I will never forget. But, in not forgetting, I will begin to speak again, begin to find the words to give to others. For the Marcies who are not past prayer.

Marcie. Marcie, forgive.

Forgive.

How Glenda Found Her Future at Harry's Hamburger Palace

What does a woman do when the only man she has ever loved is about to step out of her life forever?

This is a fantasy, a romantic fantasy. Or maybe a fantastic romance. Please notice the sun—yes, there, a crimson balloon suspended low over Harry's Hamburger Palace. It vibrates with color and warmth. It swells and envelops the world—a red-orange globe looking gargantuan beside the little blue ball of Earth. Now it returns to normal. Look. The sun perches over Harry's, where Walter and Glenda are just now strolling in the door.

Today Glenda has been especially aware of the sun. Her senses have become heightened, extraordinarily sharp, perhaps because of Walter, perhaps not. Even the atmosphere seems different today. Sometimes the air has bad breath. But today it smells of peppermint and lilacs and roses in bloom.

Walter and Glenda sit down at a booth. They are facing each other, smiling. Walter has very dark hair, nice crinkly eyes behind small rimless glasses, and a wide mouth with perfect white teeth. He could be Jimmy Stewart from a 1940s flick. He could be a dentist. But no. He is a seminary student who must return to school in two weeks to complete his final year of study. The seminary is in New York. It is 1,493 miles away.

Glenda is aware of this—of both the distance and the time, which is growing short. Walter will go away and she will be alone again. All her life she has been alone—until this summer. A momentary sadness flickers in Glenda's eyes. She has wren-brown hair, doe-sad eyes and suitable features. She could be Doris Day without makeup. She could be missed in a crowd. But since Walter, Glenda is beautiful.

On the jukebox Barry Manilow croons a love song. This is most fortunate. It could have been Led Zeppelin, Alice Cooper or Rolling Stones. Glenda and Walter appear to be listening to the music. They sit at attention, shoulders straight, hands folded properly on the table. Their eyes rove cautiously over the crowd. They look everywhere but at each other. They are still smiling politely.

"Menu?" The waitress, appearing from nowhere, beams a Pepsodent smile and drawls in her Georgia accent. They take their menus as if receiving a gift, unexpected. They glow with appreciation.

"Special on the chili dog and fries. Two-fifty. Three if you want the soft drink."

Walter and Glenda exchange quizzical glances, considering this.

"Well, what do you—?" he begins.

"I don't know, Walter. A chili dog—?" She glances up at the waitress for approval. The waitress is looking elsewhere, chewing gum, indifferent.

"You don't have to have the chili dog," Walter is quick to assure her.

"Oh, well, I do like them, but—"

"There's always the ground round platter."

"Five ninety-five," interrupts the waitress. "It's not today's special."

"Hummm. The ground round platter?" muses Glenda.

"With onion rings and a salad," Walter adds enthusiastically.

"Well, I—"

"I can come back later if you want more time," offers the waitress, her Southern drawl noticeably clipped with impatience.

Walter and Glenda turn into reprimanded children. They shrink in their seats. They become barely three feet tall. Everyone in Harry's Hamburger Palace has turned to stare at them. The whole world is waiting for Glenda and Walter to make up their minds.

"The ground round but hold the onion rings," they say at once.

"And two iced teas," adds Walter.

That settled, the waitress nods, scribbles something on her pad and leaves abruptly. The Palace moves with life once more. Walter and Glenda, duly chagrined, resume their normal size. They laugh.

When their laughter thins, they link glances and laugh again. Their faces are flushed and alive. Barbra Streisand is singing now. Something soft and lilting. And very romantic. Romantic enough to make them feel like Jimmy Stewart and Doris Day. Yes, this could be a romantic comedy. Or a funny romance. Harry's Palace swells with laughter and song, the buzz of voices, the warm, sweet delirium of the crowd, the pastel blur of Harry's marvelous patrons.

Glenda and Walter relax, soothing their slightly bruised egos with private glances that hint of romance. So far they have only hinted. Neither has ever dared to speak of love. That would require them to step out into deep water, over their heads. One of them, or both, might sink. Heaven forbid, they might even drown.

All summer Walter and Glenda have remained where the water is shallow and safe. They have waded together, hand in hand, delighting in each other like pleased, cautious children. Their conversations have always been casual, undemanding. Glenda has been somewhat of a diversion for Walter who has spent several unrelenting years as a bookworm. Glenda has been a temporary amusement. All his life Walter has seen himself as rather a self-sufficient giant. He has needed nothing, no one.

Oh, his faith, of course. Preparing for the ministry, he has been scrupulously aware of his human frailties and foibles and, therefore, his need for total dependence on God. But not since childhood has he felt the need to depend on a woman. Surely now he does not feel the need to depend on plain, beautiful Glenda.

She, too, has lived rather an independent life, securing a degree in elementary education, preparing now for her fifth year of teaching lovable, dimple-cheeked kindergartners. Her steady faith in God has seen her through the loss of her parents and grandparents and at least one close girlhood friend. Glenda has lived alone since her youth, gleaning satisfaction from her full, if singular, social life at church.

Until Walter. Now she finds it extremely pleasant to be two instead of one, to say *we* instead of *I*. She cannot imagine sunrises and sunsets without the possibility of hearing

Walter's voice. She cannot conceive of God selecting any other man on earth for her besides Walter.

But tell Walter.

"Tell Walter, Lord," she has prayed in early morning devotionals on sleepy knees and during lengthy midnight supplications. *Tell Walter...if it is Your will,* she has always added dutifully.

But so far Walter has no idea.

The ground round platters arrive. "Which one of you ordered medium rare?" quizzes the waitress, pushing her gum into a corner of her cheek.

"Mine was well done," answers Walter.

"And mine—"

"Yeah, I know, medium rare," the waitress drawls, quickly distributing the items of food and drink. "And no onions."

They are settled now, these two—Walter and Glenda—eager, yet anxious, anticipating a scrumptious meal. Harry never lets a patron down. While Walter seeks God's blessing on the food, Glenda entreats His blessing on the evening.

Yes, it is evening now. The sun has set. The sky is darkening outside the Palace windows. Prussian blue is spreading across the heavens.

"Your ground round okay?" asks Walter solicitously.

"Yes, just right. Is your—"

"Great. Good old Harry. Never lets—"

"—You down," she finishes, laughing lightly.

"You're reading my thoughts," he accuses teasingly.

"No, I—I really can't." (Blushing.)

"I was just kidding. Teasing you," he assures her.

"Oh, but of course. I knew you were."

Walter dabs at his mouth with his napkin. "Well, there won't be any Harry's Hamburger Palace back in New York."

"No," she agrees. "Better fill up now—"

"On chili dogs and fries?" (A little joke.)

"No, of course not. You won't miss those!"

"But I'll miss...you."

Glenda looks up startled. The earth pauses in its rotation, the music stops, and her heart hesitates, refusing to interrupt this moment by pounding needlessly. "What?" she queries.

"I'll miss these great times we've had together," Walter responds pleasantly.

No, that's not what he said the first time. His first comment might have pushed him over the edge. How carefully he avoids the drop-off. Perhaps he's afraid to swim. Or maybe he doesn't know how to begin.

Glenda's heart resumes its disappointed ticking. "Oh," she replies, her voice hardly there. Actually, she is scarcely present either. She feels herself becoming invisible. She struggles with her precarious self-esteem, fighting off the impulse to vanish.

"Did I say something wrong?" Walter inquires, seeing that he has wounded her.

But Glenda is swift in binding her wound. Over her hurt expression she slips a very cordial, very proper mask. With a perfectly painted Gleem grin, she asks, "What did you say, Walter?"

"I said, did I say something wrong?"

She blushes. "Why would you think—?"

"Well, you looked...you looked peculiar."

"No, Walter, I'm fine. Goodness! Don't be silly."

He removes his pocket watch and glances at the time. It is a gold watch, a very old watch, an heirloom, an antique. It belonged to his father and grandfather before him. Walter would never go anywhere without his cherished watch. "My, it's getting a bit late," he remarks. "Do you want dessert—pie, ice cream?"

Glenda pushes back her plate. "No, Walter, I'm fine. Unless you—?"

"Oh, no, I'm stuffed too. Besides, we should be going. I was thinking that I might start packing tonight."

"Packing? This soon? But you still have a week!" Glenda scrambles to keep her cheery mask in place. This time it has very nearly slipped off.

"You know how fast a week will pass," he reasons.

"Yes, I know," she answers, her countenance dismal beneath the mask.

"You will write, of course—"

Glenda nods cautiously. "If you want me to..."

"Want you to? Why, of course. Why would you think I—?"

"I don't know. I just figured...I mean, you never mentioned writing...or anything."

Walter leans forward intently. His gaze has never been so direct. "You don't think that I intend to let things end here, do you?"

"I don't know," Glenda responds faintly. She feels herself hanging in midair, suspended perhaps from Walter's watch chain. Jimmy Stewart would never keep Doris Day hanging like this. Time is ticking away and Glenda is holding on for dear life, dangling helplessly back and forth, back and forth. She wonders, *When Walter releases me, will he drop me upon a—a cloud? Or over a precipice?*

"You must know I'm fond of you," Walter persists. "Or am I speaking out of turn?"

Glenda lifts her hand in alarm. "Oh, no, Walter, I'm fond of you too." She is still hanging on fiercely, holding her breath. It is such a terribly long way to fall.

"Then you think it's possible—?"

"Think what?"

"Possible we have more than friendship going for us?" he suggests.

"Possible?" she whispers in amazement.

"Something more permanent perhaps?"

"Oh, Walter—"

"There's so little time left, but—"

"Walter, I—" She feels herself beginning to fall. *Oh, please, Walter, a happy ending! It's what Jimmy and Doris would want.*

"I don't know if you would even like New York," he remarks. "It's so much colder there than here."

"I love winters," she cries, floating deliciously downward.

"There's your teaching too," he adds. "You've signed a contract for the fall. Your little kindergartners—"

"There are kindergartners in New York."

"You'd have to pack—"

"So will you."

Walter brightens. "Glenda, does this mean—?"

"I don't know, Walter. What are you trying to say?"

Walter pauses to consider this. At last he speaks, choosing his words precisely. "I think I'm trying to tell you I don't want to go to New York alone. Glenda, uh—dear, I believe I want to marry you and take you with me."

"But why?" she pleads, still airborne and drifting. By now her mask of pretense has utterly dissolved.

"Why?" he echoes uncertainly.

"Yes, Walter, why!"

"Because...I love you."

Glenda's landing is perfect. The cloud is glorious. She breathes the perfume of euphoria. "Walter, darling, I love you too!"

In a pastel haze of stardust and dreams, the happy couple sit spellbound, speechless, seeing each other for the first time ever in their lives. Their hearts beat as one; they drown deliriously in each other's eyes.

As Walter and Glenda clasp hands across the table, the world steps back into the shadows, hushing itself. The spotlight turns to the lunch counter at Harry's Hamburger Palace where the New York Philharmonic orchestra performs Chopin's splendid Polonaise in A-flat. Now New York beckons not only Walter, but Glenda too. New York will be their home!

At last Harry's Hamburger Palace throws open its doors and releases the joyous twosome. As the symphony music crescendos, Glenda and Walter float hand in hand into the moonlight, flanked by rows of trees standing at attention, accompanied by galaxies of stars applauding their romance, and welcomed by a mighty, triumphant ocean congratulating the blissful couple for finally taking the plunge.

Ah! Eat your hearts out, Jimmy and Doris. You never had it so good!

Bitter Saturday

What does a woman do when she can't stop physically abusing her own child?

Saturday, 6:00 A.M.: The alarm is ringing, the baby crying. I bury my face in my pillow until I remember what day this is. My mother is arriving tonight by plane for her first visit in four long years. So already, strike one against the day.

I turn off the alarm and grab the baby before she wakes Sarah and Bobby. Sarah's four and the quiet one, with silky blonde hair and blue eyes that could charm the fuzz off a peach. Bobby's seven and a holy terror, with red hair and freckles and the stubbornness of a pint-size mule. Sometimes I think it'll be a miracle if I survive his growing up years; in fact, it'll be a miracle if he survives too.

While I warm Carrie's bottle, I push away cobwebs of sleep. My head is dream-fuzzy, my tongue tastes like green moss, and that awful, nameless weight is still in my chest—a feeling of dread, almost a panicky sensation. As much as I care about my mother, she's the last person on earth I want to see.

For the next half hour I give Carrie her bottle. She's a good baby—plump and rosy-cheeked and easily soothed, not like Bobby who always cried no matter what I did. As I rock Carrie, I calmly recite the things I must do today—the last minute cleaning, the shopping and baking, the children's baths, and a perfect dinner on the table when Scott arrives home with Mother.

Scott is on one of his three-day runs, but he promised to be home by four today. I told him I'm not dragging three little kids to a crowded airport. I reminded him with stinging words I now regret that it's not easy being married to a truck driver who's away from home so much. "How would you like raising three kids single-handedly?" I challenged. "You should be here, helping with the kids. Especially Bobby. It's a man's job to watch his son." I really poured it on, but it's how I feel. It's the truth. So he promised he'd go to the airport and get Mother for me.

Now, if I can just get through this day. I want things to be right for my mother. It's crazy, I know. Why, after all these years and all we've been through, do I still need to impress her and win her approval? What's she ever done for me?

Saturday, 10:00 A.M.: The phone is ringing. I switch off the vacuum cleaner and answer more gruffly than I should. It's my neighbor, Janice Shaw. She goes to the same church we've attended a few times and she's got it in her head that my kids belong in Sunday School every week. Does she have any idea what it takes to get three kids ready on time?

Actually, I like Janice. She's been more of a friend to me than I'll probably ever be to her. She has driven the children to Sunday School while I stayed home and slept, brought them homemade chocolate chip cookies, and taken them home for an afternoon when I was just too tired to care. Would you believe? She talks as easily about Jesus as she does about her husband. Sometimes I envy her, she's so good-natured and easygoing. But she baffles me too, always saying things like, "Jesus loves you, Donna." Sometimes I wonder, is she for real, or what?

Now she's calling to tell me she wants to take Bobby and Sarah to Bible school next week. She says they'll learn how much Jesus loves them. I tell her we'll wait and see. My mother, who has no time for religious things, will be visiting all next week.

I hang up as quickly as I can, explaining I have a cake in the oven. It's true. But also a good excuse. I don't always feel comfortable chatting with Janice. She talks about God as if He were her personal friend. Come on, get real, I say.

And sometimes she pokes her nose where it doesn't belong. One day she dropped in without warning and saw bruises on Bobby's arms and legs. I told her he fell off his bike, but I know she didn't believe me. She started telling me how God can help a person when the pressures get too bad and the stress builds up. Boy, did she set me off. I really lost it. I told her I had things to do so she'd have to go home. I was trembling. My voice was shrill. I told her I wasn't going to have anyone implying I hurt my own son.

But Janice wasn't the least bit offended. Smiled and said she'd keep praying for us. She still calls and chats as if we were close friends, even when my voice is cold enough to freeze water. There's something unnatural about a person like Janice. Like, what planet is she from?

Saturday, 10:30 A.M.: The phone is ringing again! I bark, "Hello," then quickly retreat. It's Scott. "Where are you?" I cry. "Cincinnati? But you're supposed to be home in a few hours. You're kidding! The truck broke down? Tomorrow morning? Oh, Scott, no! I need you here. Tonight! I can't face Mother alone. And you know how I hate that drive to the airport! You did this on purpose, didn't you? To punish me! No, I won't listen to reason. I don't care if you and your blasted truck never come home!"

Angrily I hang up on Scott, then instantly regret everything I've just said. Somewhere in the back of my mind I know the delay isn't his fault, but the rush of disappointment is too great to be quelled. It's a torrent sweeping over me, waves of bitter emotion that engulf all reason. How I dread being home alone with the kids and my mother.

In frustration I pick up one of Carrie's plastic toys and slam it against the wall, shattering it. Bobby and Sarah are watching cartoons on TV. Donald Duck and Pluto. Sarah looks at me with a stricken expression on her face, then looks quickly away, as if she's seen nothing. Bobby looks up too and is already on his feet running over to the fragmented toy.

"You broke it! You broke it!" he screams accusingly. "You broke Carrie's toy!"

"Shut up!" I shout back. "It's not a good toy. She doesn't even play with it."

"Yes, she does!" he insists. "It's her best toy and you broke it!"

The anger that erupted in me moments ago because of Scott's delay still simmers hotly. I reach out and grab Bobby's arm and shake him furiously.

"Stop, you're hurting me!" he screams. Even as my fingers dig into Bobby's flesh, from somewhere in my mind emerges a crude child-rhyme...a faded, sad little memory:

Mama, please don't hit me.
I promise I'll be good.
Mama, why you crying
when I'm the one who should?

I release Bobby and order him to his room. I am trembling, weak inside. I keep telling myself this won't happen. I should be able to control the rage. Trouble is, I don't have time to prepare, to gather my reserves of control. The emotions just knock me flat and leave me feeling helpless, devastated. *Oh, God, it isn't like this for other people. Why is it like this for me?*

Saturday, 3:00 P.M.: I am shopping at the Kroger store, pushing a cart from aisle to aisle, clutching my coupons and tossing in soups, cereals, hamburger, bread. I am watching for the specials on brownie mix, tortilla chips, sliced beets and coffee. But my mind keeps wandering off. My thoughts are scattered in several directions at once. I'm thinking of Bobby, of Scott, of my mother. I feel so guilty. They all make me feel guilty, each in a different way. Why did I hang up on Scott? Why was I so angry with Bobby? Why do I have such mixed feelings about seeing my mother again?

I am determined to make it up to all of them. I select their favorite foods—porterhouse steak for Scott and chicken legs for Bobby. And for Mother, fresh sweet corn and broccoli. And of course, her favorite chocolate cake is waiting at home. I frosted it just before leaving for the store and it turned out perfect. A real masterpiece.

I realize suddenly that I have been in the store for over an hour. Too long. The only sitter I could get was Shelly, the 12-year-old next door, a giggly little airhead who thinks a telephone is a natural extension of her arm. But surely she can hold down the fort for an hour or so.

Saturday, 3:45 P.M.: Both my arms are loaded with groceries, so I kick at the door with my shoe. Sarah opens it a crack, then wordlessly scurries back to the TV. Sure enough, Shelly is on the phone. She hangs up promptly and hurries over, taking the grocery sacks while I fish in my purse for the cash

I owe her. "Where should I put these, Mrs. Cochran?" she asks.

"In the kitchen, Shelly. Thanks."

After she has gone, I go to the kitchen to put away the food. "Hey, you guys, I could use some help!" I call, reaching into a bag on the counter. "Bobby, Sarah, did you hear—?" I stop in mid-sentence and stare in horror at the table. Where my perfect cake once sat, now a chocolate catastrophe covers the tablecloth. My beautiful creation has been mauled and thrashed and the icing smeared everywhere.

I am too shocked to speak or react. I simply stare in mute fascination at the horrible mess. Then a small voice murmurs, "I didn't do it."

I look down at Sarah, cake crumbs still on her lips. "Where's Bobby?" I demand.

"In the bedroom."

I fly to the bedroom propelled by an energy that transcends excitement or rage. Bobby, sitting on his bed, looks up at me defiantly.

"Why, Bobby, Why!" I cry. "Why did you destroy my cake!"

"Sarah was hungry," he replies evasively.

"But you wrecked it, Bobby. Why!"

"You broke Carrie's toy," he explains with his stolid seven-year-old logic, "so I broke your cake."

I yank him up by both shoulders. "You were a bad boy, Bobby. Say you're sorry or you'll get the spanking of your life!"

He squirms out of my grasp. I lunge forward and pull him up short and slap him hard across the face.

"Don't, Mommy!" he screams, cowering.

But it's too late. I'm over the edge. I strike him again...and again. I feel a monumental sense of vindication, of justification inside me. I'm giving this child what he deserves. It's as if my actions are on automatic drive, as if my hand has a will of its own. I am blinded by the lightning bolts; the flash flood of rage has my senses reeling.

I hear myself shriek again, "Say you're sorry!"

Then, with a terror that snatches my breath away, I realize Bobby can't say anything. He is lying in a heap on the floor, blood running from his mouth and ear.

"Oh, no. No! Oh, God, help me," I whisper in disbelief. "I'm not that kind of mother. I'm not!" I stoop down and gather Bobby's limp body into my arms. I cradle him and weep and kiss his puffy, bruised face. "I love you, Baby, I love you," I tell him over and over. "Why do you push me, sweetheart? Why do you make me hurt you? Oh, Baby, I didn't want to hurt you!"

Sarah's crying jolts me out of my self-absorbed grief. She whimpers, "Is Bobby going to die?"

Seeing her, hearing her sad little voice, I spring into action, wrap Bobby in a blanket, and carry him to the car. I go back for the baby and scoot Sarah out the door. "Come on, honey. Bobby hurt himself. We've got to drive him to the hospital."

Sarah stares back at me without blinking. I see in her eyes that she does not believe me.

Saturday, 6:00 P.M.: I am in the gray, dingy waiting room at Memorial Hospital. Sarah is sitting beside me looking at a *Sesame Street* picture book. Carrie is asleep in her infant seat.

When we arrived at the emergency room, the nurse took one look at Bobby and summoned the doctor. They rushed my boy away on a stretcher, the doctor scowling. I heard him say something about internal bleeding.

"Bobby fell down the steps," I called after them.

Moments later I heard a clipped voice over the intercom announcing, "Any surgeon in the house—STAT to the emergency room!" The nurse at the admitting desk glanced coolly my way, then beckoned me over. She handed me several forms to fill out. Moments later the nurse was there, brisk, efficient, a surgical consent in her hand. "You'll have to sign this, Mrs. Cochran," she said, her voice kind, her expression stoical.

Now, as I return the completed forms to her, she asks, "What happened, Mrs. Cochran?" Her voice does not accuse; it questions. It is still tempered with kindness.

"I—I already told the doctor. Bobby fell down the basement steps. I tell him not to play on the stairs, but he doesn't listen."

"Was your son ever a patient here before?"

"Yes. Last year," I reply. "He fell off his bike and cracked some ribs. He, uh, had a slight concussion too."

The nurse scribbles something down. "We'll have to send to Medical Records for his chart," she explains. Then her hand rests gently on mine. "Has Bobby been hospitalized anywhere else?"

I hesitate, then answer quietly, "Once or twice before."

"Where? When?"

"I can't remember. I'm just too upset." I feel my pulse racing. She knows something! Weakly I ask, "How long before I'll hear about Bobby?"

"It may take awhile," she replies. "You might as well sit down and try to relax."

"But you don't understand. I have to pick up my mother at the airport."

"I'm sorry, Mrs. Cochran, but the doctor's going to have to admit your son; he's not going anywhere tonight."

I look nervously at my watch, then allow my eyes to wander around the lobby. I see a hospital security guard, a man in uniform walking my way. My mother's plane is due. I must not keep her waiting. I look back at the nurse. "Please, miss, I've got to go. Tell the doctor I'll be back in an hour."

"Mrs. Cochran," she protests, "you can't just leave."

"I'm sorry. I have no choice. My mother does not like to wait."

Saturday, 7:00 P.M.: The tense, bright, animated mood of the airport is a startling contrast to the drab, depressing atmosphere of the hospital. Here everything is bustling and noisy; there everything is silent and oppressive. Here the air is pleasant and inviting; there it is foul and antiseptic. I don't want to go back there. I don't want to hear bad news. I don't want to see the condemnation in their eyes. I want to run, escape, be free. Forget. And yet I must go back. I want to take Bobby home and kiss away his tears.

Of course, I can't run. Or forget. I am sitting here at the airport with Sarah and Carrie, waiting for my mother. The plane is due at any moment. I feel guilty about leaving Bobby, knowing what I did and not knowing how he'll be, but what else could I do? My mother is arriving; she's depending on me.

Thinking of Mother, I feel a sense of nausea in the pit of my stomach. What will she think when she hears about Bobby? She'll blame me. She'll hate me. Somehow, all of my life I've managed to make my mother hate me. We've repelled each other like the wrong sides of magnets. We've infuriated each other, frustrated each other, exhausted each other. Just like Bobby and me. Just when I want to love him, he infuriates me. Why? Will it go on like this forever—Bobby's children twisting his love into anger, and their children doing the same? Who's to blame...and where will it end?

Or will it end with Bobby? What if he dies? *Oh, God, he has to live! I was angry, but I didn't mean anything by it. Please don't punish me. Don't take Bobby away.*

For an unsettling moment I feel like a child again pleading for a reprieve from punishment. But words never worked. Mother wouldn't listen. My only salvation was ducking under a table or hiding under the bed to escape her blows. Unexpectedly the singsong phrases of that little rhyme haunt me again:

Mama, please don't hit me.
I promise I'll be good.
Mama, why you crying
when I'm the one who should?

A rumbling voice announcing Flight 409 slices into my solemn recollections. I jump up, gather the baby into my arms and grasp Sarah's hand. We hurry to the gate where the passengers are disembarking. I watch intently until I spot that familiar figure—a large-boned, straight-backed woman with sternly handsome features and cropped gray-brown hair. She spies me too and wends her way toward me. We embrace stiffly, politely; then as she welcomes the baby and Sarah into her arms, her eyes fill with tears. I am caught off guard. I have never seen her expression so tender.

Finally, looking around curiously, she asks, "Where's Bobby? Where's that little carrot-topped grandson of mine?"

"I'll explain when we get in the car, Mother."

Saturday, 10:00 P.M.: We are back at the hospital, waiting for Bobby to come out of surgery. Mother and I sit in silence, each holding a sleeping child on our lap. On our way here I told Mother that Bobby had an accident, that he fell down the cellar steps. She didn't reply. Now, something in her stony silence makes me defensive.

"Bobby's such a careless child," I remark lamely, making a stab at conversation.

Before Mother can respond, the door opens and the surgeon comes out. His expression is haggard, his eyes hold a severity that causes me to flinch. "Mrs. Donna Cochran?" he queries.

I stand up shakily, holding Carrie against my chest. "Yes, I'm Mrs. Cochran. How's Bobby? When can I see him?"

"They're transferring him to intensive care right now. It'll be awhile before he comes out of the anesthetic."

"He—he will be all right, won't he?"

"We've stopped the internal bleeding," he replies soberly, "but we had to remove your son's spleen. Things are under control, but your child is not out of danger yet." He clears his throat, then lowers his voice. "Why don't you tell me, Mrs. Cochran. How did your son hurt himself?"

"I already told the emergency room doctor. Bobby fell off his bike and—"

The surgeon frowns. "But, Mrs. Cochran, didn't you tell the nurse your boy fell down the stairs?"

I feel trapped, terrified. The bike excuse was the other time! "Yes," I whisper hoarsely, "that's what I meant. The basement steps. He's so clumsy. I've told him a million times—"

"I'm sorry, Mrs. Cochran," he interrupts, his voice ironically kind, "but we're going to have to file a report with CPS."

I stare at him dumbfounded. "You mean, the police?"

He looks almost sympathetic as he replies, "No, the Child Protective Services."

"Why?" I demand indignantly.

He eyes me with a frankness that unnerves me.

"It appears almost impossible that your son's injuries were sustained from a fall." He places his hand on mine. "Is it possible, Mrs. Cochran, that his wounds were physically inflicted by another person?"

"No!" I cry in protest. "How dare you suggest that I—!"

"Not necessarily you, Mrs. Cochran." He turns away as if to avoid saying more.

"He fell down the steps!" I insist frantically. "Why won't you believe me?"

"Excuse me, Mrs. Cochran," he says, glancing back but not meeting my eyes. "I want to look in on your son. I'll return when there's more to report."

I reach for him, nearly upsetting Carrie. "Don't make trouble for me with the authorities," I plead, my voice dismayingly shrill. "Please, doctor! They won't understand. They'll take away my children!"

The physician is already walking away from me, refusing to listen. I sink back down into my chair. The old, familiar panic is taking over, numbing my senses. "I have to go home," I tell Mother. "Let's go. Let's get out of here."

Instead of rising, Mother places a constraining hand on my arm. "How did Bobby get hurt?" she questions, her eyes penetrating mine.

"I told you. He fell down the steps."

"Listen to me, Donna." Mother's voice assumes an earnestness I've never heard before. She grips my arm with a frightening desperation. "Break the cycle now, Donna, before it's too late. Stop this curse while you can."

I look away and mutter, "I don't know what you're talking about."

"This hideous pattern of violence," she persists. "Oh, Donna, you know the truth. I abused you as a child just as my mother abused me. And now you're hurting Bobby. Only *you* can stop it!"

I begin to weep bitterly. I clutch Carrie tighter. My tears wash her fine, corn-silk hair. Never before has my mother admitted how wrongly she treated me. All my life I've blamed myself for her cruelty, condemned myself for not measuring up to her impossible expectations. Now, when it's too late, she confesses. I can't cope with her sudden burst of honesty. I counter with, "What gives you the right, of all people, to tell me what to do?"

A dark, painful silence hangs between us. Then Mother speaks slowly, with a ground swell of emotion. "You don't know this, Donna, but I've struggled with my own guilt for more years than you can imagine. Why do you think we were never close? Why do you think I always kept you at arm's length? Not because I didn't love you. Because I was afraid. I could never predict what I would do or how we might clash. I hated myself for what I did to you. I didn't want to die carrying this burden of guilt and regret, so two years ago...I began therapy."

"You, Mother?"

"I'm still in counseling. My therapist felt it was time for me to face you. That's why I'm here. I couldn't talk about it until now. And now, I see myself in you, and I know it's happening all over again, and it breaks my heart."

I don't answer. I can't. My own emotions are riding the edge. For a while neither of us speaks. The silence beats in my ears like a terrible pressure. Finally I force out the words, "How can I stop, Mother?"

She meets my gaze. "I don't know, Donna."

"I try, but I can't help myself."

"You were grown and gone before I faced myself and admitted I needed help. It was too late for me. Don't let it be too late for you."

"Then help me, Mother, please."

"I don't have the answers, Donna. But there are people. There are organizations that can help. Give them a chance."

"How do I find them? What do I do?"

"Maybe the hospital has a social worker. We could ask the doctor."

I draw back warily. "Not the surgeon. He's going to cause

trouble for me. Turn me in to Child Protective Services. The police. There'll be an investigation, Mother. Scott will be furious."

"Oh, Donna, Scott knows what's happening. He may not admit it, but deep inside, he knows."

"He'll hate me if they take away our children," I cry, pondering the unthinkable. "And when he sees what I've done to Bobby, he'll never forgive me."

"Is there anyone else you can turn to, Donna? Anyone who could help?" She rocks, Sarah nestled trustingly against her.

"I don't know. I don't— Wait. There is someone..."

"Who? Tell me, Donna."

"My neighbor. Janice. She's always so friendly. Would you believe? She actually told me Jesus loves me..."

Mother's tone is wistful. "I was never a church-going woman, Donna. Maybe if I had been..."

"I think Janice would help me, Mother, or at least find someone who can help."

"Then call her, Donna. Get help wherever you can find it."

I shift my sleeping baby—my sweet, innocent, untouched Carrie—in my arms. I know in my heart of hearts I must protect her, but I'm not sure I can go through with it.

"Mother, I'm afraid," I whisper plaintively. "What will the authorities do? What will Scott say? What will people think?"

Mother's firm voice steadies me for the long, ragged, unknown road ahead. "Aren't those fears better, Donna, than that old, secret, deadly fear of what more you might do to hurt your children?"

I press my cheek against Carrie's fuzzy, sleeping head. Tears sting my eyes. "It's not too late, is it, Mother, for me to call my friend Janice tonight?"

Mother reaches past Sarah for her purse and nods toward

the wall phone. "I have change, Donna. Don't wait until morning. Call her now from here."

She hands me the change, and for an instant our fingers touch. We clasp hands. Mother and daughter. Connected by time and pain, nightmares and dreams, desperation and hope. Our eyes say it all. Wordlessly I place Carrie in her arms beside Sarah. Mother's embrace tightens around both of my daughters, securely, lovingly. I stand, my legs wobbly, and go make my call

Shopping at the Safeway

What does a woman do when she is sure the world beyond her door is the enemy and certain death awaits if she leaves her home?

She woke at dawn when the world was still painted in sepia tones and knew that this was the day. She would do it or die.

She lay in bed, still as a rock, listening to the slightly audible whoosh of her own breathing, listening to the clock ticking on her bedside table—a dogged rhythm, jarringly loud, like a drumbeat in her ears. She realized her own heartbeat was in sync with the terrible ticking. Imprisoned by it—the two beating as one—unrelenting, unstoppable, eternal.

It was beating out her name. Katie Saunders...*Katie Saunders!*

She feared her own heartbeat more than she feared its cessation. She feared the sound of it pounding out her name to the world at large, where strangers might hear and look her way and wonder what manner of person she was. Who was this woman, Katie Saunders?

She was nobody. She was anonymous. She didn't exist.

Except in this house. In the closed, secret womb of this house.

She climbed out of bed, walked to the bathroom and peered at her face in the mirror. An ordinary face, pale, too angular, with sunken eyes and a mouth drawn too thin to be pretty. There was something beyond the eyes that she couldn't read, something to be unlocked, a secret self that she hadn't discovered; or perhaps there was nothing more; perhaps she was fooling herself to imagine a real person behind the face.

She splashed her skin with cold water and ran a brush through her short brown hair. It had no style, no curl, only a gentle wave where it meandered over her forehead and down her neck. She had never been a beautiful woman, although George must have seen something in her, a certain remote attractiveness; he had married her. And even now, never knowing what he would find, he always came home again.

She shuffled to the kitchen and stuck a ceramic mug of water in the microwave, then stirred a spoonful of instant coffee into the boiling water. She sat at her small dinette table and stared through the chintz curtains at the yard, the street. She had forgotten whether they were real—actual trees, houses that were more than facades, a street that went somewhere. Or were they merely movie props placed there to make her believe there was still a world beyond her windows.

It was time to find out.

Was she up to it? Would she actually do it today, or would she just go through the motions as she had so many times before, doing it halfway, getting to the door or halfway out the door, then retreating, the panic as distasteful as castor oil in her throat?

She had a feeling today would be different. She would make it today. Her courage was up; she felt better than she had in weeks, maybe months. And if she failed, who would know? George was gone on his business trip to Toledo until tomorrow. If she failed, she would have a whole day and night to recover. He would never know, never think to ask if she had tried it.

She sipped her coffee—black and strong; it burned down her throat and grew sour in the pit of her stomach, but she needed it. She needed more but no—no pills; she must do this herself. She must remain clear-headed; she must stay in control and she would be okay. Yes, God, help her, she would be okay.

She returned to her bedroom and examined her wardrobe. She hadn't bought a new outfit in over two years—not since Aunt Amelia's death, not since the estate sale. Or was it the funeral? Yes, she had bought a black dress for the funeral.

Since then, George had begged her to go out shopping; he had bribed her with promises of gorgeous dresses and stylish suits, cashmere sweaters or a fur coat, whatever she wished. He would take her wherever she wanted to go—Nordstrom, Bullocks—it was up to her. But, of course, she hadn't gone anywhere, hadn't bought a single new outfit, and now she realized how little she had to choose from.

But perhaps that was best. A simple tailored shirt and slacks would do—nothing too showy or bright; nothing to call attention to itself. She showered, then dressed with painstaking care, her fingers trembling as she worked the buttons. She examined herself in the full-length mirror in her narrow hallway and decided this would do. She looked like anybody, like nobody, like any normal person.

Except her face. Her features faded into the glass; her

reflection seemed smudged somehow, her eyes mere dark spots against a chalky complexion. She returned to her bathroom and fished through her cosmetics drawer for foundation and blusher and an eyebrow pencil. If she were going to do this properly, she must do it all the way. She must look the part and play her role without attracting anyone's attention.

Just Katie Saunders, normal person.

"Sweet Jesus, let me do this today," she prayed aloud. She knew she was being foolish and hysterical, but she added urgently, "And don't let me die. Please don't let me die!"

Of course, she would not die. No one died from this. No one was crazy enough to think that doing this would kill them.

Perhaps that was the difference between her and the rest of the world. She could not stop thinking that this, this thing that she must do, would kill her.

Even so, she had decided. And she felt a certain fatalistic pride in knowing that even if she did not survive, she had risked everything in the attempt. And George would be proud of her. He would know she had done it as much for him as for herself.

She finished her makeup with a touch of lipstick—a pale, pink shade, not red. Heavens, nothing garish. It wasn't on even, but she hoped no one would notice. She wiped her teeth with a tissue and licked her lips. Her mouth was already dry; she would have to remember to carry mints in her purse. Pray God, she wouldn't have to speak.

Oh, yes, she would need her checkbook. What a calamity if she made it all the way and forgot her checkbook!

She found her purse by the bureau and looked inside. Yes, her wallet was here, her car keys, checkbook and driver's license. She was ready to go. She walked around the house and made sure the doors were locked and the windows shut; she knew they would be; they always were. Still, she checked. Then she straightened her shoulders and walked to the door.

She remembered then that she should have made out a list. She glanced toward the kitchen and mentally inspected her cupboards and refrigerator. That would have to do. If she took time to make a list, she might change her mind and all the torment of this morning would be in vain.

With trembling fingers she opened the door and hesitated as the cool breeze swept her face and the sunlight exploded in her eyes. She was glad it wasn't a cloudy day, nor a dark day threatening rain like the day of the estate sale two years ago—the day men came and dragged all her aunt's possessions into the yard, the day the rains came down like an indictment from God, and strangers swarmed over the place buying her aunt's cherished, rain-soaked treasures for a song.

No, she must not think of that day. Not now. Not if she hoped to survive the next few hours. She stepped back momentarily and looked away, then forced her gaze back toward the front yard, the driveway, her waiting automobile. George always left the car here for her when he flew off on his trips—his quiet way of saying he believed in her.

Gritting her teeth, she stepped out onto the porch, shut the door behind her and tried the handle. Yes, it was locked. She was on the outside now. She had come too far to go back.

She walked to her car and climbed in. Stuck the key in the ignition, started the motor, listened to the uneven hum, and fastened her seat belt. It felt strange and yet eerily familiar to be behind the wheel again, to feel the power of the automobile converging in her fingers. She drove slowly, with excruciating precision. Above all else, she wanted to look like an ordinary driver out for an ordinary ride.

The Safeway store was less than a mile away. As she drove she couldn't quite believe that this was happening. Katie

Saunders in a car again, out on the open road, heading somewhere. She felt as if she were someone else, someone anonymous, standing at a distance, watching herself, watching every gesture, every move. She felt detached, passive, uninvolved with this woman at the wheel. Who was she? And why did she feel that her life was at stake?

As long as Katie remained detached, she could keep the mushroom cloud at bay—the debilitating panic. As long as she stayed in control, she would be all right. She glanced down at her watch. Only ten minutes had passed. She would have guessed hours. Hadn't she already traveled a hundred miles?

At last—the Safeway store. She found a satisfactory parking spot and sighed, relieved she wouldn't have far to walk. She had considered parking even closer in the handicapped space, but no. No one would believe she was handicapped. Her handicap didn't show.

For a long while she sat in her car and watched the store, watched people coming and going, ordinary people wheeling carts of groceries out or carrying plastic bags of stuff in their arms. They looked so perfectly normal, so wonderfully normal. It all looked so easy, so deceptively simple.

But then that day at the estate sale had been deceptively simple too. Katie had watched the men carry all her aunt's furnishings outside—love seats and tables and chairs, paintings and books, dishes and heirlooms. She had chatted with the men, joked with them—and with the customers who came in droves. She had watched the storm clouds gather and the rain pour down, drenching all the objects her aunt had loved. She watched in mute fascination as the people gathered around those treasures under their colorful umbrellas while the auctioneer sang out his slippery spiel: *Who'll give me ten I got ten who'll give me twenty, twenty, who'll make it thirty, going once, going twice...*

Going, going, almost gone.

No, it would not happen again. She wouldn't let it happen. She had come this far. There was no turning back. She would kick herself forever if she turned back now. If she simply made herself go and do it, it would all be over in an hour. Somehow she would live through it, and everything in her life would be different. Transformed.

But if she failed—if she got inside the store and it started all over again—the blinding, heart-pounding terror—if she failed this time, then it would all be over, and she knew she would never try again. And it would be the same as dying, only worse, because it would be the end of Katie Saunders. She would never recover.

"Sweet Jesus, don't let me think negative," she whispered. "Help me. You're in me, part of me. Make it go right."

She climbed out of the car and took quick strides toward the Safeway. She was moving too swiftly, she realized, glancing around anxiously, acting suspicious, like someone being followed. Someone with something to hide. Slow down, she told herself. Walk slowly, calmly, with your head erect.

Better. She was inside the store now, her ears tuning in to the low hum of voices, the buzz of commotion, the whir of air-conditioning. She looked around and blinked. The supermarket was larger than she remembered, assailing her vision with a plethora of mingled objects and colors. A service deli and bakery, a video tape rental counter, a display of fresh cut flowers, a wagon with loaves of freshly baked bread. The signs everywhere were too bright, the aisles too long, the shelves stocked too high. She would never manage. How could she navigate a shopping cart through these crowds, through this chaos? She turned and looked back longingly at the automatic door. It was an entrance only. The exit was somewhere else. She would have to press on.

She latched on to an empty cart and gripped the bar as if

embarking on a roller-coaster ride. White-knuckled, she pushed toward the nearest aisle. BREADS AND CEREALS. She stared helplessly at the vast selection of rolls and buns and rye breads and whole grain, and white and wheat and sliced and sandwich style, and natural and raisin, and— "Oh, help me," she uttered.

She would skip the breads and try cereals. She groaned. How could she have forgotten how many varieties there were? Trix and Cheerios, Rice Krispies and Corn Flakes, Raisin Bran and Special K. And odd names she had never heard of. Cereals that looked and sounded more like Saturday morning cartoons.

She grabbed a box of oatmeal and threw it into her cart. Her heart was pounding. She could hear it in her ears, inside her head. No one else could hear it, but it was only a matter of time. She must hurry; she must quell the pounding before anyone noticed, before everyone turned her way and realized the truth.

Remember at the auction how it all began—the rain, the auctioneer droning on, strangers carting off the bits and pieces of Aunt Amelia's life? Dear Aunt Amelia—the woman who had practically raised Katie. Remember another day dimmed by the passing of years when another house and other lives were dismantled?

No! It was a child's memory. It meant nothing.

Nothing.

Katie steered her cart perilously down one aisle and up another, dodging scores of blank-faced consumers moving their carts mindlessly through her orb. She could no longer tell one face from another; they all blurred, took on the same anonymity she sensed in herself; they were all remote, crowded together, moving with a synchronized rhythm. All mute strangers without connections.

Like the people at Aunt Amelia's estate sale.

Like the people who came and took apart my life after Mommy and Daddy died.

The panic was starting deep in her stomach, a vise-like grip sending spasms of pain up through her chest. Tension. It was only tension, she told herself. Still, she nearly doubled over, then caught herself and straightened, forcing herself to maintain control. She was biting her tongue, keeping back the sound that was already gathering deep in her throat. She couldn't hold on much longer. Perhaps she ought to leave her cart here and flee. No one would be the wiser. There was still time to save face, to survive.

No. She must see this through. She would select a few more items and head for the checkout stand. She sucked in a deep breath and pushed on, one aisle after another, reaching mindlessly for produce and dairy products and canned goods and detergents. She tossed in Velveeta cheese spread, Colgate toothpaste, Star Kist tuna, and Mr. Clean.

She was in the homestretch heading for the checkout counter when it happened. Her cart rammed Mrs. Crocker's, her neighbor down the block. The thick-jowled woman eyed her for a moment as if she couldn't quite place her, then beamed with the light of recognition. "It's you, Mrs. Saunders! Why, I hardly recognized you. You look so thin."

Katie stared back open-mouthed, speechless.

"I talked to your husband awhile back," the stout woman rushed on cheerily. "Asked him why we never see you anymore. He said you'd been ill. We were all so sorry to hear it."

"Thank you. I'm better now," Katie managed.

"Well, that's wonderful. It's so nice to see you out and about. Of course, your husband was rather vague about your ailment. A virus perhaps?"

"Uh, something like that."

"Well, dear, it must have been a nasty one to keep you in

the house well over a year. Hasn't it been that long since we've seen you?"

"About a year. I couldn't—" The words died in her throat and the throbbing in her head drowned out Mrs. Crocker's words.

Remember the estate sale. The rain. Hands grasping. The auctioneer's garbled fountain of words. I wanted to buy Aunt Amelia's portrait, but I didn't know what to say. I spoke but no one heard. I began to scream. Couldn't stop screaming...

Katie careened her cart toward the checkout stand and began unloading her groceries, frantically dumping the items onto the counter.

Mrs. Crocker followed close on her heels, a geyser of words gushing from her lips. "I might as well tell you, Mrs. Saunders, there have been rumors in the neighborhood about you. I'm not one to gossip, mind you, but I think a body has a right to know what's being said, don't you?"

"I—I can't—"

"Well, I hate to say this, naturally, but several unkind souls have hinted about, er, a nervous breakdown. One of those emotional disorders that keep a body prisoner in his own home. What do they call it? Agoraphobia? Something like that. Now, I don't believe a word of it, of course, Mrs. Saunders, but I thought you'd want to know..."

"Yes, thank you, I'm fine...tell them I'm fine..."

The cashier was ringing up her purchases, passing each item over an electronic scanner and repeating each price in a dull monotone. A bag boy was asking whether she wanted paper or plastic. And Mrs. Crocker rambled on, dribbling a putrid stream of dark insinuations.

Amid it all the heartbeat pulsing inside her skull boomed with a life of its own, the sound drowning out everything around her. She could no longer contain it; the drumbeat echoed against the walls and vibrated through the towering

Safeway superstructure like a low-rumbling earthquake. She gripped the counter for dear life. The inevitable was happening: She was dying before their eyes. Her knees had turned to jelly, her muscles had liquified; she was going down for the count.

I am at Aunt Amelia's estate sale. I watch her life being dismantled before my eyes...just as strangers dismantled my own home when my parents died...

"That'll be $56.98," said the cashier. "Unless you got coupons."

"No. No coupons."

I was only five. I thought it was all my fault. I was sure I was going to die too. What could I do with the anguish...except scream?

"Mrs. Saunders, are you all right?" asked Mrs. Crocker.

"Did you hear me, ma'am? That'll be $56.98," repeated the cashier.

"My checkbook," said Katie. "It's here somewhere." She searched her purse. She could feel the color draining from her face. How long did she have? Minutes? Seconds? "Yes, here. See? I have it. My checkbook."

The cashier handed her a pen and waited with a small, patient smile for the check.

"I'm sorry," said Katie. "Can you read it? My handwriting isn't what it used to be." She was growing faint, fading fast.

I'm dying...going, going, nearly gone...who'll give me ten I got ten who'll make it twenty, going once, going twice...

"I can read your handwriting okay, ma'am, but I need some identification."

"Identification?"

"Yeah, you know. Driver's license. Credit card. Visa. Check guarantee. Something that shows who you are."

Isn't that exactly the problem? I can't put my finger on who I am. I've come this far to prove my identity, to prove I do exist, that I have a life beyond the confines of my own home, and now, I'll be turned back, denied my purchases, denied my very existence because I don't have the proper identification. It was a mistake to come here, a mistake to think I could ever rejoin the world. Can't they see? I'm in the midst of my own death throes!

"I'm sorry," Katie stammered, her panic mushrooming, pulse racing, palms wet with perspiration. "I shouldn't have come!"

She was about to bolt and leave her ordinary treasures behind when, over the terrible thundering of her heart, she heard the cashier ask, "Did you check your wallet, ma'am?"

"My wallet?" Of course. Everything would be there—her driver's license, credit cards, all the pieces of paper and plastic she needed to define her fragile personhood. Trembling, she seized the proper cards and thrust them triumphantly at the cashier.

"Thank you, Mrs. Saunders," said the girl, smiling as she handed her the grocery receipt. "That was simple enough, wasn't it?"

Simple? Is it possible? I'm not at the estate sale. I'm not five. I'm not watching beloved lives be dismantled. I'm here. Shopping at the Safeway.

Katie nodded, tucking the receipt into her purse.

As she turned to go, Mrs. Crocker reached out and clasped her hand across the shopping cart. "Nice seeing you again, Mrs. Saunders. Now don't you be such a stranger, you hear? If it's okay with you, I'll stop by and visit one of these days with some of my homemade bread."

"All right," Katie managed, her voice rising precariously over the throbbing tom-tom of her heart. Sweet Jesus, she was still alive and the panic was receding, drawing back in on itself, like an atomic bomb reversing itself in slow motion, shrinking, becoming contained. "Sweet Jesus," she whispered reverently under her breath.

Her senses bristling with electric energy, Katie gripped her brimming cart and steered toward the exit door with the awkward gait of a fresh-born colt.

The Best Gift

What does a woman do when she has no Christmas spirit amid the holiday hustle and bustle?

It was the day before Christmas and all through the house every creature was stirring—especially me! Sound familiar? Would you believe, at dawn five-year-old Kristy bounced into the bedroom, squealing, "Is it Christmas yet?"

My husband, Jim, turned over with one eye open and hissed, "Go back to bed. It's still dark."

"When is Jesus' birthday?" Kristy persisted, burrowing under the covers between us.

"Tomorrow," I said, getting out of bed. Visions of the day's chores danced in my head. Christmas Eve, and I had a million things to do! Where had I gone wrong? Hadn't I started preparing for the yuletide holidays even before we consumed the leftovers from the Thanksgiving turkey?

Still groggy, I poured myself some coffee and made a mental list of the day's activities. First thing that morning I had to pick up the gifts of food from the neighbors on the block. Each year we gathered groceries for a needy family in the neighborhood and presented our gift on Christmas morning. This year Jim and I would do the honors.

Hopefully I would have the food gathered and be home in time to fix an early lunch for Kristy and Janice, our eight-year-old. In the afternoon I would clean house, wrap gifts and put a ham in the oven to bake while I went to have my hair done. At six Jim's parents would arrive for dinner. Everything would have to be ready, perfect for my hard-to-please in-laws.

The morning passed smoothly enough. I arrived home at 11:00, the trunk of the car loaded with boxes and sacks of canned goods, cereals, bread, powdered milk, pastries, and even a turkey.

"Where's the loot?" asked Janice when I entered the house carrying only the turkey.

"In the car," I answered, looking in the refrigerator for a place to store the turkey.

"Where's the food *we're* giving?" asked Janice, following me into the kitchen and taking two cartons of milk I handed her.

I removed several Tupperware containers, stacked leftover peas and fruit salad on top of the egg carton, and squeezed in the turkey. "The groceries we're giving are in your old Easter basket in the pantry," I answered patiently.

"Easter basket, Easter basket!" squealed Kristy, running to open the pantry door and clapping gleefully.

"Shut the door," I said.

"Who gets the stuff this year?" asked Janice.

"The Clarks," I said, shutting the pantry door.

"The ones with five kids?"

"Yes. Mr. Clark has been sick and out of work almost six months."

"Why do they get our food?" asked Kristy, reluctant to move away from the door.

Opening a can of spaghetti for lunch, I explained, "When it's Christmas, we give gifts to others to show our love for Jesus."

"But that's our good food," Kristy argued.

"Of course," I said. The spaghetti was sticking to the pan. "Jesus gave all He had for us, so we should always give our best to Him."

"But our food—"

"Kristy, please!"

She was quiet a moment, then chirped, "What can I give Jesus?"

"You don't have nothing," teased Janice, going to turn on the TV.

"Mommy, I love Jesus," Kristy continued eagerly.

"That's wonderful, darling," I said, dishing up the spaghetti. "Now go wash your hands—and tell Janice to come eat."

"Jingle Bells" blared from the TV.

"Hey, Kristy," called Janice. "Come see Rudolph the Red-nosed Reindeer!"

After lunch I dusted the furniture, vacuumed the carpet, straightened the kitchen and baked a cake. Then I hid out in the bedroom wrapping packages—Kristy's "Big Bird" from *Sesame Street*, a CD player for Janice, dresses for both the girls, a shirt and tie for Jim. And the gift I was proudest of—a beautiful pendant watch for Jim's mother. How I had scoured the stores for just the right gift, something for the woman who has everything. At least it seemed to me that my mother-in-law had everything. What did she lack in possessions, in graciousness, in talent? Somehow, by comparison, I felt awkward and incomplete.

"It's your imagination," Jim would tell me whenever I complained of feeling all thumbs around his mother. Nevertheless, I felt compelled to make everything as perfect as possible for her. And that included tonight—Christmas Eve!

"Now where's the good wrapping paper?" I said, perplexed. All I could find was orange tissue paper and a silver foil with little pink angels riding burros.

I went into the living room where the girls were watching a cartoon version of Dickens' "Christmas Carol." Scrooge was ranting, raving and verbally flaying his lowly clerk, Bob Cratchit. "Have you seen my good wrapping paper?" I called above the noise.

Scrooge screamed on; I shrugged and went to the kitchen where my cake sat cooling. I decided to frost it and then look for the paper. I was putting the last touches on the cake when Kristy skipped blissfully into the kitchen, the pendant watch spangling around her neck.

"Kristy!" I shouted, nearly defacing my glistening chocolate masterpiece with the frosting knife.

"Look at me, Mommy," she purred, her face beaming.

"Put that back," I cried. "That's a very expensive Christmas gift. It's not to play with."

Kristy looked disconcerted. "Is it the *best* gift, Mommy?"

"Yes!" I snapped. "Now put it back."

I glanced at the clock and saw with alarm that it was time to put the ham in to bake. And I had only half an hour before my hair appointment. Would I ever have dinner ready by six?

Jim arrived home from work just before it was time for me to leave for my appointment. I kissed him hello and whispered, "Did you get the stocking stuffers for the girls?"

He nodded. "In the car."

"The ham should be all right but keep an eye on it, okay?" I said, kissing him good-bye.

"What time will Mom and Dad be here?"

"Six. Have the girls put on their good dresses—the red ones hanging on the closet door."

"Will do. It's starting to snow. Looks like we'll have a white Christmas."

"I noticed. If I'm not back in an hour, turn the fire on under the potatoes."

"This is a terrible time to get your hair done," said Jim.

"I know, darling, but it's the only time Angie could take me today, and I want to look nice for your folks."

"I don't know why you worry so much about what they think."

"I just want to look my best," I said defensively, going to the door.

"'Bye, Mommy!" called Janice from the living room.

Kristy came running to kiss me good-bye, a piece of orange tissue paper in one hand, several crayons in the other. "How do you spell 'Jesus'?" she asked breathlessly.

"J-E-S-U-S," I answered, leaning down to kiss her.

"I'm making Him a card," she said, holding out the paper for me to see. "How do you make a 'J'?"

"Ask Daddy," I said, and escaped out the door.

Already darkness was beginning to mute the sky. Christmas carols rang joyously from the car radio and dazzling snow flurries floated earthward in a spiraling, slow-motion ballet. I tried to summon some fragment of Christmas spirit, but alas, all I felt was exhausted.

I was Angie's last appointment for the day. She worked quickly and efficiently, talking nonstop all the while. I sat under the dryer drooling over Christmas recipes in a woman's magazine. Occasionally I wondered, Would Jim turn on the fire under the potatoes? Was he watching the ham? Would his parents arrive early?

While Angie combed my hair she told me in detail what she was giving each of her relatives for Christmas and what she hoped they were giving her. We each said, "Merry Christmas!" as I left the shop, going out into the darkness and the bright cold taste of new snow. On the way home I stopped at K mart and bought the best foil wrapping paper I could find.

At home the girls were properly dressed, the house was clean, the ham and potatoes were done, and happily, Jim's parents had not yet arrived. Quickly I set the table, cooked cauliflower and made cheese sauce. I was stirring the gravy when the doorbell rang. I heard Jim say, "Merry Christmas," then his folks echoed the greeting. I took off my apron, put on a smile and went to welcome them.

Actually the dinner went very well. Everyone ate heartily and laughed frequently. It seemed that I had forgotten nothing. The girls were well-behaved, and Jim's mother complimented me on handling everything so well.

After dessert, Kristy and Janice opened their presents, squealing with delight. Finally they hung their stockings on the fireplace, kissed everyone good night and went to bed. The rest of us had coffee in the living room. The lights from the tree were vivid with color and the room was warm and cozy. I felt great.

Then I remembered the pendant watch. I hadn't wrapped it yet. As unobtrusively as possible I excused myself and stole to the bedroom. I spread the expensive foil paper out on the bed and went to get the watch. It wasn't on my dresser. It wasn't in any of the drawers. It wasn't on the floor or under the bed. It wasn't anywhere in the room! Panic rising in my chest, I hurried to the girls' room. In the darkness I groped among their things, looking for the watch. I couldn't find it. I looked in the hallway and the bathroom. Nothing.

Jim called me. I returned to the living room and glanced about furtively.

"When are we going to open our gifts?" he asked. "The folks are anxious to get home before the snow gets worse."

"Soon," I said hopefully.

"Is anything wrong, honey?" Jim looked at me intently.

"No, not at all," I said, glancing behind the couch.

"Did you lose something, dear?" asked Jim's mother with concern.

"I don't think so," I said, taking her empty coffee cup. "May I get you more coffee?"

I scurried into the kitchen and searched countertops, cupboards, and corners. I found nothing except several pieces of Kristy's puzzles and a recipe I had lost months ago.

Disheartened, I returned to the living room with the filled coffee cup for Jim's mother. Taking it, she said, "You poor dear, you're so busy. When will you have a chance to sit down?"

"In a minute," I sighed, and in desperation I rushed to the bedroom and wrapped a set of lavender towels I had planned to give my sister.

Jim's mother seemed delighted with the towels, but I felt absolutely deflated. Jim gave me a questioning glance (What happened to the watch?), but I looked away, smiling brightly, and told Jim's dad how much I liked the cuff links Jim picked out for him.

At 10:30 Jim's folks left, driving away carefully into a winter wonderland of soft fallen snow. I considered the possibility of collapsing into the nearest chair. "What happened to the watch?" Jim asked as he unbuttoned his shirt.

"I have no idea," I lamented. "I must have misplaced it. And I wanted everything to be so perfect!"

"It was, honey," said Jim, kissing my cheek. "We'll look for the watch tomorrow, okay? Merry Christmas."

"We still have an hour to go," I mumbled, about to cry. Instead, I blew my nose and went to the kitchen where the dinner dishes sat in stacks ready to be washed.

"I'll fill the stockings," said Jim. "Then I'm going to bed. How about you, hon?"

"As soon as I finish these dishes," I told him.

It was nearly midnight before the dishes were done and put away. Jim was already asleep and the house was dark except for the soft glow of the kitchen light.

Here it is nearly Christmas, I thought, *and all I feel is depressed*. Somehow, looking back, the day seemed almost wasted. It had been so filled with activities and yet now it seemed that I had missed something. Or something was missing in me. The Christmas spirit? Yes, but something even more important than that. What was it?

With this vague emptiness inside me, I dreaded thinking about the morning—the girls' glee and excitement as they opened the rest of their gifts, the hurry and bustle as Jim and I took the boxes and sacks of food over to the Clark family—

The Clark family?

A practical thought occurred to me then. I had better take our basket of food out of the pantry or we might forget it in the morning. Opening the pantry door, I reached for the basket, then hesitated as I saw something unfamiliar nestled among the canned goods. A package. Clumsily wrapped in newspaper with an orange tissue paper card attached. I stared at the card: A crude, whimsical drawing of a Christmas tree and underneath, in awkward letters, the name "Jesus."

Quickly I tore open the newspaper wrapping, knowing already what I would find. Yes. The pendant watch. Kristy's gift to Jesus. Of course. The best gift. The best gift for Jesus.

I sat down and stared out the window at the snow-covered yard. For the first time that day I thought about Jesus my Lord, and my heart began to fill with love for Him. With the love came an ache as I realized how seldom I ever gave Him the best of myself. I was so concerned that I do my best for everyone—except for the One I loved most of all.

Now it was midnight. Christmas. Christ's birthday. I had spent myself preparing for this celebration, but no time had been spent on Him. Or with Him. Nothing for Him.

Yet Kristy wanted God to have her best. She found what she thought was the best gift, wrapped it, made a card and placed it in the basket as her offering to Jesus. In her own way she had been more faithful than I.

In the quiet of my kitchen I began to pray softly, asking God's forgiveness, asking Him to take first place in my life again. Then I rejoiced, praising God for His gifts to me, for His willingness to forgive and renew my heart.

Impulsively I wanted to wake up Jim and the girls and tell them it was Christmas and that the secret to having the Christmas spirit is Christ—His presence, His fellowship, *His* Spirit! But I would have to wait until morning. For tonight, all I could do was gently, lovingly, return Kristy's gift to its rightful place in the Christmas basket.

Home to Southfield, Mourning

What does a woman do when her father's death underscores her emotional distance from her husband?

They were driving from Hillsdale to Southfield, returning home after a week of mourning, of attending to familial tasks and obligations, of offering and receiving the bleak, distracted comfort of the grieving. Anna's father was dead and buried. During the final days of his illness his children and their families had swarmed back to their birthplace like stunned but dutiful bees, unwittingly enmeshing themselves in one another's lives, bumping abrasively as each sought to cope with death and the tedium of everyday living.

During that week rituals and habits clashed unmercifully. Silences loomed, TV blared, and conversations were cliche-ridden, unfulfilling. Now, the week over, with friends and relatives emptying out of the old homestead back to their separate, anonymous lives, Anna, exhausted but intact, could reflect on the past seven days and their significance.

It was perhaps too soon to analyze events and feelings. Anna still felt shell-shocked, her reactions anesthetized by incredulity and pain. But now, riding over familiar ground—the rural landscape somehow reassuring—and with Gil comfortably beside her in the driver's seat, Anna could afford to breathe again. Needed to breathe. Needed to reaffirm her life. And Gil's.

Gil had said little all week. Anna had felt his presence, his quiet support as she sat paralyzed and tearless by her father's deathbed. Gil had demonstrated amazing efficiency in helping with the funeral arrangements, gathering information for the obituary, and handling a hundred unexpected details. Still, he remained somehow at a distance, remote.

It had not mattered until now. Anna had been too busy, too preoccupied. She had spent herself on the demands of a dozen others—first her father, afterward her mother and her younger brother and sisters and their families. The list seemed endless, the responsibilities exhausting. Why had she found no comfort, not from her family, and now she realized not even from Gil? In spite of 20 years of marriage, he had been as much a stranger as anyone in her father's house. The realization was disturbing.

Anna glanced at her husband from the corner of her eye. *Thoughts are skimming through his mind a mile a minute,* she mused, *and yet I can't read one of them.* She forced her eyes back to the road. *There's no one on earth I really know,* she thought. *Not my parents, nor my brother and sisters. Not even my own husband!*

To distill the terrifying implications, Anna blurted a banality she immediately regretted: "It's a beautiful afternoon for driving, don't you think, Gil?"

He nodded absently, and she wondered if he had really

heard her. She tried again. "We're making good time, aren't we?" Another absurd remark. Could she say nothing worthwhile? She had spent a week politely receiving the condolences of others, answering with the proper phrases, maintaining an acceptable balance of grief and control. She had succeeded in camouflaging her real emotions and reactions, the irritations and negative impulses. She had kept the mask of propriety in place against her will.

Soberly now she recalled some of the incidents of last week. When her brother and sisters argued over who would keep their father's valuable coin collection, she remained silent. When, on the night of her father's burial her sister's children played the TV at full blast, Anna swallowed her anger and said nothing. When thoughtless friends and relatives dropped by at all hours expecting to be fed and then remained to chat, Anna did what she could to feed them, though both the food and conversation were sometimes meager. Anna's mother flitted about like a wounded butterfly, helpless and confused but still fluttering. Anna squelched her impatience (most of the time) and strove to assist the broken, baffled woman who bore her.

Anna rationalized now that she had done well. Who could criticize her? And yet had she really communicated with anyone, even once? After a week of such meaningless verbal exchanges, she ached for real words.

"Hungry?" asked Gil, his gravelly voice shattering the silence.

"No," she said without thinking, then added, "but it's time to eat, isn't it? Go ahead and stop if you see a nice place."

It occurred to Anna that a pleasant atmosphere and good food might be just what she and Gil needed. What a welcome change to be served a delectable meal, to be free to smile again, to reaffirm their lives. After all, she and Gil were survivors. Thank God for that!

"How about Tom's Grill?" suggested Gil, slowing down and pointing across the road.

"Is their food good?"

"Truck drivers apparently like it. Won't hurt to try it, I guess."

"All right," she said, wanting to say no.

The place was just what she had expected, what she dreaded. A hole in the wall, a dreary rundown truck stop. Anna felt irritated with Gil for even choosing it. Was he so insensitive to her needs that he failed to see she desired a bright, attractive atmosphere tonight, something to confirm that life was indeed still beautiful?

Tom's Grill. The screen door was full of holes and the walls were gray with grease and grime. Torn posters of long-dead movie stars—John Wayne, Clark Gable, James Dean—were tacked over cracked plaster, along with dog-eared signs advertising specials of the week. The place was stifling, lacking air conditioning, and the little air that could be had was tainted with onions and garlic. On the jukebox Waylon Jennings was crooning something about a love gone wrong.

"I didn't know it would be this bad," murmured Gil as they sat down opposite each other in a narrow booth.

"It's okay," she said, kicking herself because it wasn't. She realized this was the story of her life. She never said what she really felt. Did Gil?

"This heat—!" he began, wiping his forehead. She nodded. Already she could feel perspiration beading on her upper lip. Gil pushed the menu her way. She glanced at it halfheartedly, feeling snobbish, reluctant to accept anything the place had to offer.

A coarse, chunky woman in a tight red dress came to take their order. Gil waited for Anna to order first, so she said, "Iced tea. And the roast beef sandwich." Gil ordered a steak sandwich and fries. *It'll be tough,* she predicted silently.

When they were alone again, she caught Gil's gaze and held it momentarily. She couldn't get beyond his eyes though. Had she ever really tried? She loved him, but how often had she risked the pain of really knowing him and exposing her inner self as well?

"Are you all right?" Gil asked, looking puzzled.

"Yes," she said. "I was just wondering—about my mother, how she'll get along now."

"She's always had a life of her own. She'll manage better than you think."

It was true. Anna understood that her mother had never really been close to her father. They had gone their separate ways, been involved in their own interests and activities for years. They had shared little more than a house and a bed. And yet now her mother seemed so devastated, as if the hub of her life had been removed.

"We're a lot like them, aren't we?" Anna murmured, momentarily bold.

"Like who?"

"My folks. We have our own lives, come and go as we please, just like they did."

"I suppose," Gil said noncommittally as the waitress brought their food. They ate in self-absorbed silence. But the mashed potatoes were instant and the roast beef tough and dry, so Anna pushed her food aside, half-eaten. Doing so, she caught Gil's glance. His expression told her he took the rejection personally.

"I just wasn't hungry after all," she said defensively. But she *was* hungry, suddenly starved, for something that had no name, for a closeness with Gil that did not exist, an intimacy between them that might give meaning to her grief or at least make it more tolerable.

Not once this past week had she genuinely touched anyone she loved, nor had they touched her. *Why?* she wondered now. *Are we too selfish to spend ourselves on one another, too proud to risk being vulnerable? Instead of caring we build up grievances. If it's that way in a family, what chance is there for the rest of the world?*

Someone was playing a Johnny Cash song on the jukebox now, and the music jarred Anna out of her reverie. Gil was finishing his sandwich. Anna noticed with distaste that the salt and pepper shakers were greasy and a fly was probing the gravy on her discarded plate. Her stomach turned, and she made a gesture of revulsion.

"What is it?" said Gil, sounding mildly irritated.

"Nothing," she said. He was flying out away from her, farther and farther away. Panic moved in her. She could be dying just as her father died, and still Gil would not know how to reach her. Just as she had not known how to reach her father.

"Do you know what my father and I talked about before he died?" she said aloud, abruptly.

Gil looked up quizzically.

"The weather," she said with a small ironic laugh. "We both knew he was dying. It was the most terrible and the most significant moment we had ever faced together, and all we did was try to kill time—like two strangers waiting for a bus."

Gil shrugged. "It's always hard at a time like that."

"And my mother," persisted Anna, wrestling a mushrooming desperation. "I should have been able to help her more. We never talked. All I did was get impatient when she fluttered around so much."

"That doesn't mean anything," Gil murmured, glancing around and signaling the waitress for the check—his way of ending this one-sided conversation.

"It was the same with my brother and sisters," Anna rushed on, pinning Gil with her gaze. "We went right back to being bickering children under the same roof. We took one another for granted. We weren't available to comfort or share." Anna shredded her paper napkin into tattered snakes. "What's more, even their children irritated the life out of me."

"Their kids were spoiled brats," Gil noted dryly.

"That's not the point."

"Then what is?"

"Nothing," replied Anna shortly. *What's the use?* She slid out of the booth, stood up, and said politely, "I'm going to the rest room. Be right back."

The rest room was a drab, airless, foul-smelling closet. The walls were scarred with lipstick and ink. Anna glanced into the mirror and was stunned by her image. The heat had wilted her. Her face appeared puffy, unsettled, unattractive, and her gray-streaked hair fluttered about her head as if befuddled. She looked as distraught as she felt.

Impulsively, she pulled open the door and fled. Back to Gil. Back to their table. Back where there was at least a sanctuary of sorts and the possibility of—something.

Anna stared at the booth where she and Gil had sat. The table had been cleared of dishes and wiped clean. Everything was gone. Even Gil. He was gone.

It's as if we never existed, she thought, horror-struck. *As if our meal together, our words, our glances were simply erased. Will our lives be that way too—erased as swiftly, as senselessly, as my father's?*

Blindly she ran out of the grill, an irrational panic coursing through her veins. She ran. Breathless. Past incoming customers. Out into air, elusive salvation. The door slammed shut behind her. Late afternoon sunlight burst her vision, sent her mind pinwheeling.

She collided with Gil. He was coming back into the restaurant and caught the weight of her body full force. Recognizing him, she sank instinctively against his chest. He slipped his arm around her and led her gently toward the car.

"You were gone," she murmured weakly.

"I just came out to look at the tires before we start on the road again," he said.

He helped her into the car and climbed in behind the wheel. She began to cry. "I haven't cried all week," she said, hiding her tears in her handkerchief.

Gil looked down the road. She could tell he wanted to get going. "Go ahead and cry," he told her. "They say it's good for you."

"I was no help at all to my mother," she confessed miserably, knowing he didn't want to hear it again. "And I was so inadequate saying good-bye to my father—"

"You did the best you could, Anna."

"Did I?" she cried. "By talking stupidly about the weather?"

"What did you want to say?"

"I—I should have told my father...I loved him."

"Why didn't you?"

Anna twisted her handkerchief in a gesture of futility. "I didn't know how. Our family has never been good at putting our feelings into words."

Gil's voice was mildly scolding. "Anna, you've got to stop torturing yourself like this."

There was a moment of silence before she blurted, "Gil, it's not just my father I grieve for. It's us."

"Us?" he echoed in obvious disbelief.

"How long has it been since we really said anything to each other? How long since I really wanted to know what you thought or felt? Or since you truly wanted to know me?"

Gil glanced down self-consciously. "Anna, it can't happen just like that—I mean, suddenly we tell each other our deepest thoughts? It doesn't come that way."

He stuck the key in the ignition and turned it. The engine

flared, then began to hum rhythmically. Anna spoke over the drone of the motor. "Then how, Gil? What can I do? There's an emptiness yawning inside me like a gulf. I don't have enough tears to fill it."

"We'll talk," he assured her, putting the engine in reverse and glancing out the back window. "We'll talk, just give us time."

"Time is a thief," she argued plaintively. "How much do we have left?"

"I guess there's never enough, is there?" He patted her knee, as if she were a child threatening a tantrum. "Remind me to have some air put in that left front tire again tomorrow."

"Tomorrow is your appointment to pick up your new glasses," she told him.

"That's right. I nearly forgot."

"Me too," she said.

Through the early evening dusk she stared long and hard at her husband, seeing him new all over again, storing his features in her memory. She would begin now to collect such treasures, preserving them like precious gems against the day...*some day...*

Instead of pulling out into traffic, Gil stopped and looked at her and smiled. Their eyes held. He reached for her hand.

"I hurt, Gil," she whispered over the painful egg in her throat.

"Yes, Anna, I know," he whispered back. "I hurt too."

"You, Gil?"

He nodded. "I'm going to be an old fool and tell you something I haven't admitted before. When we were at your father's house, I hoped you would need me. I don't mean just to run errands or make arrangements. I mean, really need *me*. But you never once turned to me, Anna. I felt useless, unnecessary."

She stared at him in surprise. "Oh, Gil, all I really wanted was your touch, your understanding. I wanted you to hold me, to comfort me. But you kept your distance like the rest of my family. Sometimes I felt like screaming. We all sat there insulated against one another, staring forever at that hideous TV screen. We fixed meals and ate and washed dishes in silence. Gil, if we were all hurting so much, why didn't we ever talk? Why didn't you and I talk?"

"Maybe we were afraid."

"Afraid?"

"Afraid of revealing ourselves, exposing too much...risking rejection."

"But why, Gil? Why couldn't we just be honest?"

He shrugged. "Maybe we're afraid of what other people will see in us—the weaknesses, imperfections. We erect barriers, hide behind walls until we feel safe. Our isolation becomes a habit, a selfish, comfortable indulgence."

Anna nodded. "But we miss so much behind those walls. I suppose I was so afraid of tarnishing my self-sufficient image, I couldn't admit I needed anyone, even you."

He gazed tenderly at her. "You don't have to be afraid, Anna. I love you."

"I love you too, Gil. It's not too late to tear down those walls, is it?"

He smiled at her with his eyes. A warm, lingering smile as his hand tightened on hers. "Know what, Anna, my girl? I think that's what we've just been doing."

A Proper Funeral

What does a woman do when divorce seems like her only option?

The President, in his State of the Union address to a joint session of congress, declared that the impact of the recent recession...

Martha aimed her remote control device at the TV and flipped from the Channel Six Noon News to a mindless game show on channel four, then to a "Love Boat" rerun, and finally back to the news. But she was weary of hearing about the troubled economy, the Middle East crisis, and the dangers of toxic waste. For crying out loud, she was sick of the whole thing—the world and its crises and catastrophes, so she flicked off the TV and tossed the remote control onto the sofa. The room was disturbing with its silence, leaving her face-to-face with her own problem: her decision to divorce Bert.

She sat down in Bert's chair. They called it that because it was a large, overstuffed, comfortable recliner, not at all like the sleek, modern furniture she had selected for the living room. He had a right to be comfortable. He worked long hours. She owed him that much recognition. He spent hours at the school, struggling with an over-crowded classroom of 5th graders. But when he came home, he made a beeline for the recliner. Bert always sat there after dinner watching his favorite cop shows and sitcoms and usually fell asleep before they were over. She hated that about him. Why couldn't he either watch his shows or not watch and go to bed if he was tired? Why did he always fall asleep in his chair so that she had to shake him and say, "Wake up and go to bed"? It even sounded stupid, like *Wake up and go to sleep*. It made no sense, like so many things in their marriage. "But no, this isn't the time to rehash old gripes," she said aloud, pushing away the irritation that stirred in her again.

Today of all days Martha wanted to stay calm. *Relax,* she told herself. *Stay in control*. Yes! Everything was at stake today. Today she must show herself to be a strong, no-nonsense woman. A take-charge lady, her mother would say. It was the only way to go. But, sitting now in Bert's chair, she felt lost and small. Her hands were shaking. She hadn't noticed it before. She had been too busy dusting, loading the dishwasher and then straightening Mark's room, lining his toys and games and stuffed animals neatly on the shelf. She liked having everything in its place, everything just the way it was supposed to be.

But now, with only two hours before her appointment with the lawyer, Martha could feel her tension mounting. The accumulated stress had become a fiber weaving through her muscles, making her ache. She wondered if she would ever relax again.

It hadn't helped that her mother had called first thing that morning harping again about the divorce. Martha could still hear her mother's strident voice declaring, "I'm not going to say I told you so, but I told you Bert wasn't right for you in the first place. No gumption, no get-up-and-go. Thank goodness, now you know and you're finally going to do something about it."

Martha had cut her off, telling her the bath water was running. But she knew her mother would call again. Even as the thought crossed her mind, Martha heard the familiar ring. She waited, letting the phone ring four times, then five. Her mother wouldn't give up. Or maybe, possibly it was someone else. Bert. Or the lawyer. Maybe the meeting had been cancelled. She reached for the cordless phone on the table and said hello. Her heart sank.

It was Mama, just as she had known it would be.

"Martha, listen, I've been thinking. You know, you've got Mark to worry about now and that's not going to be easy. He's just a baby—not even five yet. Have you thought about what you're going to do with him? I suppose I could take him for a while when you go back to work, but you know my health. And you can't trust these day-care centers. Maybe a private nanny—"

"Mama, please," she protested, "I don't want to think about nannies. Right now I've got enough to worry about with the divorce."

"Well, let me tell you, it's a real weight on my mind too. Don't you dare let Bert off easy. With no-fault divorce and crazy judges awarding men alimony and custody of the children, you can't be too careful these days. You make sure Bert pays you plenty. Get every penny of alimony you can. You can do it, just like I did from your dad. I made sure I got my fair share—"

"Mama, please, let's not talk about it. This whole thing is my fault as much as Bert's. I'm the one who wants the divorce—"

"That doesn't matter, Martha. He still owes you. You gave him eight years of your life!"

"Did I, Mama? Sometimes I don't feel like I gave him anything."

"Don't talk like that, Martha. You tried to make it work. Bert just didn't give you anything to work with. You needed a man with a good future, someone who could give you the kind of life you deserve."

"Yes, Mama, I know. I've heard it all before. Listen, I've got to go. My appointment with the lawyer is at two. I've got to get dressed and drive Mark over to the sitter's."

"Well, the sooner it's over the better. After George left me, my nerves got better immediately. Of course, you were too young to remember..."

"Good-bye, Mama. I'll call you when I get back from the lawyer's."

"Bert will be there, won't he?" her mother asked skeptically.

"Yes, he's taking the day off from work. But I won't let him talk me into anything. It's just a formality. You're supposed to talk to the lawyer before you go through with anything. You know how it is, Mama."

Hanging up the phone and settling back into Bert's chair, Martha realized what she said wasn't exactly true. She didn't have to see the lawyer with Bert. It was Bert's idea—his idealistic attempt to save their "happy home." He wouldn't let things be. No, he had to go searching below the surface of things, probing around for causes, reasons for this or that kind of behavior. You couldn't just be afraid of something. You had a phobia or a deep-seated anxiety. You couldn't just be tired of trying to make a go of your marriage; there had to be some psychological problem. You would think he had majored in psychology in college, the way he carried on about it sometimes.

She'd liked that in him at first—his way of looking beneath the surface of things, trying to understand what made people like they were. In spite of herself, it was easy to remember those first days they spent together, even that first wonderful evening.

Bert had been a junior at State when they met. He was majoring in elementary education. She was studying business at the local junior college and had a part-time secretarial job with Harper's Savings and Loan just off Main Street. Bert was there one afternoon to see about a loan to help with his college expenses. She couldn't remember what they had talked about, but before he left they had a date for that evening.

It was a nice date, pleasant but vague in her memory, except for the last part of it. He hadn't taken her right home. Instead, they drove to a quiet place near Moncrieff Lake where Bert stopped the car in a remote glen. She hadn't expected this. Fingering her purse strap nervously, she wondered how far he would try to go.

But Bert only wanted to talk. That was all. So they talked. That is, Bert talked—about his classes, himself, his family (he was one of five children)...and about her. In fact, he guessed more about her than she would have thought to tell him: that she was an only child of divorced parents with a spunky, independent spirit, and that she was spoiled and had probably never loved anyone in her life.

In spite of his blunt remarks or perhaps even because of them, she began to love Bert. Not with lightning bolts and flames of passion. Rather, he was her port in the storm, her safe haven. Maybe she loved him because he was genuinely interested in her as a person rather than as a sexual conquest, or perhaps just because he stood up to her, telling her what she was, yet loving her anyway.

Bert was easy to be with. Having grown up alone, Martha found it difficult to be at ease and talk freely with others, but with Bert it was different. He didn't demand more from her than she was willing to give. She loved him for giving and not demanding, for accepting her as she was, for making her feel cherished and protected.

Of course, her mother was against the marriage. Bert still had another year of college and teaching positions were few and far between. "Who ever heard of a man teaching grade school?" her mother demanded. "What kind of money will he make? Chicken feed! He's just like your father, Martha, a long way to go and slow to get there!"

"He likes kids. He'll be good with them. And I'll be working too," said Martha. "Almost all families depend on two incomes these days."

"Well, you'd do better to get a husband who's already established, like that nice young doctor I go to for my arthritis. He's single—and quite a catch, if I do say so myself. You don't listen to me, Martha, but you're used to nice things, and who's going to buy them for you if you marry Bert?"

Martha didn't want to admit that her mother was right. Really, her marriage had been good at first. But the money never lasted, and when Mark was born, Martha gave up her job to stay home with the baby, and their finances took a nosedive.

Still, money wasn't the real problem. It was more than that. She sensed something inside herself, an unwillingness to open up, to give and share herself, a resistance to committing herself to anything, or anyone. She thought Bert would be able to help her break through that shell, but neither he nor Mark had succeeded. In fact, lately her feeling of isolation had increased, along with her critical spirit. Nothing pleased her anymore. Nothing was quite right. So what was the use of going on with a farce? The least she could do was be honest with Bert. He deserved so much more than she could ever give him.

But she remembered what had happened when she tried to explain her feelings to Bert a few weeks ago. She tried to make him understand, but he was as stubborn as she usually was, and he made her feel little and stupid.

"Bert, can't you see that what I'm telling you is the truth?" she had pleaded. "I love you and Mark as much as I can love anyone, but it isn't enough. I'm not happy and neither are you."

"Just what do you suggest we do about it?" he had challenged.

"Let's just face the fact that we made an honest mistake—"

"And...?" She had never seen such intensity in his face before.

"And get a divorce." She barely whispered the words.

He turned on her then, and his eyes were cold, hard coals. "I told you once you had never loved anyone in your life. Well, how right I was. That goes for now too!"

She felt like a helpless little animal curled up on the sofa, but now she was fighting back. "You're wrong! I did love something once! I did!"

"What? What was it?"

She retreated. "I don't know. I don't...remember."

Bert looked drained. "Right. Take the easy way out. The story of our lives."

She sat there small and silent, hugging herself defensively, musing over the idea of something she had once loved. Looking up at Bert, she saw in his eyes that he wanted her. Oh, how he wanted her. But he turned abruptly and left the house, letting the door slam behind him.

The phone was ringing. Again! Martha's fragile memories shattered like expensive crystal. She realized she was still sitting in Bert's chair waiting for her appointment with the lawyer, and—oh, yes, the phone! Heaven help her. Her mother again.

"Dear, I know you didn't want me to call again, but I was thinking about this lawyer you're going to see. Didn't you say he's a friend of Bert's? Well, you know, it's customary for each party to have his own lawyer—"

"I know, Mother. We've been through this before. I told Bert I don't want my own lawyer. I'm sure this one will be more than fair."

"But if he's a friend of Bert's, you may have trouble getting anything out of Bert at all. Martha, are you listening?"

"Yes, Mama. You don't have to worry. Bert wants to do what's best for Mark and me."

"Sure, that's what he says. But, Martha, you know I have one of the best lawyers in town. If those two pull any monkey business, you let me know and I'll call my attorney for you."

"No, Mama. No! Bert got the lawyer. Let things be, Mama, okay?" She tried to sound firm, but she suddenly wanted to cry.

"I'm only thinking of you, Martha, but if you don't need me..." The older woman's voice trailed off.

Martha was beginning to feel that tight, upside-down roller-coaster feeling in her stomach that she often felt when talking to her mother. "Mama, I gotta go. I'm not dressed and I've got less than an hour before my appointment. And Mark's still outside playing. I'll talk to you later."

Martha felt a weakness in her knees as she dressed, and it was difficult to apply her makeup evenly. Still, she was a little freer with her mascara and blusher. It never hurt to make a good impression. With only a half hour before she must leave, she was glad she had dressed Mark for the sitter's before sending him out to play.

She went to the front door and called him now, her eyes urgently scanning the wide grassy yard. Strange, he was nowhere in sight. "Mark? Mark, where are you!" she shouted, panic rising in her chest. She hurried down the porch steps and ran around to the backyard, screaming his name.

Thank God, there he was sitting in the dirt, his straw-blond hair wind-tossed, his stubby, chubby frame huddled over something on the ground.

I'm upset, she told herself, *and I must not take it out on my child.* Walking closer, she saw the streaks of mud on his best Sunday school shirt and trousers. He was carefully scooping the earth away with one grimy hand. In the other he tenderly held the remains of a dead bird.

Suddenly, she had had enough.

Grabbing his arm, she pulled him to his feet. In the same moment she tore the puff of flesh and feathers from his fingers and flung it hard into the grass. Still clutching his arm, she turned him toward the house. "March, mister!"

Then she looked down into his face. She had never before seen horror written on a child's face. More than horror. Worse than horror. Hurt. Hurt deep like a wound that would never heal.

She was screaming at him now. "It's dead! Don't you realize that? *It's dead!*"

His eyes remained steady on hers and full of sorrow. He didn't understand at all. Suddenly she felt as if a secret place in her heart had been torn open. Kneeling on the ground and pulling her son into her arms, she held him against her and sobbed into his mussed hair, remembering the something she had once loved.

With Mark it was a bird. With her it had been a mongrel pup. Rocking Mark in her arms, she remembered how it had been, how her five-year-old mind had seen it those many years ago.

From her bed she had heard her parents quarreling in the living room. They had quarreled before, but this time it was worse. Their fighting always made her feel frightened and alone. If only she had Dowie—yes, that was his name—what she had called all animals as a child, and the name had stuck with him. Dowie, her happy little terrier pup. He was in the garage now, but if she could only get him and bring him back to her room, she was sure she would be all right.

She reached the hallway in time to see her father go striding out the door. She heard the garage door open and the car engine start. Her mother was already in the doorway shouting and crying, hardly noticing her child slip through the doorway to the porch. The car screeched backward into the street, its headlights flashing by, its great orbs of white blinding her in the doorway. And then she heard it: the sickening scream of a dog struck by automobile wheels.

For the first time since her childhood she could remember every detail of that scene: she, a fragile thing in a pink nightgown sitting near the curb clutching the bleeding remains of Dowie, the wet night grass clinging to her arms and legs like tentacles of a hideous nightmare.

"Let go of him. He's dead! Can't you see that, you crazy child?" her mother had screamed at her, prying her hands from the animal and dragging her back into the house.

After that night, her father never came home again. Dowie was gone and her mother was never the same. Martha never knew whom to blame, but she suspected she must have done something horrible to be so suddenly alone. Even at five she sensed that she must never again love something enough to risk being hurt by its loss. Until today, she had never understood, but now it was clear. How early she had been taught to close her heart to love!

Dear Lord, this she had almost done to her own child!

Mark was still huddled against her breast, quieter now. She looked at his face, blotched and red with tears, no doubt like her own had been so long ago. She took the corner of her dress and wiped them away.

"Baby, it's okay. Really, Mark, it is okay." She hugged him quickly and released him. "Come on, Mark. Let's look for your bird and give him a proper funeral. You know, he was a lucky little bird to have someone like you to love him." She helped him to his feet and held his hand firmly. "We'll find a nice little marker for your bird. Then we'll look for his family and give them some bread crumbs."

Even as she led Mark through the grass, she heard the phone ringing inside. "Stay right here," she told her son. "I'll be right back. I promise."

She ran inside and caught the phone on its fourth ring. She should have known. Her mother again.

"Martha, I'm so glad I caught you before you left. I just thought of something else. Listen, when you talk to that lawyer—"

"Mama—Mama, listen. I'm busy. I'll call you later, okay?"

"Don't tell me you're still getting ready."

"No, Mama. Mark and I are—well, we're involved in a little project in the backyard."

"The backyard? But your appointment. You're supposed to be there in 20 minutes."

Martha looked up at the clock. Almost two. She smiled. That upside-down roller-coaster feeling was gone. Something else had replaced it—the warm glow of hope. "I won't be keeping my appointment with the lawyer, Mama. I've got something more important to do here."

"More important? Martha, what could be more important than your divorce?"

"My son. We have something we need to take care of together. In fact, we're going to be rather busy, Mother, so please don't call back. When I have something to say, I'll call you."

"Well, certainly, if that's the way you feel. I was only trying to help, you know."

"I know, Mama. But I'm a big girl now. It's time I made my own decisions."

"But what will Bert say when you don't show up for your appointment?"

"Oh, I think he'll understand, Mama. After I've told him what happened today, I think he'll understand perfectly."

The Baby-Sitter

What does a young woman do when helping someone puts her own life in danger?

Fran Smith's baby is sitting in his high chair smearing icky prune stuff over his forehead and elbows. He gurgles contentedly, watching me through prune-dotted eyelashes. In frustration I whisk the dish and spoon out of his hands and run for a washcloth. I scramble around breathlessly, wiping purple globs out of Randy's hair, swishing the cloth over his face and arms. Momentarily startled by this sudden cleansing, Randy's pink, scrubbed face puckers (yes, like a prune!) and he lets out a terrible yell.

"Stop that!" I insist, but he doesn't hear me.

Baffled, I jerk the grimy tray forward and remove my small, squalling charge. "Is this any way to earn a living?" I quip to no one in particular. Of course, I have my university scholarship, but it's baby-sitting that puts spending money in my pocket and gives me extra study time when the little darlings are asleep.

I set Randy in his playpen in his room and hand him a plastic rattle. He scrutinizes the toy, whimpering a little, and decides at last that it is an object worth chewing on. With relief I go back to the kitchen to see whether four-year-old Peter has finished his spaghetti. I catch him holding a strand at arm's length and sucking it into his mouth.

"Use your fork," I tell him, trying to sound reasonably authoritative.

His forehead ripples into a frown. "When's my mommy coming home?"

"Later, after you're in bed. You'll see her in the morning."

"Where'd she go?" he persists, sucking in another spaghetti strand.

"Stop that," I say again, with little effectiveness. "Your mommy went bowling with your Aunt Jackie. Didn't she tell you?"

"Why didn't she go with my daddy?" says Peter, ignoring my inquiry.

At Peter's question, I draw back involuntarily, unable to think of a thing to say.

"Why doesn't Mommy go places with Daddy anymore?" Peter continues, his round, dark eyes peering insistently into mine. "Why doesn't she, Robin?"

"Didn't she explain that, Peter?" I ask cautiously, stalling.

"She said Daddy doesn't live here anymore. How come, Robin?"

"I don't know, Peter."

"Doesn't he love me anymore?"

"Oh, I'm sure he loves you very much."

Peter shakes his head solemnly. "No, he doesn't. I know he doesn't."

I lean down and, in the light breathless voice of someone sharing a marvelous secret, I whisper, "I know Someone who loves you very much, Peter."

He juts out his little chin. "Who?"

"Jesus."

Fran Smith is explaining about the jars of baby food lined up on the counter. Her makeup is bold, maybe even a little bawdy, and her bleached, permed hair is teased into a frizzy cotton-candy froth. She reminds me of Bette Midler, only taller and slimmer.

"Give Randy the strained chicken and carrots first, when he's hungriest," she says. "Then applesauce instead of prunes. You said he made a mess of them last time, right?"

I nod, smiling agreeably, looking alert, while Fran goes on to explain something else. I call her Fran, not Mrs. Smith, because we're not that far apart in age. I'm almost 20, she's maybe 25. It's hard to imagine, but she must have been pregnant already with Peter when she was my age. I'm just glad I'm single and still looking. Sometimes I feel like Fran and I are the same age, and sometimes I feel older, wiser than Fran.

Like right now. Fran is talking excitedly about something. She laughs nervously, stopping in the middle of a sentence to laugh. I don't know what she's saying. My mind is on something else, someone's words that have echoed so often in my brain lately they have become my own thought. *You don't have to go to a foreign field to be a missionary. Begin right where you are.*

My pastor said that just a few weeks ago. And we talked about it in my college-career class at church. I can't get it out of my mind. I'm studying to be a missionary someday, maybe in Russia or China, but that time seems so remote, so far away. I stare at Fran, at Peter, at Randy. It's true. A solemn, secret knowledge. *I am already a missionary. This is my mission field.*

"Did you hear me?" says Fran, sounding faintly exasperated.

"No, I'm sorry, Fran," I murmur.

"I was telling you about this man I met at the bowling alley. Oh, wow, wait'll you meet him. He's totally cool. You'll see. He came up to me right out of the blue and asked me out. Just like that. He's nothing like my ex-husband, thank goodness."

"You're going out with him tonight?"

"Sure, he'll be here any minute. Ralph looks just like that actor Clint Eastwood, only a little heavier. And he's smart too. He's a used-car dealer, has his own car lot and everything. Real possibilities, you know?" Fran rolls her eyes meaningfully, her bright orange lips drawn into a grin. She glances into a mirror, suddenly absorbed by her reflection.

"I figure one of these days my luck's got to turn, you know, Robin? Anytime now things will start going my way. What do you think?"

I shrug, not wanting to dampen Fran's enthusiasm. "I don't exactly think of it as luck..."

The doorbell rings and Fran hurries to welcome Ralph somebody—a tall, red-haired man with massive shoulders. Fran introduces us and he grins at me through colorless, watery eyes. *Clint Eastwood?* I muse. *Get real!* His nose and cheeks are so ruddy and glistening that I can hardly focus on his eyes. His voice is loud and booming, although he seems to exert no effort when he speaks.

"Hi, gal," he drawls, chewing on a fat cigar and shaking my hand heartily.

We exchange small talk while Fran goes to get her purse and coat. He asks about my college classes and I ask about his used-car dealership. He rambles on in a deep, monotonous voice about Blue Book prices, inept personnel and sagging sales figures until it dawns on him suddenly that my interest is strained; so he pauses, chuckling over something. Then, muffling his amusement, he says, "Did you hear the one about the used-car dealer with the 40-year-old wife? He traded her in on two *twenties!*" He guffaws noisily, unruffled by what must be a stiff, pasted-on expression on my face.

I am relieved beyond words when Fran returns. In a delighted, possessive manner she takes Ralph's arm and moved dreamily toward the door. "We may be late, Robin, honey. You don't have any early classes tomorrow, do you?"

"No. Nothing till eleven. You two have a good time."

After Fran and Ralph leave, I sit down on the rug with Randy and build a tower of colorful blocks. Randy chortles gleefully until Peter comes over and topples the tower with his foot, scattering the blocks everywhere. "Look at my trucks," he demands in his small, pouting voice.

At bedtime I hold Peter on my lap in the rocking chair and sing "Jesus Loves Me." Peter's pride in being four and too old to be held on someone's lap is overshadowed by his need to be comforted and loved. Again and again he asks me to sing the song about Jesus loving him, until finally he sings along with me, knowing the words by heart. I rock Peter in the chair until he sings himself to sleep.

"What's this about you teaching my kid church songs?" Fran asks, eyeing me suspiciously. She is working on her makeup, outlining her mouth with a bright peach lipstick. "How can I have you sit for my kid if you teach him stuff that confuses him?"

Dumbfounded, I mumble, "I—I figured all little kids know 'Jesus Loves Me.' I didn't think you'd care."

Fran stiffens her upper lip and carefully blends her lipstick with her little finger. Without looking away from her mirror she replies, "It's not just the song, Robin. You got Peter talking about Jesus and begging to go to church. Would you believe he wants me to take him? Me! I'm supposed to get up at the crack of dawn on Sunday and take my kid to church. Come on, Robin, get real!"

"I'd be glad to take him with me sometime, Fran. You're only a few blocks away. It wouldn't be any trouble."

"Hey, hold on. You're really into this church business, aren't you? When I want my kid to learn about religion, I'll teach him, understand?"

I hesitate a moment, then ask gently, "What will you teach him, Fran?"

She turns and gives me a withering glance. "I suppose you think you've got the market cornered on religion, huh? Well, I'll have you know I believe in God just like everybody else. And no matter what anybody thinks, I'm just as good as most people. Maybe even better!"

In my mind I pray urgently for just the right words. Carefully I explain. "My faith isn't based on what I do, Fran—."

"On what then?"

"On what Christ *did.* He knew I could never be good enough to deserve His salvation so he made it a free gift. All I had to do was accept Him."

"Free?" she mocks. "So Jesus is free!"

"Please, Fran, the Lord Jesus means more to me than the whole world."

"Hey, this isn't 'My Favorite Sermon' on TV, you know," Fran jokes ironically. Examining her teeth in the mirror, she briskly wipes away lipstick smears with a tissue. Satisfied at last that her smile is perfect, she gives me a long, appraising glance. "Aw, don't get upset over what I said. I mean, you're a terrific sitter and I trust you with my kids. I'm sorta glad you're—religious. I know you won't be bringing wild guys in or having beer parties, stuff like that. So if I sound irritable it's just that I got things on my mind. Like Ralph."

"Ralph?"

"Yeah, right." Fran nods as if her thoughts must be obvious. "I like him a lot, already, you know? I want things to work out, but I don't know. Ralph's a funny guy. He likes to drink and then he acts—well, different. Maybe I'm too fussy.

Or scared maybe. I don't want another one like Randy and Peter's old man."

I listen silently, sympathetically. I can't help but think of Peter and how much he misses his daddy. Evidently Fran notices the sober expression on my face because she immediately brushes off her confessions of anxiety with a frivolous laugh. "Don't look so serious, Robin. I'm just overreacting, that's all. What do I have to worry about? I can take care of myself. I've had to long enough." But the laughter escapes from her voice when she adds, "All I ask, Robin, is that you cool it on the religion bit, okay? Peter doesn't need it and neither do I."

"Come on in, Robin. We're running late tonight, so you'll have to get Randy's food out of the cupboard." Fran's face looks strained; she sounds preoccupied. Peter clutches at her leg, whining. Randy sits on the floor chewing on a rattle.

Ralph is already here this evening, looking impatient, pacing about with a sour expression on his face. "We're going to be late, Fran," he mutters under his breath.

Fran nods distractedly. "I know, Ralph, but I gotta take care of something first." She glances at me with a strange, startled look on her face. "Robin, sweetie, I want to tell you—" She pulls me aside, pressing her hand against my arm. Her voice is pinched and accusing. "Robin, you didn't listen to me, honey. How come?"

"What do you mean?"

"I mean what you've been telling Peter. He talks about Jesus all the time. I told you not to dwell on that subject with him."

I feel a tight, unexpected disappointment wrench inside me. "I haven't, Fran. I've only answered his questions. That's all, believe me."

"Well, I don't know. Maybe so, but listen, I talked with my

sister Jackie the other day, and really there's no reason she can't take care of the kids from now on. It might be better all around. You understand, don't you, hon?"

I am too stunned to say anything, so I nod blankly. My face feels twisted in an expression of anguish, but Fran doesn't seem to notice.

"Well, good, that's settled then," she says in a voice tinged with relief. "We'll talk some more when I get home, if it's not too late." She picks up her purse and turns to Ralph. "Okay, sweetheart, I think I'm ready."

After they leave, I busy myself in the kitchen. All evening I feel close to tears. I hadn't counted on the reprimand.

Be a missionary. Begin right where you are.

I keep asking myself if I was wrong to consider Fran Smith and her children my mission field. Didn't I pray for them every day? Were my prayers, my efforts wasted? Was I too eager, too aggressive, too persistent? Was my pastor wrong about average people like me being a missionary right where we are?

I put Randy and Peter to bed early and force myself to spend the remainder of the evening working on an English lit assignment.

Around midnight I doze off in the rocking chair. It is nearly one A.M. when I wake with a start. For a moment I feel groggy and confused. Disoriented. My body feels stiff, achy. All I want to do is go home and climb into bed. Then I realize what woke me—the sound of voices on the porch. Although the sounds are muffled, I recognize Fran and Ralph—arguing! Then suddenly the door flies open and Fran enters, her expression strained with—anger? Fear? Terror?

Obviously, something is dreadfully wrong. I bolt out of my chair. "Fran, what's the matter?"

She stares at me as if she doesn't quite see me. There is a frenzied, distraught quality about her, but she tries to cover it with a grim smile. "Nothing, Robin. I'm fine. I—well, Ralph and I—we had a little disagreement. But it's okay now. Really. See? Okay."

I nod uncertainly and begin to gather my handbag and books. "The kids were real good, Fran. Randy ate all his strained beef and most of his spinach—" My words break off as a thunderous noise sounds on the porch. Fran and I stare at the door. A terrible, insistent hammering shatters the silence of the night.

"Ralph!" cries Fran, looking stricken.

"Ralph?" I echo without comprehension.

"He's drunker than a skunk. He got rough with me tonight, slapped me when I wouldn't let him come in and stay."

"What—what can we do?"

Ignoring me, Fran cowers near the door and shouts, "Go home, Ralph. Go home and sleep it off!"

Ralph bellows back in rage, "Open this door or I'll take it off its hinges. Woman, I oughta kill you for this!"

Fran presses her hands against her temples in a gesture of despair, frantic. She screams, "Go away! Leave me alone!"

I shudder as Ralph bombards the door, heaving himself against the frail wooden frame like a maniac. "I'll kill you!" he roars. "I swear I'll kill you!"

As the door begins to splinter, I run to the phone and dial 9-1-1. "Help! We need the police! A man's breaking in!"

The words stick in my throat as the door springs open, banging against the wall. Ralph barges in, rampaging like a wounded beast. He grabs Fran by both arms and shakes her like a rag doll. "No one says no to Ralph, you hear me, Fran? Not even you, Doll. Not even you!"

I am frozen to the spot, gaping like an idiot. I can't believe this is real. It can't be happening. I open my mouth to speak, to scream, but there is nothing there. No sound. My mouth is like sandpaper. I am too numb to flex a muscle. A hideous vision flashes in my brain. What will Ralph do to Fran? To me? To Randy and Peter?

"Nobody says no to Ralph," he repeats, slurring his words. His huge hands fasten around Fran's throat now, squeezing. The color drains from her face.

Instinctively I leap onto Ralph's back, knocking him off balance. He releases Fran and stumbles. We both nearly fall, but he steadies himself and whirls around to face me. His eyes narrow menacingly. "So, the baby-sitter wants to play rough too. Okay, Babe, you asked for it!"

I step back, bumping into a chair. He reaches for me, misses and reaches again. I feel his fingers graze my blouse and I begin kicking desperately. A sob rises in my throat as the truth strikes home: *Nothing will stop this man. Nothing!*

Then seemingly from nowhere a baby screams. Randy. The sound appears to diffuse the intensity of Ralph's attack. The thrust of his anger wavers as he shakes his head dazedly. "What's that?" he demands, a hint of uncertainty coloring his voice.

"Randy, my baby," replies Fran, rousing herself and stepping between Ralph and me. "You woke him, you brute. And now, big man, you stupid drunk, you're trying to kill us!"

"No, Baby, no." As Ralph takes a faltering step toward Fran, I hear the sound of footsteps on the porch. A deep male voice shouts, "Police!" Several officers bolt inside and swarm around Ralph, holding him down while they search and handcuff him.

"Thank goodness, you're here!" Fran cries. "Ralph got so drunk and mean, we didn't know what to do."

"Well, he won't bother anyone anymore tonight," the officer declares as he pushes Ralph toward the door. "We'll need a full statement, ma'am. We'd like you to come downtown tomorrow and file a complaint."

"I'll be there," Fran promises.

Later, after the police have taken Ralph away, Fran makes a pot of tea. We sit together at the kitchen table trying to relax and unwind. We're still trembling, slowly easing ourselves away from the edge of hysteria. Fran plays nervously with the handle of her teacup while I drum my fingers on the table. Gradually our panic subsides.

Fran's voice falters as she talks about herself, her life. "I never once found anyone I could love or trust, except maybe the kids," she murmurs dismally. "Maybe I sound bitter or silly to you, huh? But it's the truth. You wouldn't know what it's like, would you, Robin?

"I—I guess not."

"And you have your—faith," Fran adds significantly. "I never had anything like that." With her fingernail she traces an imaginary line on the tablecloth. "Well, anyway, thank God the police got here in time."

"I am thanking God, Fran."

"Yeah, well, I suppose you would." She manages a smile and lifts her teacup to her lips. "You're a strange girl, Robin. Real different. And brave too. The way you jumped in there and tried to rescue me. You could have gotten hurt, you know."

"I didn't think about it. I just knew I couldn't let him hurt you."

"Well, thanks. You're a lifesaver."

"No, Fran, God's the lifesaver."

"Yeah, right. I guess I owe Him one. In fact, if I don't watch it, you're going to have me talking about this Jesus of yours just like Peter does."

"That would be *all right*," I reply, joy warming my face.

From the bedroom we hear Randy begin to whimper again. Fran gives me a wry little smile and says, "How about you looking in on him, Robin? We might as well keep him used to you. After all, I figure you'll be around here quite a bit. What do you say?"

"I say...terrific!" thinking I'll have another chance to talk to Fran and her children about Jesus.

Fran is still speaking. Her words startle me. I pause in the door to the baby's room.

She repeats her question. "That Jesus song of yours—maybe you could teach me to sing it, too. Would you?"

I am trembling again, but not from fear. "I would like that," I answer. "I would like that very much."

Woman on a Bus

What does a woman do when nothing in her life fills the emptiness inside her?

Emily sat formally, stiffly, her hands folded in her lap, wondering if women still applied for jobs wearing a hat and gloves. She hoped not. She was hatless, gloveless. She turned her gaze out the bus window toward the sun perched high and distant in the sky, an unspectacular globe. Meanwhile the bus groaned and creaked as if all its parts could not quite decide to work together.

Emily was all together (so she kept telling herself). True, she was wound tight, her mind ready to spring at the least provocation, but she was intact. She was stepping out, doing something, groping toward a reasonable solution. With utmost discretion she stole glances at her fellow passengers, allowing herself a measure of pity for them. They did not look as if they were going anywhere. They appeared static, as if this bus ride had been their only goal, and having achieved it, they were satisfied to sit back, assume a blank expression and dismiss all thoughts from their minds.

Emily's mind was constantly in motion. It seemed at times that people must certainly hear the inner workings of her mind, the intricate machinery manufacturing reams of questions to baffle the vast computers of her brain. Emily was aware of the sound, a familiar whir like a fan, providing a continuous background for the questions. Actually, the questions were Emily's greatest source of irritation, although she treasured them too, because they represented something about herself she had not yet discovered. They had no words—these questions—no logic, no explanation. They did not bother her by their presence but rather by the space the question marks left inside her. A vacancy she did not know how to fill.

This emptiness had propelled Emily down a dozen roads, into far countries and near tragedies. She had traveled to Japan the summer before graduation from college; she had switched her major from elementary education to Oriental art; she had a broken engagement and then met and married Martin after graduation. In the years following she had given birth to Debbie and Darren.

But even as a wife and mother, Emily was aware that something was missing. She wasn't using her education; she wasn't tapping her real potential. Every day Martin went off to a challenging job working among interesting people; he was an advertising executive with a prestigious firm that helped create award-winning television commercials. Meanwhile, Emily stayed at home and slaved—washing diapers and dishes, scrubbing dirty faces and floors, facing no greater challenge than to persuade Debbie to eat her carrots or to help Darren capture fireflies in a mason jar.

Was this all there was to life? Emily wondered time and again. Was there no greater purpose, no all-transcending reason to exist? Somewhere there had to be something that gave life continuity, meaning, value beyond the mundane and the humdrum. But when Emily expressed her thoughts—these nagging questions—to Martin, he merely dismissed her concern as frivolous female restlessness.

"You think too much," he chided. "You're not a dreamy-eyed college girl anymore with worlds to conquer. Settle down and enjoy your family. Appreciate what you have."

Martin's attitude infuriated her. For that reason—and in response to those wordless, persistent questions—Emily gave her husband an ultimatum, packed the kids off to preschool, and was now in determined pursuit of a career to establish her identity as a person. A person as opposed to nonperson, for obviously the void created by the questions was a result of her lack of "fulfillment" as an individual (weren't feminists still making that claim these days?). She had missed the boat somewhere along the line—in spite of travel, education, marriage and motherhood. All of these had merely skirted the issue, dodged the questions like nimble children playing ring-around-a-rosy. But the childish chant always ended with the chilling phrase, "all fall down." Emily sensed that it was necessary, *vital* in fact, to learn the meaning of the questions—and the answers—or everything about her might indeed "fall down."

Wasn't her marriage and her relationship with the children already strained, the delicate seams of communication fraying and at times threatening to split apart? Perhaps they in their own ways were pursued by the same wordless questions, haunted and driven by the same nagging void. But this was not something Emily wanted to consider. For all the bother, the sounds and questions were her own. She could not imagine them belonging to anyone else.

Emily's mind had done its job—had kept her properly occupied until she reached her destination. Now she was vaguely aware of the bus shuddering noisily to a stop. Stirring life into her limbs, she escaped its stuffy innards, moving as if in a dream, awaking suddenly on the sidewalk in the bright sunlight. She blinked. The sunlight confused her. She had grown too accustomed to the half-light of the bus. She could not handle the light. She squinted and turned her back to the sun, walking in the direction of the La Farge Towers.

Suddenly, without warning, an energetic young man approached and thrust something into her hand. She looked up startled as he said, "Ma'am, have you ever given Jesus Christ a chance in your life?"

"I beg your pardon," she snapped, shrugging off the booklet.

He pressed it into her hand.

"My name's Jerry."

"Jerry?"

"I just want to share my Savior with you, the Lord Jesus."

"I have an appointment," she announced impatiently, looking past him, willing herself away from the impulsive youth.

"Please, just read it," he said urgently.

She glanced suspiciously at the pamphlet. The title read, *Gospel of John*. Confused, embarrassed, she stuffed it into her purse and hurried past him.

Emily walked briskly to the La Farge Towers, entered, went directly to the elevator, stepped tentatively into the cramped, airless cubbyhole and pressed the fifth floor button. Her thoughts were righting themselves, settling down after the brief episode with the young man, a radical, religious fanatic in ivy league clothes.

It irritated her that he had interrupted her, nearly knocking her off course with his strange enthusiasm. Couldn't he see that she knew where she was going, that she had a destination, an appointment to keep? Emily quelled the impulse to yield to anger. What was the use?

The elevator jerked to an abrupt halt and the door yawned

open. Emily stepped out promptly, her gaze taking in the long narrow hallway of doors. *Which one holds my future?* she wondered as the click of her heels echoed down the corridor. She stopped in front of the door lettered *Jerome Coats, Architect*. Taking a deep breath, she went inside and approached a neat young woman who was busily working at her computer. Cautiously Emily said, "I'm here about the job...the one advertised in—"

"You want Mr. Richardson, over there." The girl had scarcely glanced up and now she was absorbed again in her work. Summarily dismissed, Emily wandered in the direction of Mr. Richardson's office. Moments later he offered her a chair and stared benevolently at her from across his wide desk. "Just what is it you are looking for?" he said.

Emily was outraged. He was asking her her own question! *I'm here because I want to find out what it is I'm looking for,* her mind screamed at him. When she did not answer, when her face only grew strained and tight and brittle, he said again, less patiently, "What are you looking for?"

"A job," she replied evenly.

"Well, yes, of course. What I meant was..." His words drifted off as he reached into a drawer and brought out an employment application. "Fill this out over there," he said, gesturing toward a table outside his office.

"Is the executive assistant's position filled?" asked Emily.

"Not yet." He brushed her off with, "Naturally we must consider *all* the applications." He made a move to stand.

"Don't you have to interview me or something?" Emily persisted.

She noticed that he had become dreary and dour-faced while waiting for her to get up and go. "The application first," he told her.

Obediently Emily went over to the table, sat down and began to fill in the blanks of her life. Name: Emily Ross.

Address, telephone number, educational background, skills, previous employment.

Emily hesitated, conscious of the devious tentacles of rage creeping in again, agitating the steady flow of facts from her brain centers. Why was she bothering to record this superfluous information? What really did it have to do with anything? With her? She knew these bits of trivia as she knew the planes and angles of her own face. It was worthless stuff, unrelated to the real, wordless questions, the inexplicable hollow inside her. Emily's precise hand gave way to spurts of rapid, unintelligible scribbling as she pushed resolvedly through the questions, finishing in record time. Like a dutiful school girl, she delivered the completed form into Mr. Richardson's hands.

He scanned it rapidly, then in a noncommital voice replied, "We'll be in touch, Mrs. Ross. Thank you for coming in."

In desperation Emily said, "I type very well..."

Mr. Richardson thumped his fingers rhythmically on the massive desk. "That's well and good, but—" He paused meaningfully, then added, "We would prefer someone with a business background, Mrs. Ross. You studied elementary education and, uh, Oriental art. Hardly the preferred qualifications for an executive assistant."

"I learn fast," Emily offered pleadingly.

"We'll call you if something works out," Mr. Richardson replied, standing up and shaking her hand.

Emily walked out with her composure surprisingly intact. But behind the steady, unblinking eyes, her mind was on a rampage. *Why, why, why! Why did I think this was the answer?* She knew, without knowing how she knew, that this job didn't really matter, that even when she landed the position she wanted, it still wouldn't fill the empty space in her life. There would still be the wordless questions, the restless search for meaning, significance.

Emily made her way to the bus stop, passing the same young man handing out his *Gospel of John*. He recognized her and said, "God bless you."

Venting her irritation, Emily snapped, "How can you do this, stand here like this? Don't you get tired? Don't you ever want to scream?"

"No," he said.

Emily fled. She collapsed into a backseat on the bus, barely conscious of the steps and the tremendous effort that had deposited her there. The sounds, the questions reeling in her head buzzed precariously now, bouncing off the walls of her mind, flying blind. The noises exhausted her. She stared into space, her expression sagging.

Then one question seemed to separate itself from the others and clothed itself in words that could be formed into a thought. The thought was: *What do the questions matter?*

It's true, Emily realized suddenly, dismally. *Nothing matters. When all of this is over, I'm going to die anyway...*She cut off the thought, left it stillborn in the stale air.

She turned her gaze to the window. The late afternoon sun hovered low in the sky, large, brilliant, shimmering with color. The sunlight was penetrating, nearly blinding in its intensity. As she watched, the sun pressed in on her, seemed to envelop her. Her pulse quickened and she fumbled in her purse for her sunglasses.

Then something fell. Emily glanced down. The pamphlet from the young man was at her feet. It was all right, she told herself reassuringly. It was nothing that belonged to her. She was about to kick it under the seat, out of the way, but she stopped and looked down again. The title of the booklet stood out in bold letters: *Gospel of John*. That was from the Bible. She couldn't kick the Bible.

With effort she reached down and picked it up. Brushed it off. Flipped through it. Strange. The sun seemed to vibrate on the pages, making the words come alive. She turned to the first page and began reading.

In the beginning was the Word, and the Word was with God, and the Word was God.

Emily, bone-weary and at the end of herself, rationalized that after all she had been through today, she needed something diverting. So she continued to read.

In him was life; and the life was the light of men.

What did these words mean? Who was the Word and what did He have to do with her? A puzzle, strange, perturbing. Emily read further.

As many as received him, to them gave he power to become the sons of God...

Emily marveled. Something was working inside her, provocative and tantalizing. An odd sense of anticipation was stirring. Was it possible that here in these words was the answer to those nameless, gnawing questions inside her?

For God so loved the world...

Did He? Really?

Or was she being foolish, succumbing to the siren song of a fantasy, a myth, a primitive yearning for something—or someone—beyond herself? Someone to make sense of things? Someone like God to love her? Even God Himself?

Was it crazy? Hoping a God in heaven loved her?

She didn't know.

Her common sense told her to put the little booklet on the seat beside her and forget it. Concentrate on her next interview, on Martin and the children at home, on carving out a satisfying career for herself. Yes! Concentrate on things that were real and what they claimed to be...

But what if Jesus is real and what He claims to be?

Something told her she was treading on dangerous ground now, letting the wordless questions take on real words.

But something else told her to keep reading, that an honest quest for truth brings truth...

Emily read on hungrily.

She read all the way home.

"Woman on a Bus" was originally published in *FAITH for the Family*.